CATHERINE

CATHERINE

April Lindner

poppy

LITTLE, BROWN AND COMPANY
New York   Boston

Poppy

Hachette Book Group
237 Park Avenue, New York, NY 10017
For more of your favorite series and novels, visit our website at www.pickapoppy.com

Poppy is an imprint of Little, Brown and Company.
The Poppy name and logo are trademarks of Hachette Book Group, Inc.

The publisher is not responsible for websites (or their content) that are not owned by the publisher.

First Edition: January 2013

Library of Congress Cataloging-in-Publication Data

Lindner, April.
Catherine / by April Lindner. — 1st ed.
p. cm.
"Poppy."
Summary: In this retelling of "Wuthering Heights," Catherine explains how she fell in love with a brooding musician and left her family to return to him, and her daughter describes searching for her mother many years later.
ISBN 978-0-316-19692-5
[1. Mothers—Fiction. 2. Love—Fiction.] I. Brontë, Emily, 1818–1848. Wuthering Heights. II. Title.
PZ7.L6591Cat 2013   [Fic]—dc23   2011043402

10 9 8 7 6 5 4 3 2 1

RRD-C

Printed in the United States of America

To Eli and Noah, with love

Chelsea

As I hurtled toward New York City on a Greyhound bus, I'd imagined my destination would be a gleaming ultrachic high-rise or a brownstone full of cousins, aunts, and uncles who would gather me into their arms, thrilled to discover the long-lost relative they never knew they had. So the reality was a shock: a hulking windowless concrete block on the corner of Houston and Bowery, painted a forbidding black. There wasn't so much as a doorbell beside the locked front door. Big jagged silver letters spelled out THE UNDERGROUND. Whatever it was—a restaurant? a comedy club? a warehouse?—it looked about as welcoming as a maximum-security prison.

I froze on the front stoop, unsure of what to do next. Had my mother really grown up here? Two doors down a woman with fluorescent-yellow hair and a zebra-striped minidress was arranging thigh-high boots in a boutique window, and a mural of a fire-snorting dragon on the side of the building vibrated with color. Though cars blasted past me down the wide street, the sidewalks were surprisingly empty, except for a guy in a long black apron smoking against a wall and a couple of skaters propelling their boards in my direction.

Could I have gotten the address wrong? I dug in the front pocket of my backpack for the letter I'd found last Tuesday, the letter that had changed everything—my past, my present, my future. The return address, in my mother's loopy handwriting, assured me I was in the right place. I pulled it out and unfolded it, hoping for some clue I'd managed to miss.

Sweet Chelsea Bell,

By the time you get this letter, I hope you're old enough to understand and forgive me for leaving. As I write, you're probably sleeping in your bed, what's left of your favorite blue blankie clutched to your face, and it hurts to think that the next time I see you you'll be older, bigger. Maybe you'll barely remember me.

Maybe your dad is reading this letter to you, or maybe you're old enough to read it on your own. Or maybe—if I'm really lucky—we'll be together soon and you'll never need to read this at all. Still, I'm writing it just in case.

You're the best daughter I could imagine, better than I deserve. And your dad's a good, kind, responsible man. I need you to know I'm not running away from him. I'm running toward something. Does that make sense?

I can't explain exactly why I went away, but here's the main thing: I've been given a chance to undo the biggest mistake of my life. That's why I've come back to New York City, to the home I grew up in. I don't know yet how long it will take. There are some people I need to talk to in person. One of them is Jackie, my best friend from high school. I hope you'll meet her someday, because I know she would love you, and I bet you'd feel the same way about her.

Though I'm far away, everything I see makes me think of you. Like today, out on the street, I saw a woman in a pink suit being pulled along the sidewalk by a pack of five identical white poodles. I know you would have laughed at the sight of her flying along, her fussy little pink high heels barely touching the ground as the dogs raced her down the street. You have the greatest laugh, like lots of bells ringing all at once. At night, when I'm trying to fall asleep, I close my eyes and I can see your face and hear that laugh.

Remember me always,

Mom

No matter how many times I read the letter, her words still sent a jolt through me—an electric current of love, sadness, and even guilt, because my memories of her had worn away, vanishing like that tattered blue blanket. All I could summon was warmth, the tickle of her hair on my face, and the scent of her perfume—cut grass and little white flowers.

My discovery of the letter had been completely random. I'd had the day off from slinging crullers at Mr. Donut, but it was the worst kind of day off, with nothing to do and nobody to do it with. I finished the last of the mystery novels stacked beside my bed, and the thought of walking to the library to get more in the ninety-five-degree heat gave me a headache. My best (and only) friend, Larissa, was stranded on a family vacation in a part of Cape Cod so remote it didn't even have cell-phone service. She'd be gone for two whole weeks, and though it was pathetic that I had only one real friend, that's what moving every couple of years will do to a person. By the time Dad and I arrived in Marblehead, I'd grown so tired of starting over that I couldn't make myself try very hard to fit in. Luckily, Larissa transferred from private school in the middle of freshman year, and she was in as dire need of a friend as I was. But with her out of town, I might as well be a complete pariah.

I could have used a ride to the beach, but of course my dad was at his office, teaching. He never used to teach in the summer; when I was little, he'd take me to the beach or the movies, or even to his office, where I would spin around in his chair, make long paper-clip chains, and draw with fluorescent highlighters. But at some point I got too old to hang around with my dad, and he started shipping me off to summer camp to be a counselor in training. This summer I flat out refused to be sent away—I wasn't one of those hard-core camp types who lived to make lanyards and fight color wars. I applied for the job at Mr. Donut so I'd have a reason to stay home all summer for once.

So I'd gotten my wish, and there I was, hitting refresh at the Nico Rathburn fansite every fifteen seconds, waiting for someone else to make a post. When nobody did, forcing me to face the fact that everyone in the world but me had a life, I decided to look around in Dad's closet in search of our old family photos, something I do every now and then so I won't forget my mother's face. She died when I was three, or so my father had always told me. *Of a brief illness,* he would say, to anyone who asked. His face would go all pale and solemn, and you could tell whoever asked was sorry they'd brought it up.

I riffled all the way through our box of family photos, and somehow it still wasn't enough. Dad's closet was packed with cartons and shoeboxes; there had to be something else interesting in one of them, but most of what I found was unbelievably pointless. A stack of old bank statements. A yellowing manuscript from a textbook Dad had helped edit. Manila envelopes full of tax documents. I'm not sure why I didn't give up. I must have been *really* bored.

But then I hit the—pun intended—mother lode: a shoebox at the back of the highest shelf, where I'd never have stumbled on it by sheer accident. There wasn't much stuff inside, but all of it was new to me. My birth certificate. My parents' marriage license. Mom's old passport, stamped in Italy, France, Greece, the Netherlands, and other places too blurry to make out. The next thing I found set my heart racing: a snapshot of my radiant, glossy-haired mom in a beret and a man's flannel shirt. The picture was cut crookedly in half. She'd been standing beside someone—an old boyfriend, probably. Part of a hand was still holding hers.

I dug a little deeper and found a few more cut-in-half portraits of Mom. She looked a lot younger—maybe my age. She was dressed a lot younger, too; I saw none of the pastel shirts and denim skirts she'd worn in my baby pictures. Even in a black Pretenders T-shirt and torn jeans she looked regal and confident in a way that had unfortunately passed me by, no matter how alike my dad always said we looked. In another photo she wore a short skirt, motorcycle boots, and a leather bomber jacket, the missing somebody's tan, slender but muscular arm draped across her shoulders. In that one, she was glancing to the side, toward the person who'd been chopped out of the picture, her blue eyes laughing.

But the next thing I found blew me away: an envelope addressed to me, Chelsea Rose Price, care of my dad, Max Price. Something about the handwriting on the envelope made my heart beat faster. The blood whooshed in my ears as I read it and the truth became clear. There hadn't been a "brief illness." And Dad hadn't sprinkled my mother's ashes off the coast of Falmouth, the way he'd said he had.

She hadn't died at all. She'd run away from us, and he'd been lying to my face about it for years.

Of all the lies a father could possibly tell his only daughter, this seemed an especially cruel one—letting me believe my mom was dead when she wasn't. But why hadn't she come home to us, the way she'd wanted to? Had she changed her mind? Or had Dad not let her? What else had he been hiding from me?

When I could trust my shaking legs, I ran for my laptop and typed my mother's name into Google. I found a Catherine Eversole Price in Des Moines, Iowa. A florist posed beside a prize-winning arrangement of tropical flowers, she looked nothing like my mom. One Cathy Eversole turned out to be a fifty-something real-estate agent in Bakersfield, California, and another was a fluffy blond newscaster in Indianapolis. On the next page of hits, I found what I was looking for—a four-year-old story in the *North Shore Ledger.*

Woman's Disappearance Still Unsolved

Ten years since a Danvers wife and mother went missing, police are no closer to solving the mystery of her disappearance. On an ordinary weekday, Catherine Eversole Price vanished from her suburban home without a trace. A wife and mother of a three-year-old daughter left a brief note saying she had business to attend to in New York City and would return shortly. Her husband, Max Price, declined to be interviewed for this story, but police records show he assumed his wife had taken a spontaneous trip to her hometown to visit old acquaintances. Price, at the time a visiting professor of economics at Harvard, said he thought his wife would call him from New York and return home within a day or two.

Letters sent from lower Manhattan reassured Mr. Price that his wife was safe, and he resolved to wait patiently for her return. "Cathy always seemed reliable and sensible. I'm sure Max had no reason to think anything was wrong," a former neighbor of the couple told the *Ledger.* But Price grew alarmed when days passed without a word, and he went to the police.

An exhaustive search uncovered few leads, and

Price criticized investigators for what he perceived as a slow and ineffective response to his wife's disappearance. Now an associate professor of economics at Salem State College, he resides with his daughter in Marblehead. A former Danvers neighbor still recalls seeing Mrs. Price wheel her young daughter's stroller through town to the local playground. "Cathy was so devoted to that little girl of hers. I can't believe she went away of her own free will. I'm afraid she must have met with some kind of foul play."

A yearlong investigation yielded no leads. "We've done everything in our power to locate Catherine Price," County Sheriff Dan Stevenson told the *Ledger*. "If a person wants to go missing, New York City is the perfect place to hide." He declined to answer questions about why Mrs. Price might have chosen to run away. "That's a private matter," he told the *Ledger*.

My heart sped up as my eyes traveled down the screen. So the county sheriff thought my mom was still alive somewhere in New York! It seemed at least as likely as any other possibility. What if all these years she'd been hoping I would figure out the truth and come find her? Then again, why hadn't she simply come to me? If she'd really been alive all this time, and hiding out somewhere, why not call and tell me she was okay?

But maybe she *had* tried to get in touch. Dad's job-hopping and our moving around from one town to the next would have made it hard for her to track us down. And our phone number was unlisted ("So students won't call and wheedle me to change their grades," Dad had said). Of course Mom could have found Dad's work number online. But what if she hadn't wanted to talk to *him*? What if she knew he was trying to keep me away from her? He'd kept that letter from me. Plus, the article said my mother had sent "letters," which meant there must have been others.

Unable to sit still a second longer, I paced the house on shaky legs, every familiar piece of furniture suddenly strange, as though I'd woken up in somebody else's life. On the living room bookshelf, the framed photo of Dad and me goofing around at Wingaersheek Beach might as well have been a photo of two strangers. Who was that man—his blond hair dripping with salt water, his eyes the same clear green as the ocean sparkling behind us? Some guy who had been lying to me for fourteen years straight.

At first I rehearsed the speech I was going to give when he got home, muttering the words as I paced. I would expose him for the liar he was. *How can you live with yourself? Don't you think it's time you told me the truth?*

But as soon as I'd figured out exactly what I would say, I realized it was no good. I knew he'd say he'd only been trying to protect me, and I wasn't in the mood for his excuses. No: What I wanted was to get away from him. I wanted to find out the truth for myself. And more than anything, I wanted my mother.

Dad stayed at his office even later than usual, so I had a long time to piece together a plan. The first step was obvious: I had to get to New York City. I would start with the letter's return address, knock on the door, and figure out where to go from there.

Luckily, my seventeenth birthday was just a few days away. I knew Dad would give me a check, the way he'd done since I turned twelve and stopped wanting Barbie and her Dream House; I guess after that, he couldn't figure out what to get me anymore. That was around the time I quit doing the things he wanted me to—swim team, piano lessons, and getting straight As—and we stopped having much of anything to say to each other, to the point where all he ever wanted to talk about was why I hadn't made a list of colleges to apply to and why I didn't already know what I wanted to major in. How many times had I heard about my mother's great sense of purpose and direction, how she'd always known she wanted to be a writer and go to Harvard, and, sure enough, she'd applied herself and gotten in? How many times had I asked myself why I couldn't be more like my perfect mother?

Well, the joke was on Dad. I was about to become a whole lot more like my mom. Now I had a purpose—finding her—and a direction—as far away from him as I could get.

As it turned out, I was right about getting a check for my birthday. Dad handed me the envelope and stood in the kitchen doorway waiting for me to rip it open. He was on his way to his office, of course. He fidgeted in his checked shirt and dorky tie as I read my card and examined its contents. Five hundred dollars. More than I'd expected. I should have been glad—after all, I needed the money—but I couldn't help feeling let down that it wasn't something more personal or fun—an iPhone, maybe, or a boxed DVD set of *The X-Files*, something that showed he had thought even the tiniest bit about what I wanted and who I was.

Even so, as I thanked him and let him kiss me on the cheek, I felt a twinge of sadness. I knew he would worry about me when I was gone; he *always* worried. As I inhaled the familiar scent of his aftershave, I was seriously tempted to blurt out how I'd found the letter and give him a chance to explain himself. I opened my mouth to speak.

But Dad stepped back, took a look at his watch, mumbled something about being late for work, and bolted. It was my birthday, and even so he couldn't wait to get away from me. I looked down at the check in my hand and felt the anger flood in again. *Thanks, Dad,* I thought. *I'll use this money to buy myself something you could never give me: a new life not based on lies.*

The very next day I slipped out of my house before dawn. That's how I came to be stranded in front of 247 Bowery, without a clue what to do next. Would The Underground eventually open its doors? And what on earth would I do with myself in the meantime?

I looked around, taking inventory. Across Bowery, well-lit and glowing like The Underground's polar opposite, stood a health-food café. I crossed the street and ducked through the door. Behind the counter a youngish woman with crayon-red hair and hennaed hands was manning the juice machine.

I waited my turn, ordered a banana-coconut smoothie, and asked, "So, that place across the street? Is that some kind of restaurant?"

She gave me a look as if to say *Well, duh.* "That's The Underground. THE Underground."

"Oh. Right." Apparently I was supposed to have heard of this place because, after all, New York is the center of the universe, and THE Underground is the center of New York. "When does it open?"

She shrugged. "Different times. Six, maybe. Or seven thirty."

Great. It was only noon. The guy in line behind me was breathing down my neck, and I could tell the girl wanted me to move along, but I had about a thousand questions. "Do you know who owns it? And how long it's been there? Like if it's been there about fourteen years or more?"

"Of course. It's been open since the seventies." She sighed and turned away from me, firing up the blender and drowning out any further conversation.

So much for that strategy. If I wanted to learn more about The Underground, I was going to have to find it out on my own. I took my smoothie and set up shop at a table in the corner. Luckily, the place had free WiFi. I googled *The Underground* and clicked on the first hit. Punk rock started blaring out of my speakers, drowning out the café's wind chime-and-synthesizer mood music. One table over, a lady with floaty gray hair and pink overalls shot me a dirty look. The website's jagged silver lettering—just like the lettering across the street—told me I'd found the right place.

I plugged in my earbuds and clicked to enter, and a collage bloomed in front of me—picture upon picture, all of punk rockers. I'd never seen so much leather, so many tattoos and body piercings and Mohawks in one place. Had my mother grown up in a punk nightclub? This didn't mesh with what little I knew about her—mostly the things my dad had told me. She'd had a 4.0 average at Harvard before she'd left school to have me. She baked sourdough bread and made birthday cupcakes from scratch. Most of all, she'd married my dad, who listened to Bach and Brahms and whose idea of a wild night was having a glass of red wine before he dozed off in front of *Law & Order* reruns.

I examined the evidence in front of me—a sea of unfamiliar faces sprinkled here and there with one or two I recognized: Blondie, The Ramones, Green Day. A link took me to The Underground's history, a formidable block of text in red letters on a black background. *The Underground has outlived its competition— even the famous CBGB—and remains THE place to catch cutting-edge underground music....*

This was all very interesting, but I was scouting for information I could actually use. I found it in the second paragraph. *Visionary founder Jim Eversole...* Could that be an uncle of mine? I did the math quickly and realized he was about the right age to have been my grandfather. *After Jim's untimely death, the torch was passed briefly to his son, Quentin, who remade the site into an upscale steak house. But The Underground's original vision was revived by its current owner, Hence, former frontman for Riptide....*

What kind of name was Hence? Was he a relative of mine, too? I scanned the screen for my mother's name but didn't see it. No matter. I had a strong feeling I was on the right track. I couldn't waste the rest of the afternoon waiting around for The Underground to open. After all, how much time did I have before my father guessed where I'd run off to and came looking for me? I'd been careful not to leave any clues. Still, I could imagine Dad getting home from work, finding me gone, and going on a frenzied search. How long would it be before he thought to look for the letter, found it missing, and guessed where I'd gone?

Back at The Underground, I tried pounding on the front door until my hands ached. Nothing. I walked around to the rear of the building, stepping over fast-food wrappers and broken beer bottles. I found another door with an actual doorbell beside it. I pressed it and heard a buzzer ring inside the club. No answer. I rang again.

Just as I was about to give up, the door opened and I came face-to-face with a guy exactly my height and slender, with brown bangs that fell in his eyes and splotches of pink on his cheeks. We stood for a moment, staring at each other. This couldn't be the club's owner; he was too young—around my age, or a little older. He wore paint-stained cargo shorts and a faded purple T-shirt with black letters that read PUNK'S NOT DEAD. Head cocked questioningly, he looked at me, not saying anything.

He was probably just an employee, but my hopeful side wondered if he could be related to me—maybe a long-lost cousin? "Hello. I'm Chelsea Price." Would my name mean anything to him?

It didn't seem to; his head remained cocked. "We're not open yet."

"I'm looking for the guy who owns this club. Is he here?" When he didn't answer, I tried again. "Hence. That's his name, right?"

"He'll be in later tonight," he said, reaching for the door. "I'm not sure when." And he started to close the door on me.

"Wait! Please..." I could hear my voice getting higher, the way it does when I get upset. "I took a bus all the way from Massachu-

14

setts to see him. I've been dragging this backpack around since five this morning...."

He hesitated. "I don't think Hence would like me to let you in."

But something about his hesitation gave me hope. I leaned forward a little, so that to close the door he'd have to slam it in my face. "My pack is heavy," I said. "And it's so hot out."

The guy sighed, but he didn't shut the door on me. "You want to fill out an application? I'll give it to him when he gets in...."

"No! I'm not here for a job. I'm looking for my mother, Catherine Eversole."

The expression on his face changed.

"You've heard of her?"

His response was tight-lipped. "I know the name."

"You do?" I asked. "Is she related to the guy who founded the club? She's his daughter, isn't she?" I was pretty pleased with myself for having figured this out, but he didn't answer. Still, he swung the door open and let me in.

I followed him down a long hallway that reeked of fresh paint. We passed a door that led into an industrial-looking kitchen and another that opened into a room stacked high with mixers and musical equipment, its walls smeared with graffiti. So this was what a nightclub looked like.

"This way." He opened another door and flipped on a light switch, illuminating a steep staircase to the basement. I followed him down the creaky steps. At the bottom he clicked on a bare lightbulb dangling by its wire from the ceiling.

The basement's floor and walls were stark cement, adorned only by a poster of some band I'd never heard of called Black

Watch—three bare-chested guys in eyeliner and tartan plaid pants. A metal cot was covered with a few scratchy-looking blankets and a lumpy pillow. Against the foot of the bed leaned a battered electric guitar. "You can stay here until Hence gets in." He turned to leave.

"Is this where you sleep?" I asked his retreating back, not wanting to be left alone for God knows how long. "Wait!"

He paused. Before he could disappear again, I asked, "What's your name, anyway?"

"Cooper," he said. "Coop."

"Are you Hence's son?"

He laughed, as though I'd said something funny. "No. I work here. And I need to get some painting done. I'll let you know when Hence gets home." He took the stairs away from me two at a time.

When he was out of earshot, I allowed myself a heavy sigh. I perched on the cot's crinkly mattress, with nothing to do but wait. The small, ancient TV in the corner got about four stations, all of them too staticky to watch. I thought of the phone in my pocket, but I couldn't exactly call anyone. Larissa was still on the Cape, and even if she hadn't been, I couldn't trust her not to crack under my father's interrogation.

After at least an hour had passed and I was about to die of boredom, I started poking around Cooper's stuff. Not that there was much of it—a heavy English lit textbook under his cot, and a battered trunk plastered with stickers and stuffed with a tangle of jeans and T-shirts with names of bands I'd never heard of. I fought the urge to fold his clothes for him—that would have just been weird.

Instead, I picked up his electric guitar, slung the strap over my

16

shoulder, and stood in rock-star stance, giving it a strum. Not that I knew how to play. Those piano lessons Dad had forced me to take revealed I wasn't the prodigy he'd hoped for, and in a few months he'd gotten tired of nagging me to practice. Now, wondering if my mother had been musical, I ruffled my hair and drew my lip back in a sneer, trying to look like the pictures on The Underground's website. I gave one last muffled, tuneless strum. According to my watch, it was five thirty. What if Cooper forgot his promise to come and get me? Would I have to stay trapped in this basement all night?

And then I started worrying about Hence. Cooper had seemed nervous about my being here, like his boss would bite his head off for letting me in. Why else would he be hiding me in the basement? But if I really *was* the granddaughter of the guy who founded The Underground, didn't that make me something like rock-and-roll royalty? Why wouldn't the current owner be happy to meet me?

Suddenly tired, I thought about lying down on the cot, maybe crawling under the blankets, but they smelled like boy and probably hadn't been washed in months. Instead, I dug into my backpack, zipped on a hoodie for warmth, and put a T-shirt between my head and the grungy-looking pillow. Earbuds in, I hit play on my iPod and shut my eyes.

When I opened them again, groggy and disoriented, someone was standing over me, watching me sleep. I bolted upright, struggling to recall where I was. The someone was a guy, familiar and strange at the same time, looking down at me with a wry little smile, like I was a puzzle he was working out how to solve. I yelped, scrambling to my feet, and our heads collided.

"Ouch!" The pain jolted me back to the present, and I remembered where I was and how I'd gotten there. "Geez! What were you looking at?" It didn't seem fair, watching a person like that while she slept.

"I came to get you." The flush on his cheeks deepened. "I was trying to decide whether I should wake you up."

"You scared the crap out of me." I didn't mean to be rude, but I'd always been cursed with a tendency to blurt out the first thing that pops into my head. It was something I'd been meaning to work on.

"Sorry." The flush on his cheeks deepened.

I felt bad for snapping at him, so I changed the subject. "Anyway, is Hence here?"

Cooper nodded. "He's not in the best mood."

I shook the hair out of my eyes and slipped my hand into my hoodie pocket to make sure the letter was still safely there. "That's okay. Neither am I."

"No, seriously. He can be prickly. It's easy to get on his bad side." He paused to look me squarely in the face with eyes that were midway between blue and green. "And I'm guessing you can be prickly yourself."

True as that was, I didn't much like hearing it from a complete stranger. "I'm not prickly." I drew myself up to my full height. "And I'm not afraid of your boss." Because, really, how bad could this Hence character be?

"Hokay." Cooper's mouth twitched, like he was holding back a grin. "Don't say I didn't warn you." And with that he led me up the creaking staircase, into the heart of The Underground.

Catherine

My life changed forever on an ordinary Tuesday. I was rushing home from school so I could get together with Jackie and start on our homework assignment. The school year had barely begun, and already I was feeling frazzled and more than a little frustrated—I wanted to be doing my own writing, not some lame collaborative book report. It was a hot, sticky afternoon, the kind of late-summer day that made me want to hang out in a sidewalk café with an iced tea and a fresh pad of paper, eavesdropping on the conversations around me and jotting down every crazy idea that popped into my head. It felt wrong to be wearing an itchy school uniform and lugging a backpack, and even more wrong to have homework.

When I took the corner, I saw him right away: a slender guy with shaggy black hair camped out on my front stoop next to a guitar case and a big duffel bag. My first thought was *Oh, no, not another one.* One of the most annoying things about living above a nightclub—and believe me, there are plenty—is the musicians who are always trying to introduce themselves to my dad, hoping to convince him to put them on the bill. It's a waste of time, of course; Dad books his acts a year in advance, and he knows exactly who he will and won't let play in the club. A band not only has to be great, it has to be on its way up, about to go national. "The Underground has to stay relevant. We're more than a place to hear music. We're tastemakers"—that's how he puts it. He's not exactly humble when it comes to The Underground, but why should he be? The place is kind of famous, and Dad's a legend in the rock-and-roll world. Or so everybody has told me all my life, to the point where I get a little tired of hearing about it.

Really, I'd gotten so sick of coming home and finding stray guitar-god wannabes on the doorstep that I was thinking about sneaking around to the back door so I wouldn't have to talk with this one. He was staring down at his feet—lime-green Chuck Taylor All Stars—so I could have slipped right around the building without him so much as noticing me, except he happened to glance up as I was passing, and the look on his face stopped me. He was striking, with dark eyes, glossy hair, skin like coffee with extra cream, and the sharpest cheekbones I'd ever seen, but it was more than that. He looked hungry. Literally. Like he hadn't eaten in days. I had this feeling he needed someone to be kind to him. It was written all over his face: He was on the verge of losing hope, and he needed someone to urge him to keep going, to fight for what he wanted.

It was the strangest thing. It's not like I'm usually good at reading minds. If anything, I'm the opposite—dense about what other people are thinking and feeling. But something flashed between me and the guy on the stoop—a kind of understanding. So I went over to him and he scrambled to his feet and dusted his hands off on his jeans. He held out his hand and I shook it—like we were executives meeting at a business luncheon. His touch surprised me; the palm of his hand was dry but hot—almost feverish.

"Do you work here?" His voice sounded hopeful, but right away his gaze shot back down to his sneakers, as if he didn't dare meet my eyes for long.

It was a strange question, considering I was wearing my school uniform and carrying a knapsack.

"I live here." I threw my shoulders back and brushed a stray lock of hair from my eyes.

"You live in The Underground?" Now he was looking at me in disbelief, as though I'd claimed I lived in the Taj Mahal or Buckingham Palace.

"Not in it. Above it." I fumbled in my knapsack for my keys. "My father owns the place."

"Seriously? You're Jim Eversole's daughter?"

I had to hand it to him; he'd done his homework. But the hope in his voice made my stomach lurch. Like all the others, this one would turn out to be way more interested in my father than in me. Why had I thought, even for a moment, that there might be more to him?

"You want Dad to book you." It wasn't a question.

"That's not why I'm here." He sounded defensive. "I know I'm not ready for that yet. For now, I just want a job. Any job. Waiting tables, maybe." From closer up, I could see the faint scruff above his upper lip and along his chin. Despite the heat, he had on a black denim jacket, and under it his faded blue T-shirt was speckled with small holes, one wash away from dissolving into shreds.

"I don't think my dad needs any more waiters."

"I'll wash floors. I'll even scrub toilets. I just want to get to know the place from the inside." He dug his hands into his front pockets and looked back down at his sneakers, as if he knew he was asking for a huge favor and didn't want to pressure me one way or another.

Maybe he wasn't like the others who had tried to worm their way into The Underground. I paused a moment, weighing my options. When I opened the door, stepped inside, and beckoned for him to follow, I wondered if I was making a big mistake.

I usually hate giving tours of the club to my friends. Call me paranoid, but I get the feeling that where I live is more important to most people than who I am. But showing this guy around made me see the place through new eyes. First I took him through the main room. As we approached the stage, he paused for a long moment, staring like he could see the ghosts of all the acts who'd played there. So I waited beside him, recalling some of the bands I'd seen—The Magnetics, The Faithful, and Hot Jones Sundae were a few of my recent favorites—and I had the feeling that if I grabbed his hand and squeezed my eyes shut I could share my memories so that he'd have them, too.

But I didn't. What would he have thought if I'd tried it? Most likely that I was crazy—or hitting on him.

Instead, I cleared my throat and led him onward, into the mixing room with its tangle of wires and crates. I let him take a peek at Dad's office, and at his wall of glossy photographs of bands who'd come through the club. I saved my favorite spot for last: the dressing room where so many rockers had graffitied the walls into a multilayered, psychedelic mess. I pointed out a doodle drawn by Joey Ramone, and he studied it closely, as though trying to decipher its secret meaning.

"Thanks," he said when the tour was over. "For letting me take up your time. And for giving me a tour."

I shrugged. "No problem." There was nothing more to show him, really, but I wasn't ready to head upstairs and start dinner just yet. "I'm Catherine." And when he didn't reply, I said, "You have a name, right?"

"Hence."

It took me a while to wrap my mind around that one. "Hans?"

His answer came through gritted teeth, like he'd been asked that question a thousand times. "Hence. Like *therefore*."

I wanted to ask him if it was short for anything, and whether he had a last name, and where he'd come from, but he crossed his arms over his chest and cast a glance toward the front of the building. I got the distinct sense he was about to bolt. "You want to leave a phone number? In case my dad wants to get in touch with you? If he's hiring?"

Hence grimaced again. "I don't have a phone," he said. "I'm not really staying anywhere. I'm...I'm looking for someplace." He swallowed hard and I remembered the impression I'd had earlier, that he was on the verge of giving up. Had he been sleeping on the streets? Or in a shelter?

So I did something I probably shouldn't have. I invited him up to our apartment, into the kitchen. At my urging he sat down on one of the stools along the counter, perched uneasily like a stray cat who wasn't sure if he was going to be stroked or shooed. I cooked him one of those make-it-yourself pizzas heaped with everything I could find in the fridge. He practically swallowed it whole, so I made him another. Either he wasn't much of a talker or he was too busy eating to make chitchat. To fill the silence, I talked about myself—about how I wished I were musical but couldn't carry a tune in a bucket, so I wrote poetry instead, and how most of the girls at school thought I was weird because I liked vintage clothes and would rather spend an afternoon reading than shopping. I went on and on until I noticed I was whining about my relatively nice life to a guy who probably didn't even have a roof to sleep under.

The realization brought a blush to my cheeks.

"No," Hence said, frowning down at his plate. "Keep going. I'm interested."

"I'd like to hear about you." I stole a glance at the kitchen clock. It was 4:15, and Dad had told me that morning to expect him home at about five. My father's pretty cool about most things, but even so I didn't want him to come home and find me alone with a boy whose last name I didn't even know. Same thing goes for my brother, Quentin, who was due back from school any minute, and who could be a bit overprotective and big-brothery sometimes.

"There's nothing to tell," Hence said. "I've always wanted to

24

come to New York to see The Underground. I've read about the seventies punk scene, and the place is legendary.... But you know that already." And he stopped, as though that's all I could possibly have needed to know about him.

If I hadn't been worried about the time, I would have pressed further. I needed to get him safely outside, but I didn't want to let him disappear into the night, not before I at least tried to help him. I reached out—slowly, so I wouldn't startle him—and tugged his jacket sleeve. "I have an idea."

I sent Hence out, telling him to return around six thirty. Less than ten minutes later, Quentin burst through the front door without so much as a hello. A bag of fast food in his arms, he took the stairs up to his room two at a time and locked the door behind him. Q had been cranky a lot lately and, judging by the expression on his face as he blew past me, that night was no exception. Good thing I'd gotten Hence out in time.

Twenty minutes later Dad turned up, and—surprise, surprise— he was in a bad mood, too, after a long, frustrating meeting with his investment broker. He lumbered into the kitchen, kissed me on the cheek, loosened his tie, and tossed his jacket over a chair.

"I started a nightclub so I'd never have to deal with money-grubbers again, and look at me now." He opened the refrigerator and stared absently at the shelves as if something delicious would magically appear in front of him. "Completely at their mercy."

"I'm making pizza," I told him. "Pepperoni and mushroom. Your favorite. I'll have it ready in ten minutes if you'll sit down and get out of my way."

He grabbed a can of club soda and shut the door. "I don't deserve you, Cupcake." Dad had called me that for as long as I could remember, and despite being too old for it I didn't have the heart to make him stop. Though he was busy almost all the time and could be a bit distracted, he still had the softest heart imaginable.

While I cut the pizza and shoveled slice after slice onto his plate, I told him about the nice guy who had come to the club looking for a job as a busboy or janitor because he'd read books about The Underground and wanted to see it for himself. Of course, Dad wasn't a total pushover. He took hiring very seriously, so I made a big point of saying how trustworthy Hence seemed, and how honored he would be to work even the most menial job, to the point where I was worried I was laying it on too thick, but Dad just kept nodding, with that faraway look that meant he was either listening thoughtfully or musing about something else completely.

Luckily, it turned out he was listening, and by the time Hence knocked on the front door, Dad was completely primed. After introducing the two of them, I ducked into the hallway and hovered nearby, ready to pretend I was on my way upstairs if Dad noticed me. All Hence had to do was shake hands and talk music, and the job of busboy/janitor was his. The other part was trickier. Hence thanked Dad, then looked so uncomfortable I started to worry he'd get all the way out the door without mentioning he had no place to sleep. Finally, I couldn't stand it anymore: I stuck my head into the club and gave him a pointed look.

"There's one other thing, sir...." he began.

"Sir? I'm not royalty, Hence. Call me Jim, the way everybody else does."

"I don't have any place to sleep, Jim," Hence blurted out. "Can you, um, recommend a place nearby—a hostel, maybe, or a boarding house?"

Dad did just what I hoped he'd do—he said if Hence was willing to clean out the basement, he could stay here. We'd taken in stray musicians before, so I had a feeling he'd be cool about it, and I was right. Before long, Hence, his guitar, and his duffel bag were in the basement. I would have slipped downstairs to say congratulations and help him shift crates around and set up the metal folding cot, but as Dad helped me load the dishwasher, he seemed to be watching me more closely than usual.

"Why are you so interested in this boy, Cathy?" he finally asked, a bemused smile on his lips. "It's not like he's the first ragtag guitarist to come knocking on our door."

"He's so intense. I feel like he wants the job more than any of the others did." I paused. "Plus, he desperately needs our help, don't you think?"

Dad threw an arm around my shoulders, squeezed, and kissed the top of my head. "That's my Cupcake," he said. "Kind to a fault." Satisfied, he let the subject drop, eager to settle into his favorite armchair with the day's newspapers and to let me go off and do my homework.

Another father might have hesitated to let a good-looking stranger move in under his roof. As I rearranged my backpack, emptying out the heavy books I wouldn't need to lug all the way over to Jackie's, I thought about how great my dad was—and how much he trusted me. What intrigued me about Hence wasn't his good looks—I'd been burned by one too many gorgeous musicians. It was his intensity—that dark hunger in his eyes—coupled with that hurt look of his, the way he had of averting his glance as though he'd been kicked hard by someone he trusted and didn't dare let down his guard. I knew he must have stories to tell about the past he was fleeing and the future he'd planned for himself. I've always liked mysteries, and now one had landed on my doorstep, just begging to be solved.

Chelsea

∞

The club was busier than before. A burly guy was unloading crates from a dolly and whistling to himself in the kitchen, and a woman with a shaved head fussed with a coil of electrical wires. I followed Cooper to the end of the hallway, into a long room with a stage at one end and a curved and gleaming bar at the rear. The walls were rough, exposed brick, bare but for a blue stripe of neon light that shot down their length, giving the space a watery glow.

By the time I noticed the man lurking in a patch of shadow we were almost on top of him. He stood at the bar with his back toward us, pouring himself a shot of Jack Daniel's. He wore a businessman's jacket, and his dark hair was cut short. Though he must have heard our footsteps, he didn't turn or move. His stance was casual, commanding, like he owned the place. This had to be Hence.

Coop drew to a halt a few feet away, his arm out to keep me from getting any closer. The man finished pouring, then downed his shot in one gulp before turning to face us, an ironic smile—actually, more of a smirk—on his face. When his eyes landed on me, the smile vanished.

We gaped at each other. His dark hair was silver at the temples, and his skin was the color of caramel. He was scruffier than I'd expected, with a two-day beard. As older men's faces go, his was handsome, but it wasn't friendly or nice.

When he finally spoke, his voice sounded choked. "My God. You look just like…" Then he seemed to collect himself. "There's nothing of your father in you at all."

I stood up a little straighter. All the people who had known my mother—my father, my grandmother and aunts—liked to tell me how much alike we looked, but never in this tone of voice: a mixture of disbelief and wonder, and then, in that crack about my father, something like disdain. I struggled to keep my tone even. "So you did know my mother," I said.

He chuckled. "I knew her, all right." His tone implied he'd known her in ways I'd rather not have to think about. "A long time ago. What do you want from me, little girl?" He poured himself another shot.

Who did this guy think he was? "I only wanted to ask you a few questions. About her." From the corner of my eye, I could see Cooper hovering anxiously nearby, as though he thought I might need rescuing from his boss. Or maybe he was flat-out eavesdropping.

Hence smiled, but not nicely. "Okay, what do you want to know?"

What didn't I want to know? This guy might not stand still for a whole lot of questions, so I decided to start with the most important one: "Do you know how I can find her?"

He was silent for a moment, something like sadness crossing his face. "She's not buried around here. Her body was never recovered."

"But she's not dead!" I insisted. "I mean, I found this letter she wrote, and there's a good chance she might be alive. She sent it from here."

His eyes bugged. "A letter? Written when? Sent from here?" He took several steps forward and, involuntarily, I backed up. Hence was starting to scare me.

"Fourteen years ago."

"Fourteen years ago?" He ran a hand through his hair and gaped at me. "You think she's been in hiding for *fourteen* years?"

"The police investigators think so," I said.

"They're incompetent fools."

I narrowed my eyes at him. "That's why I'm looking for her myself." I reached into my hoodie's pocket for the envelope.

He practically grabbed it from my hand, pulling the letter out so roughly I was worried he would rip it. I watched his face as he read, trying to decipher the emotions that passed across it. Surprise? Sadness? Hope? I thought I saw all three, but they vanished so quickly I couldn't be sure.

"Chelsea…" he said finally. "So that's your name. Just like Catherine, to name you after her favorite neighborhood." Was that really where my name had come from? "She and I used to spend time together there."

"Who are you, anyway?" I asked. "Who were you to my mother?"

"Sit down." He gestured to a barstool, and I complied. "And you"—he motioned to Cooper—"get back to work."

Cooper retreated.

"How did you get here? You don't look old enough to drive." He looked me over appraisingly and a vertical line deepened between his brows.

"I'm *seventeen*," I told him. "I took a bus."

"Does your father know you're here?" Hence pulled up a barstool and lowered himself onto it. "Never mind. There's no way in hell he would let you come here to see me." He held the letter out, grudgingly, I thought, and turned back to the bar, as if he was completely done with me.

When I couldn't stand the silence anymore, I broke it. "My dad kept this letter hidden from me. He told me my mother was dead."

Hence turned to face me again. "I guess it goes without saying he never mentioned me." He looked at the letter in my hand, hungrily, as if he was thinking about taking it back. I slipped it into my pocket.

"Maybe for you," I said. "*Nothing* goes without saying for me. I grew up thinking my mother died when I was three. This letter tells me she's still alive."

"That letter is fourteen years old. It doesn't tell you anything."

"For all I know, there might be others. I read a story in the newspaper that said she'd sent letters. Plural."

He looked at me with new interest.

"My dad and I moved around a lot, and our phone number has always been unlisted. Even if my mother had wanted to reach me, she couldn't have."

"Isn't your father some kind of philosophy professor? She couldn't find him online?"

"He teaches *economics*." Hence had a point…but he didn't know everything. "Maybe she didn't want to talk to *him*. Or maybe she *did* call. Maybe he didn't tell me…or the police." I felt a pang of guilt; what was I accusing my father of, exactly? "She could have been trying to reach me for years. Maybe after a while she decided I was angry at her and just gave up." In a way, that was my worst fear—that my mother thought I'd gotten her letters and hadn't cared enough to write back.

We fell silent for a moment. The woman I'd seen untangling wires before strode into the room looking like she was going to say something to Hence, then caught the expression on his face, spun around, and was gone. For a while, Hence and I continued to sit side by side in a silence that was only slightly less hostile than before.

Finally, I dared another question. "Can you tell me about her? What she was like?"

"I can't talk about her," he said. "Don't ask me to."

This was a strange and disappointing response. Still, if he wouldn't talk about her, maybe I could at least learn something about the rest of my family. "What about Quentin Eversole? He must be my uncle, right? Does he still live around here?"

Hence snorted. "After he sold me this place, he moved upstate. For all I know he could be dead. But you didn't miss much; he was an idiot of the first order." He poured himself yet another shot. "Quentin." He spit the word out.

I waited for more.

"He despised me. Thought I wasn't good enough to hang around with any sister of his." He sneered down at my sneakers. "Jim—your grandfather—was a rich man. Did you know that?"

I shook my head, realizing how ridiculously little I knew.

"He inherited this building and turned it into a club in the late seventies. Didn't that father of yours tell you anything? A lot of acts cut their teeth here. The Chokehold. Toxic Cake. Steamtrunk." I nodded, as though those names meant something to me. "Between CBGB and The Underground, the Bowery was the epicenter of the punk movement. Bands were falling all over themselves for the chance to play here...."

I kept nodding, trying to get on his good side.

"Your grandfather turned this place from a kitchen-supply warehouse into a music mecca. I always admired him for that—the old bastard."

Uh, okay. I kept my smile frozen in place. "So what happened to him?"

"Heart attack. At fifty-eight. Then Quentin got hold of the club and ran it into the ground. It was his worst nightmare, having the club fall into my hands, but by the time he hit bottom, he didn't have a choice. It was sell out or go bankrupt. And I've built The Underground back up to what it used to be—even better. You know who played here last week?" He paused for emphasis. "The Starving Artists. *Rolling Stone* profiled them a month ago. They could be playing arenas. But they chose to come

34

here for a victory lap because we're the venue that broke them." I looked up from my hands and caught him studying me. "Not that you care. What bands do you listen to?"

I shrugged. I don't care who's hot or edgy. I like what I like—but I wasn't about to tell that to a professional music snob. "I came here to learn about my mother, not to chitchat about obscure bands." Something about Hence was bringing out the ugly in me.

He mimed shock. "My mistake. What else do you want to know?"

"Do you have any ideas about where she went? After she left me and my dad and came here?"

His black eyes bored straight into mine. "When she arrived here, I was in Liverpool. By the time I got to New York she had vanished. And believe me, if I had even the slightest clue about where she had gone, I would have followed her there. I would have…" His voice trailed off. "If she were still alive, I'd know." Another long moment of silence. "I, of all people, would know."

Was he claiming he was closer to my mother than I had been? Than Dad was? This struck me as deeply unfair. "*You* of all people?"

He inspected me, cocked his head to one side, leaned in a little, and changed the subject. "It's spooky how much you look like her. But I was wrong. You do have some of him in you, too. Around the mouth. Not that I've ever met him. I've seen his picture. Professor Max Price." He made a face like he'd bitten into a lemon.

But I'm not that easy to distract. "What do you mean, *you of all people?*"

He laughed. Then he rubbed his eyes and was silent for a

while. When he finally spoke again, his tone was cold. "Are you planning to take the bus back to Massachusetts tonight?"

I drew myself up as straight as I could. "I'm staying here until I learn about my mother," I said. "Until I figure out where she is."

"You might not like what you learn," he said, rising and rubbing his hands on his jeans.

"I'll take that risk." Anything had to be better than nothing.

Hence chuckled. "Well, okay then. I've got work to do." He started off into the hallway, but paused at the door and looked at me over his shoulder. "It's rash of you to barge into my home like this. But since you're here..." He paused for a moment before shouting, "Cooper! Get in here." His voice boomed through the empty space, and Coop appeared in the doorway, out of breath. "Take little Miss Price upstairs. She'll be spending the night."

"Should I put her in the spare apartment? You know...the one..."

"Yes, I know the one." Hence's voice was sour with impatience. "That's the perfect place for her." And he stalked out of the room without another word.

Cooper and I looked at each other. For a long moment, I fumed. "What's wrong with him?" I asked, when I could find the words. "Is he that rude with everyone? I don't know how you can stand working for him. And what did he mean when he said it's the perfect place for me?"

But Cooper just sighed and vanished. A minute later, he reappeared with my backpack and beckoned me toward the elevator. All I could do was follow.

Catherine

Between classes, Jackie asked if I wanted to come hang out at her place after school. I told her our fridge was almost empty and I'd promised Dad I'd bring home groceries, but she wasn't having any of it. She poked her lower lip out and crossed her arms over her chest. "It's that new waiter, isn't it?"

"I don't know what you're talking about." Annoyed, I fumbled my locker combination and had to start over. "And he's not a waiter." Lately I'd been spending more time around the club, going straight home from school, hoping for a chance to really talk with Hence. He'd been living in our house for almost two weeks, and I still hadn't begun to unravel the mystery of where he was from and why he'd left. When he was in The Underground, he always seemed to be scrubbing the walk-in freezer or helping the bands unload their gear; either that or he was down in his basement room, playing his guitar, the amp turned up loud enough for me to hear it whenever I passed the closed door. On his days off, he would disappear completely, taking his guitar and amp with him, then return with his spine a bit straighter, looking confident and exhilarated—almost like a different person.

"Waiter, busboy, janitor, whatever. This isn't like you, Cath." Jackie linked her arm through mine—a light, playful gesture, though her voice sounded exasperated. "You don't chase after guys. What is it about this one?"

I rummaged around in my locker, digging for my American history notebook, which was nowhere to be found. Jackie was right about one thing: I didn't chase after guys. There weren't any worth chasing at Idlewild Prep, where all the boys—and I do mean boys—lived to party. The musicians who played The Underground were more interesting—at least they had plans and talent—but they all had their own sneaky agendas, and anyway, I'd never *needed* to run after any of them. "I'm not chasing Hence."

Jackie waited for me to say more, and when I didn't, she sighed. "Then why have you been going straight home after school lately? You haven't been to my house in over a week."

I poked my head all the way into my locker. Where the hell was that notebook? "Even if I was chasing him—which, by the way, I'm not—what would it matter?"

"I'm concerned, is all. You don't know anything about this guy, Cath."

She reached into my locker and slipped my notebook out and into my arms, knowing without my having to say anything what I was looking for and where it was hiding.

The gesture made me even more annoyed. "Exactly. He's a mystery. He intrigues me." I slipped the notebook into my bag and briskly zipped it shut. "Writers are supposed to be interested in the world around them."

Jackie gave me her trademark skeptical look—one raised eyebrow, mouth quirked to one side.

"Besides, even if I did like the guy—which, I repeat, I do not—it's not like I gave *you* crap when you liked somebody." By *somebody*, I meant my very own brother; I'd listened to her obsess about him for years, and believe me, it wasn't always a picnic.

"You have too given me crap. When I was acting like an idiot. Over *somebody*."

This was true. I'd lectured her a million times about how she'd be better off forgetting Q instead of sobbing her heart out whenever he fell for a new girl in his string of foreign exchange students: Monique from Marseilles, Danica from Copenhagen, Kristina from St. Petersburg, Tessa from Bologna—Q's own version of the "it's a small world" ride at Disney World, all of them sophisticated and supermodel-skinny. With her hourglass figure, dimples, and golden-brown skin, Jackie was adorable, and Q was an ass not to see it.

"Okay. When I start acting like an idiot, you can lecture me all you want." Was it really that big a deal that I'd been spending more time at home lately? The only real difference was that instead of doing my homework at Jackie's, I'd taken to doing it in the club, sitting on a barstool, swinging my legs, chewing on my pencil, and spying on Hence while he worked. Once or twice, I'd glanced up from the page to find his eyes on me. I'd wave and he'd look away, throwing himself into his mopping as if I were his boss and had caught him goofing off.

One thing I did know so far: When it came to his music, Hence wasn't a poseur. Once, when I went down to the club to look for a book I'd been reading, as I was about to turn the corner into the main room I heard an acoustic guitar and a voice that sounded like amber and woodsmoke. I froze and listened, not wanting to startle him. Though I didn't recognize the song, I caught some of the lyrics. There was a line about hawks circling in the sky, and another about sleeping on a bus-station bench. I'm pretty sure the song was a Hence original. The melody was haunting, and I was struck by the loneliness in his voice, a sorrow that could only have come from real-life experience.

"He's an intriguing character, is all," I said to Jackie.

"An *intriguing character*," she repeated, trying to make it sound like a double entendre, which it didn't remotely.

But as wrong—and annoying—as Jackie was, I knew her heart was in the right place. "I have an idea. Why don't you come over to the club this afternoon? That way you can spy on him with me. The way we used to do with Quentin."

"We're not twelve anymore," Jackie said, but at least she was smiling. "But okay. I'll come over."

It occurred to me that maybe she was hoping to bump into Q, so I reminded her that he had a night class on Thursdays and wouldn't be home.

"Oh, I know," she said. "I mean, not that I'm keeping track of your brother's schedule. I'm not doing that anymore." She sped her words up, as she always did when she was flustered. "I just fig-

40

ured he wouldn't be around much now that he's in college. Anyway, you know I've written him off. I've moved on."

I shot her my own best skeptical look and she changed the subject to the sculpture class she'd started taking at the 92nd Street Y, and how they were working with live models, which meant a naked dude, and how that would have been okay, except instead of putting his robe on when he was taking a break, he liked to walk around the classroom, checking out the students' work and making chitchat about the weather and the Yankees, like he didn't realize he was buck naked.

Pretty soon we were doubled over laughing, drawing stares from the cheerleader and basketball star contingent, and I was remembering all over again why Jackie was my best friend. It wasn't as though I trusted or even liked a lot of people. Most of the girls at school thought I was a snob, but they were the snobs, wanting to make nice because of who my dad was or looking down at me because we lived on the Bowery instead of Sutton Place, and because I didn't spend my summers in the Hamptons—not because we couldn't afford it, but because summer was The Underground's busiest season. They thought I was strange. Maybe I *was* strange. But who wanted to be just like everyone else?

We slipped into the club, and I led Jackie to the kitchen, where Hence was filling the ketchup and mustard dispensers. He looked startled at our approach. "Hence, I'd like you to meet my friend Jackie." Okay, so it was weirdly formal, but at least it was a beginning.

"Oh. Hi." Hence glanced down at his hands and wiped them on his jeans. Then he reached out his right hand.

Jackie shot me a quick "who does that?" look as she shook it. "The famous Hence," she said.

He cocked his head to one side questioningly.

Jackie continued. "That's an unusual name: Hence. Is that your last name or your first? Where did you say you came from?" To my horror, she was going all Private Investigator on him. "Cathy couldn't remember."

Hence looked first at me, then at her. "No place you've heard of," he said, sounding annoyed. His dark gaze fell on me again, and I gave him an apologetic smile.

Before Jackie could say another word, I threw both arms around her shoulders, gave her a little warning squeeze, and laughed as though the situation weren't desperately awkward. "We're going to go hang out in Washington Square Park. I heard they're filming a movie there," I told Hence, though we hadn't made any such plan. "You must have a break soon, right? Want to come?" I gave Jackie one more warning squeeze and released her. "I promise my nosy friend here won't interrogate you any more."

"I can't." Now Hence was staring down at his sneakers, like he did the day we met. Oh, great: I was actually losing ground.

"What if we helped you with that?" I waved toward the army of yellow and red dispensers. "It wouldn't take long." Without even looking at her, I could feel Jackie's eyes boring into me, asking what on earth I was thinking, offering her up for unpaid manual labor.

"The club's expecting a delivery." Hence cast a glance around the room. "I'm the only one here."

"Some other time, then." I grabbed Jackie's hand and tugged

her toward the door. "See you around." I gave him a cheery little wave over my shoulder. He waved back warily and returned to his work.

The minute we were on the sidewalk and safely out of earshot, I released Jackie's hand and spun to confront her. "What *was* that?"

"You're asking me? I'm not the one offering to do the waiter's work for him. Oh...excuse me. Busboy-slash-janitor-slash-mystery man."

"As if it would kill you to fill some ketchup dispensers."

"That's not the point."

"You didn't even try to get to know him."

"I did try. And you stopped me." She thrust her chin out. "Why are the most basic facts about this guy such a huge question mark?"

"That's what I'm trying to figure out. Sooner or later he'll let his guard down."

"But why is his guard *up*?"

"I don't know yet. I'll find out. As long as my so-called best friend doesn't scare him off by treating him like a suspect."

"I'm not your so-called anything." Jackie sounded hurt. "He seems shady to me."

"If he was trying to hide something about himself, he could lie," I said, more to myself than to Jackie. "He could just make up a hometown, right? And a last name."

"So, why? Why be so mysterious?"

"I think he's been hurt," I said. "It's like he's escaping something."

"So you're psychic now."

"Just observant." The matter settled, I started down the street.

Jackie, hurrying after me, called from behind, "I know how you are, Cathy Eversole."

Her words stopped me in my tracks. "What's that supposed to mean?"

Jackie's voice got smaller and sweeter now, as if her tone could make up for what she was about to say. "When you set your mind on something, you don't listen to common sense. You know how you get. Like that time you got a cold because you had to climb into the fountain at Washington Square Park. In January."

"There was a thaw that day...."

"Or the time your dad took us horseback riding in the country. Remember?"

Of course I remembered. I'd pleaded for a chance to ride Thunder, the biggest and glossiest horse at the stable, despite the trainer's warnings that he wasn't for a beginner like me. My dad had made sure I got my way, and Thunder had bolted down the trail with me just barely hanging on.

"You could have been thrown," Jackie said. "You could have been killed!"

"But I wasn't," I said.

"Hence reminds me of that horse. I swear, he has that same look in his eye."

As mad at her as I still was, that last bit made me laugh. "I promise not to let him give me a piggyback ride. Now can we please, please, *please* change the subject?"

To my relief, Jackie nodded, like she'd been storing up that speech for a while and was glad to have it over with. Though we had fun the rest of that afternoon, the way we always did—poking into boutiques on MacDougal Street, trying on B-52s dresses and stiletto heels at Vintage Threads, cooling off in the spray of the fountain at Washington Square Park while watching the passing parade of street performers, drug dealers, and NYU students through our matching wraparound sunglasses—I couldn't help but notice the knot gathering in my stomach, as if something big was about to change between Jackie and me. Or maybe it already had.

As if Jackie's paranoia hadn't been enough to deal with for one day, Quentin had to go and flip out that same night. Q had always been touchy. He'd be perfectly normal one minute, then the littlest thing would set him off. His face would cloud over and his eyes would harden and you wouldn't even know he was the same person. I'd always thought of the scowling, bitter-tongued version as "Bad Quentin."

Not that long ago, Q had been his normal self most of the time, annoying but nice, still calling me Catheter (which I hated, but not as much as I hated the fact that he'd stopped) and still up for a late-night run to the video store or a game of backgammon. But since he started taking college classes, it seemed like we'd been seeing a lot more of Bad Quentin around the house.

By the time Jackie and I parted ways it was too late to start dinner, so I grabbed some take-out pad thai for Dad and me, figuring Q could fend for himself when he got home. Dad and I were eating with our feet up in front of the TV; he liked to catch the evening news, even if he mostly talked his way through it. He'd spent the day at a club in the Meatpacking District, listening to the Splendid Weather rehearse, and he was full of stories about what a prima donna the lead singer was turning out to be. When we heard the key in the apartment door, I tensed up, wondering which Q we'd be dealing with that night. The door burst open with more than the usual force and I knew right away that it wasn't going to be pretty. He swept into the room, night air clinging to his jacket, and positioned himself between us and the TV.

"Look who's home," Dad observed wryly. "Classes going well?"

I braced myself. Q wasn't what you'd call a natural born student, but Dad never concerned himself with what might set him off. I figured we were in for another fight about how Dad was paying Q's tuition and he damn well better start taking school seriously. If so, maybe I could wait till they got into it and slip out of the room without being missed.

Q shrugged Dad's question off. "School's school. I'll be glad when I'm done." Though of course Q's first semester of college had only just started.

"Want some dinner?" Oblivious, Dad peered into his take-out carton. "I've eaten most of mine, but your sister will share. Right, Cath?"

"I don't want dinner. I've got bigger things to worry about." Q took a step closer to Dad's chair, hovering over him. "That new guy you've got working downstairs. I saw him poking around in your office."

46

Dad laughed. "I asked him to straighten up my mess," he said. "He's a bright boy, and it's not rocket science."

Q bristled. "How well do you even know him? Your safe is in there."

"What did you say to Hence?" I asked, but Q and Dad didn't even seem to hear me, as focused as they were on staring each other down.

"The safe is locked," Dad said. "I'm the only one with the combination."

"What about your records? I saw him nosing around in your file cabinets. How do you know he isn't working for one of your competitors?"

Dad chuckled again, but I wasn't amused. "Are you seriously accusing Hence of being a corporate spy?" I asked.

Both of them heard me that time, and Q started like I was a piece of furniture that had just come to life.

"Because that would be paranoid," I added.

"Why should you care?" Q's blue eyes narrowed to splinters.

"He's her friend," Dad supplied, thinking he was being helpful, I guess.

"Not exactly—" I began, but Q cut me off.

"Since when?" Because Q hadn't been around much, he must not have heard the story of how Hence was hired. He hardly ever paid attention to the club unless he was forced to, so this sudden concern was more than bizarre. "How do you know him?"

I certainly didn't feel like going into the whole story. "Not that it's any of your business, but I had a conversation with him, just like you could, if you wanted to treat him like a human being."

"Since when do you hang out with Dad's employees?"

"Since when do I answer to you?"

Dad got to his feet. "The Underground is *my* business. Someday the club will be yours, and you can run it the way you see fit." Dad stood almost half a foot taller than Q, and he could be pretty imposing when he wanted to. "You didn't reprimand my employee, did you?"

Q didn't answer.

"Because if you've been causing trouble, I'm going to have to waste my night off undoing it."

"No." Q glowered. "I didn't say anything."

Without another word, Dad snatched up his empty take-out carton and strode Clint Eastwood–style from the room.

"As if I'd ever want to run this place," Q hissed, for my benefit, before stomping off to his bedroom.

Relieved the whole dustup was over, I joined Dad in the kitchen, where I helped him unload the dishwasher. "What was that about?" he asked me in an amused whisper.

I shrugged.

"With Quentin you never know what you're going to get," Dad added. "But in his own way, he was looking out for us. You know that, right?"

I didn't feel like admitting it at that moment, but I knew Dad was right. After all, when Q wasn't being Bad Quentin, he could be the nicest, most generous brother in the world. On my last birthday, he had given me a big, clumsily wrapped box, and inside, floating around, were two slips of paper—tickets to see R.E.M. at Madison Square Garden.

"Oh my God!" I flew at him and threw my arms around his neck.

"You don't have to crush me." He freed himself from my hug.

"You're coming, too, right?" I asked. "We're going together?"

"Well, yeah." Like I'd asked the world's stupidest question. But it wasn't such a dumb thing to ask, really. It's not like he was all that into music, and when he did listen, it was always to heavy metal, which I hated. R.E.M. wasn't his style at all.

But he did go with me, and we had a really nice time, even though our seats weren't the greatest and Q got bent out of shape at this one guy who had the misfortune to be sitting beside me, and who had chatted with me in a perfectly harmless way before the show.

"What are you looking so cranky about?" I asked Q when the guy climbed over our laps to get to the concession stand.

"If that jerk tries anything with you I'm going to have to deck him."

"He asked if he could buy me a soda. He didn't ask me to make out with him."

Q winced. "You shouldn't talk to strangers. Don't you know anything?"

"Nothing." I batted my eyelashes. "I'm a complete idiot." I knew from long experience that I should tread carefully whenever Bad Quentin threatened to overtake Q, but sometimes I can't seem to help myself. I guess I take after Dad that way.

Q mumbled something under his breath, and when my new friend came back with a couple of sodas, Q glowered so hard the poor guy didn't dare say another word to me the whole night. But

49

when the house lights came up, Good Q was back, bouncing around and pumping his fist, seeming almost as thrilled as I was to be there.

As great as that show was, the best part of the night was how close I had felt to Q again. Since Mom died, when I was six, it had always been Dad, Q, and me, looking out for one another. But lately Q had been spending all his time with his buddies, and acting distant and scornful on those rare occasions when he actually was home. This new wrinkle—accusing Hence of being some kind of criminal—made me wonder whether Q had completely lost his mind.

But I wasn't about to waste my night stewing over my stupid brother. Upstairs, with my bedroom door locked, I wrote in my journal, describing that day's observations of Hence. Maybe I'd eventually write a poem about him, or maybe I'd make him a character in a short story, but for the moment I was just enjoying gathering the details that might help me figure him out. *A small grave smile*, I wrote, describing the look Hence had given me that afternoon when we'd waved good-bye to each other. *As if he was touched that somebody had thought to be nice to him. As if he wasn't used to having a reason to smile.*

I filled another page before I turned off the light and slipped into bed. I'd stopped writing in my last journal after I'd left it in my sock drawer and Q had picked the lock to my room and read the entries out loud to his friends for laughs. Now that I'd started writing again, I needed a secure hiding space. By the time I fell asleep, I had figured out the perfect spot for my new journal— someplace Quentin would never think to look.

Quentin's grumblings about Hence being a thief or a spy turned out to be based on nothing but jealousy. This became clear one afternoon when I came home from school to find Dad and Hence taking a break from work, jamming on their guitars in the main concert space. "Look who's here," Dad said distractedly around the guitar pick between his teeth as he stopped to tune his trusty lime-green hollow-body Gretsch. My heart twisted in my chest. Dad didn't take his guitar out often anymore, but having Hence around must have reminded him of how much he used to love playing. Hence looked up from his guitar—a beat-up modified Stratocaster—and gave a nod in my direction.

"What's this?" I dumped my backpack from my shoulders. "A jam session? Mind if I watch?"

"Suit yourself, Cupcake." Dad gave his guitar a strum and the two of them dove into "You Really Got Me" by the Kinks. I perched on the edge of the stage for a closer view. Dad was beaming, and Hence seemed utterly absorbed. I took note of how he bit his lower lip in concentration and how nimble his fingers were on the strings.

Dad and Hence knew a lot of the same songs—Creedence, The Beatles, The Small Faces. As he and Hence worked out the live intro to Lou Reed's "Sweet Jane," Quentin came in the door, a basketball tucked under his arm, looking surprised to find us all together and having fun. Caught off guard, I patted the stage beside me, thinking he might want to watch, maybe even join in the way we used to, but from the look he shot me you'd think I'd done him some kind of rank insult. He stormed past us to the elevator and didn't make an appearance for the rest of the night.

That's when light dawned. Q has always complained about Dad being way too wrapped up in The Underground, and it was true: Dad never made it to very many of Q's lacrosse games; he was never all that interested in watching football or baseball on TV with his son, like a lot of fathers do. In turn, Q flat out refused the music lessons Dad wanted him to take, which didn't exactly do wonders for their relationship. So now Q was bugged by seeing Dad treating Hence like the guitar-playing son he'd never had.

I stayed put for the rest of the jam session, until Dad got a phone call and Hence remembered some crates that needed unpacking, but it wasn't as much fun after Q snubbed us. Afterward, I went upstairs and knocked on his door, hoping to explain that I knew how he must feel, and that I missed the way we used to hang out together, but he responded with grunts and monosyllables until I gave up and went to my room to study for the next day's history quiz.

When I got bored with that, I pulled out my journal and added to my scribblings about Hence. I tried to capture the expression on his face as he played a guitar solo with my dad looking on, an openness so different from the guarded look he usually wore. How could I break past that guardedness, I wondered, and what would I find when I got there?

Chelsea

On the slow, creaky elevator ride to the fifth floor, I kept trying to pump Cooper for information. There was so much I didn't know, so much I needed to find out. "Does Hence live above the club? Is he married? Does he have kids?"

Cooper gave me a wary look, as if I were asking for state secrets.

"What kind of name is Hence, anyway? Is it his first name or his last name?"

This, at least, got a response. "It's his whole name."

"So he's only got one name? Like Madonna?"

The elevator creaked to a halt. "Yes," Cooper said in a tired voice, like I'd worn him out. "Exactly like Madonna."

The door opened on a surprisingly cute studio apartment, with lace curtains at the windows and white bookshelves taking up most of the walls. A brass double bed sat below the biggest window, and a small kitchen held a daffodil-yellow table with two chairs. Above a blue love seat hung a painting of a young blond girl in a windswept dress clutching a bouquet of daisies. The room could have used a good dusting, but it was homey compared to the industrial gray and exposed brick of everything else I'd seen so far, and I had the unsettling feeling this little apartment had been waiting just for me.

"Whose room is this?" I asked Cooper.

Again, no answer. Instead, he plunked my backpack unceremoniously on the floor.

I opened the refrigerator—empty—and the cupboards—full of sky-blue dishes and bowls—and turned on the small TV in the corner. Still no cable. I snapped it off. Then I ran over to the bed to peek out the window for another glimpse of the traffic whooshing past and the trendy cafés and high-fashion boutiques beyond the building's black iron fire escape.

"Bathroom's over there." Cooper held up the keys he'd used to let us in. "This one unlocks the apartment door, and this one's for the front entrance. Don't lose them." He tossed me the ring.

Before he could slip away, I planted myself in his path. "Why does Hence hate me?"

Cooper looked pointedly toward the door. "I guess you have everything you need, then." He started to go, but I placed myself in the way again.

"My mother disappeared," I told him, thinking maybe I could win him over by making him pity me a little. "I'm trying to find her. If I have a lot of questions, that's why."

An ironic smile flickered across Cooper's lips. "*If* you have a lot of questions?"

"I don't have much time. I've got to figure out where she is before my dad guesses where *I* am. Maybe Hence won't help me...."

"He's letting you stay here."

"Maybe he won't answer my questions, but that doesn't mean you can't."

Cooper stood there a moment, hands deep in his pockets, light brown bangs in his eyes. He seemed to be considering the point. Without warning, he slipped between me and the door. "He's my friend," he said before he disappeared.

Feeling abandoned, I sat down on the edge of the brass bed, then jumped up again. My encounter with Hence had left me more shaken than I'd realized. Pacing the floor, I replayed our conversation, remembering his smugness about how well he'd known my mother and his certainty that she must be dead. How could he be so sure, unless—the thought chilled me—he'd had something to do with her death? He was so dour, so intense, the kind of person I could imagine committing a crime of passion.

And here I was in the guy's home. To say I hadn't planned things out very well would be a massive understatement. *You don't think things through, Chelsea.* Hadn't my dad said those words a hundred times?

But there had been an investigation, I reminded myself. Wouldn't the cops have looked into the return address on my mom's letters? Apparently Hence had been cleared. Besides, would my mother's murderer really invite me to stay under his roof? It didn't seem likely, and anyway, I couldn't afford to be afraid of Hence. If I left now, how would I ever find out what had happened to my mother?

I dropped to the bed and switched on my phone, a pay-as-you-go number Dad had bought to replace the one I'd accidentally left in the pocket of my jeans and washed. There were three voice messages, all from Dad. By now he knew I was gone. I didn't need to listen to his messages to know what they said. Guilt washed over me, followed swiftly by resentment. If Dad had been honest with me in the first place, I wouldn't have to be here, risking my life to find out what had really happened to my mom. Seriously, shouldn't this have been *his* job?

Well, it was mine now. I turned my phone off again and fished out my laptop, planning to dig up some dirt on Hence. The Underground had a WiFi connection, but it was password protected. I wasn't about to run downstairs and ask Cooper one more question he would refuse to answer. Instead, I jumped up and pressed my forehead to the window, trying to see down to the street below, feeling utterly trapped. Whose room was this, anyway, with its lacy curtains and its bookshelves? Did Hence have a teenage daughter? So many of the books were the same as the ones on my own bedroom shelves. There was a long row of familiar yellow spines—Nancy Drew mysteries. I moved in for a better look and found others I'd read and loved: *National Velvet. Anne Frank: The Diary of a Young Girl. Are You There God? It's Me, Margaret.* On an impulse, I reached for *Half Magic*, another personal favorite, and opened it to the first page. There, in the upper right-hand corner, I found my answer in familiar handwriting: *Catherine Marie Eversole.* My heart began to race.

This had been her room.

My mom had loved to read; I knew that much. She and Dad met in a used bookstore near Harvard Square. He'd ducked into the dusty little store to get out of the rain, but when he saw the pretty girl behind the register he made up random questions so he could get to know her better. Dad had told me the story once after he'd had a couple of glasses of wine with dinner: "I fell in love the minute I laid eyes on her. I couldn't help myself."

"Why? What was it about her?" This was a few years back; I was maybe fourteen or so. Though he constantly compared me unfavorably with Mom, telling me at every turn how studious, talented, and focused she was, Dad hardly ever told me stories about her, and I wanted to make the moment last.

But his eyes got wet with tears. I hadn't seen my father cry before or since, and it scared me. I didn't press the point.

Catherine Marie Eversole. I brought the book to my chest and inhaled its old-book smell. Had she read it in the bed I was sitting on, fallen asleep with it open beside her? Below her name she'd written a date in purple ink. I did the math: My mom had read this very book when she was ten years old. Holding it in my hands, I felt close to her, as though it could somehow lead me to her.

I could imagine it so vividly—a door opening and my mother on the other side. She'd be older, but still beautiful, and she would take one look at me and know who I was. She'd throw her arms around me and cry with joy. I could stay with her at Christmas and during the summer, and she would understand me the way Dad never had. Maybe her sheer wonderfulness would rub off on me and I'd become a star student, a budding writer, irresistible to every passing guy.

I flipped through the pages, looking for more evidence of her, maybe a dog-eared corner or some finger-smeared type. But that was it. I made my way around the room, tugging out a random volume here and there. *Anne of Green Gables. Betsy-Tacy and Tib. All My Pretty Ones. Sonnets from the Portuguese.* Inside each front cover I found her name and a date. The dates got later as I worked my way along the shelves, so I skipped forward in time and pulled out a thick volume with a familiar title—*Wuthering Heights.* I pawed through the pages restlessly and then...bingo! On page 139, in blue ink: *This is the truest book I've ever read.* Goose bumps rose on my arms. I did the same thing—writing little notes to myself in the margins of books I owned, registering delight or frustration when a character did something particularly unbelievable. Talking to myself. Talking to the book.

I leafed through *Wuthering Heights,* more carefully now, and on the last page I found another doodle, a little heart pierced through with an arrow, and below it, in frilly script: *Weird, weird, weird. I think I'm in love with Hence. I think maybe I have been all along?*

I stared at the words, doubting my own eyes. That was my mother's handwriting. But how could she have loved—or even liked—the grouchy man I'd met downstairs? Could there be another person in this whole city with the bizarre name of Hence? Remembering his tone when he'd admitted to knowing my mother—a tone that implied much more than their having just been friends—I flinched and shut the book. But a moment later I was picking through the next novel on the shelf, and the next.

Strange ideas pinged around in my mind like pinballs. I didn't want to think about my mother with Hence, but I couldn't help it. Had she really been in love with him? And had he loved her back? I thought of what he'd said—*If she were still alive, I'd know. I, of all people, would know*—and it seemed possible, even likely. Had she run away from me and my dad to go back to him? The woman my father had always described as practically perfect, the one I could never hope to live up to—surely she couldn't have left her husband and daughter for another man.

I spent the evening paging through book after book, pausing only to run to a nearby grocery store for Cap'n Crunch and milk. I scanned the pages until my eyes itched. Mostly what I found were elaborate doodles—of electric guitars, swans, kittens, beautiful faces with high cheekbones and big dark eyes—funky and graceful enough to be framed and hung up on a wall. Yet another thing she was great at.

When darkness fell, the building grew oddly silent. Shouldn't there be a concert or something? It gave me the creeps to think that Hence was lurking downstairs, but as much as I disliked the idea, sooner or later I'd have to confront him again. He had information I needed. I had to talk him into letting me stay in this apartment until I unlocked all its secrets, or until my dad tracked me down and dragged me home, defeated, to Massachusetts. But no—I had to find my mother. Leaving wasn't an option. I had to figure out a way to make Hence let me stay for as long as it took.

Catherine

It took something horrible to crack open Hence's shell and give me a glimpse into his personality, and I was surprised by what I saw.

The Splendid Weather was playing that night. Dad had been raving about them for weeks, and he'd given me their new album. He even suggested I sneak down to the club and check them out live. It wouldn't be the first time. Though I was underage, and technically my being there was against the law, Dad had this whole stance about drinking laws being shortsighted and oppressive. "Just stay out of the way and don't talk to anyone," he'd say.

Dad believed in me; he was wonderful that way. I didn't have a curfew, like the other girls at school. I'd always been allowed to come and go as I pleased. Dad said his own parents were like jailers, and he swore he'd never be like them; he expected us to have minds of our own. "My daughter has street smarts," he'd say proudly. "I know she'll make good decisions."

Dad's faith in me made me want to prove him right. And I did have enough sense to look out for myself. I was used to customers hitting on me, and I'd always known how to tell them no firmly and politely, just as Dad had taught me. The guy who approached me that night, with his gelled hair, superstrong aftershave, and beer breath, didn't seem all that different from the others I'd dealt with. First he asked me to dance, and I said no. Usually that would be the end of it, but when another song started, he asked again. I could tell he was drunk—they were usually drunk—so I found the dark corner I always retreated to when I wanted to hear the music but wasn't in the mood to deal with customers. But Mr. Won't Take No for an Answer followed me. I looked up, and there he was again, right in my face.

"A pretty girl like you"—he slung an arm around me—"I can't let you get away without a dance."

"Go away." I shrugged his arm off, no longer interested in being polite. "I said no."

"But you're my type, baby. You're the girl I was looking for tonight," he wheedled in that thick-tongued, self-pitying, drunken way that made me sick to my stomach. "Let me buy you a drink."

For a second I thought about telling him my dad owned the bar and I could have all the drinks I wanted, if I drank, which I didn't. But that seemed like too much trouble. I wanted to hear the band, and he was distracting me. "No, thank you," I said. "Would you mind leaving me alone?"

"Come on, baby. I'll make you feel really good." Now he was

right up against me, the front of his cheap polyester shirt brushing my chest. I took a step back and hit the wall. It occurred to me that maybe I should be careful of this guy. I tried to look for Dad or Eddy, the bouncer, who would have beaten the guy to a pulp if he could see what was happening, but he was big enough that I couldn't even see over his shoulder. He had his hands around my waist, his big clumsy thumbs trying to cop a feel, and he was planting a sloppy kiss on my mouth, except he missed and was sliming my face. I may not have been strong, but I was quick, so I could slip out of his grasp and get around him and away. As I bolted I could hear him shouting behind me, "You think you're some kind of princess?"

By that point, I'd stopped caring about the Splendid Weather. I only wanted to get out of there. So I slipped past the EMPLOYEES ONLY sign and into the service elevator, planning to escape to my room. And I almost made it; one second later, I would have been clear. But he was right behind me. His thick arm jammed into the door to keep it from closing, and before I could do anything about it he'd forced his way into the too-small elevator and the doors had clunked shut behind him.

"Where we going?" Now his voice, though still blurry, was ominously quiet. "Someplace private?" The hideous, too-muscular bulk of him was between me and the control panel, and he hit the stop button. "Princess." He said it scornfully this time. "Stuck-up bitch."

He backed me into a corner and bit my neck hard, his beefy hands tearing at my blouse, forcing their way into my jeans. Into my mind popped the self-defense tactics I'd learned in health class—poke both fingers into his eyes, jab a knee into his crotch—but he was so much bigger and more insistent, his knees pressing my legs against the wall, his thick arms pinning mine. He started kissing me, though the word *kiss* doesn't begin to describe it. His tongue kept me from screaming, and his aftershave burned my eyes.

I struggled, trying to wriggle my shoulders hard enough to shake him off me. I was beyond terrified; I'd passed into a place where I was thinking really clearly, foreseeing how upset Dad would be when he learned I'd been raped in his club. Maybe this guy wouldn't stop there but would even *kill* me, and Dad would blame himself forever, but he shouldn't because he tried to keep me safe, he taught me to take care of myself, and after all he couldn't watch me every minute of the day and night.

The man's weight shifted. His hands pulled out of my pants as clumsily as they had shoved their way in. For a second I felt relief, but then I could feel him fumbling with his own pants, and a new and useful idea popped into my mind. As he struggled with his zipper, his fat tongue still prodded mine, so I bit it. Hard.

He roared and fell backward off me. Sweating and red-faced, pants partly undone, he still stood between me and the elevator's control panel. I was struggling to think of what to do next when I noticed a crowbar prying open the elevator door, and the blessed sound of somebody shouting on the other side.

The rapist noticed, too. By the time Hence had forced himself through, the man was cowering in his corner, tugging at his stuck zipper, this time hurrying to get it back up, as if he could hide what he'd been trying to do to me.

Then Hence was in the elevator, swinging the crowbar, his face glowing with electric anger. "Get out of here. If I see you in this club again, I'll bash your head in." His voice and face were so full of rage they scared me. The rapist was gone before Hence could even get the words all the way out.

I knew I should thank Hence, but I didn't have the words. I felt for what was left of my clothes, tugging my now-buttonless blouse closed.

"Here." Hence pulled off his T-shirt, handed it to me, and averted his gaze. We were silent a long time, frozen there in the elevator.

Hence finally broke the silence. "Did he...?" His hands were still hardened into fists.

"No. He would have. You stopped him."

"You should tell your father." His mouth was set in a grim line. "He'd want to know."

"It would only worry him. Please don't say anything. Promise you won't."

But he didn't answer, his gaze fixed on the red emergency-alarm button I'd been unable to reach.

"Hence," I said. "Look at me. Please."

And he complied, his expression still grim.

"You saved me from...I don't even want to say it," I said.

"If he'd hurt you, I'd have killed him." Hence's voice was quiet, with an edge to it I'd never heard before. His dark eyes had iced over, and I realized with a shock that he meant it literally. If things had gone any further, Hence would have willingly killed my assailant.

A chill passed over me.

"You're shivering," he added in a softer tone. It was true: I was trembling with relief and terror, and something new—maybe *awe* would be the right word. Later, when the shock wore off, I would tell myself I must have imagined Hence's rage. Quiet, solemn Hence couldn't be capable of real violence. But at that moment in the elevator, I completely believed he would do anything it took to protect me, and I was grateful.

Hence pressed the button for the fifth floor. In our apartment he waited, arms crossed over his chest, as I climbed into bed. He brought me a glass of water and fiddled with the doorknob so it would lock behind him when he left.

The next morning I got up early, hoping to catch him before he disappeared to wherever he spent his days off, but he was already gone by the time I got downstairs. Now more than ever I wanted to get to know him better. Maybe someday I could find a way to pay him back, to help him the way he'd helped me.

Chelsea

The next morning over breakfast, I rehearsed the speech I would give to convince Hence he should let me stay. But when I took the elevator downstairs, the club seemed empty. There was no sign of Cooper, or any of the other workers I'd seen bustling around the previous day. Before I'd fallen asleep the night before, I'd found something intriguing: the endpaper of *Gone with the Wind* covered with the word *Riptide*—doodled about a thousand different ways. *Riptide* rang a bell; I knew I'd seen it somewhere on The Underground's website, but there was nobody around to give me the WiFi password. So with my laptop case slung over my shoulder, I set out in search of caffeine and Internet access.

The Bowery sidewalks were busier than they'd been when I'd arrived, which made me feel braver about venturing out and exploring. My path zigzagged into tree-lined streets, past funky stores unlike anything we had back home—boutiques selling high-design Japanese clothes in cartoon Harajuku colors; studded leather jackets and diamond collars for lapdogs; and ultrachic graphic tees in stark blacks, whites, and silvers—but I pressed on until I found a coffee shop with a WiFi sticker in the window. The place was crowded with tattooed hipsters. I probably stood out like the ordinary suburban girl I was, but at least I could sit in the corner and gawk while I drank my iced peppermint mocha and soaked up the free Internet.

For starters, I searched for *Riptide*, my earbuds in this time so nobody would glare when the first link I clicked on started playing music—a song I vaguely recognized. With their narrow red ties, black button-down shirts, and skinny jeans, the four guys in the home-page picture looked to be from about my mom's era. Had Riptide been her favorite band? Though that was kind of cool to know, unless she'd run away from my dad and me to become a groupie, it didn't qualify as useful information. Discouraged, I exited the page, and just as the photo began to vanish, I recognized the second face from the left.

Dark eyes, caramel skin, sharp cheekbones.

I clicked and waited, holding my breath, while the page reloaded and Hence's much younger self materialized before me. Here was a deeply uncomfortable fact: Hence had been hot once. The arm around my mother's shoulders, the hand she'd been holding in those slashed photographs I'd found? I now had a pretty good idea who they'd belonged to.

Fun facts about Riptide: They'd had one big hit album and a platinum single (presumably the song playing through my earbuds). After one whirlwind world tour, they'd disbanded. Hence had been lead guitarist and vocalist. And, judging by the website's forum pages, they still had a whole bunch of rabid fans willing to argue the meaning of their lyrics, or debate whether or not a Riptide reunion tour was on the horizon—lots of information, but very little of any use to me until I found one particular conversation on a thread about The Underground:

Hot4Hence:

This morning I scored two tickets to the Starving Artists concert in August and I'll be making the long trek from Atlanta to NYC to see the show. Even more than seeing the Starving Artists, I'm looking forward to just being in The Underground, soaking up the atmosphere, and maybe catching a glimpse of Hence. What are the odds he'll take the stage? What I wouldn't give to see him play again!

TidalWave:

You'll see him all right—introducing the bands and generally running things. But he won't get onstage unless a miracle happens. He hardly ever plays anymore.

Hot4Hence:

Why not? You'd think he'd miss the applause, not to mention the chance to play for an audience.

TidalWave:

That's the central Riptide mystery, isn't it? The band's at the top of their game, they've got a number one hit, and their album goes platinum in the US and Europe, and then, out of the blue, they split up. The other guys go on to have decent solo careers or start up new bands, but Hence, who could have had the most brilliant career of all of them, gives the whole game up. It's always driven me crazy.

LostSince89:

I hear he's a jerk. I know somebody whose sister worked at The Underground and she says he's a nightmare to work for—demands perfection from his entire staff, and goes berserk when the tiniest little thing goes wrong. You'd think he'd be a happy camper, but something or someone has soured him.

punkchik:

Maybe it was that ex-wife of his? By all reports she was a vindictive shrew. Has Hence even had a serious girlfriend since her? Here's my theory: She's spoiled him for all women forever.

Hence had an ex-wife? I did another search and found a picture of her right away, on the Infamous Groupies website: a busty redhead in a sheath of turquoise satin, eyes hidden behind cat-eye sunglasses. The caption read: *Sexy siren Nina Bevilaqua changed boyfriends as often as she changed her hair color. Linked to Richard Linklater of the Hopping Johns, Skeeter Freeman of the Tumbling Dice, and Dane Slater of Pineapple Crush, she retained her swinging single status until she married Riptide frontman Hence, a tempestuous union that landed them both in divorce court. With her groupie days long behind her, Bevilaqua now lives a much quieter life far from the Lower East Side.*

Next I tried searching for an address or phone number for this Nina Bevilaqua, figuring she'd know a thing or two about my mom—her ex-husband's ex-girlfriend—but her number was unlisted, and I couldn't turn up an address. Another dead end. The other person who could maybe help me, the Jackie my mom mentioned in her letter, was an even longer shot, seeing as how I didn't know her last name.

Hopped up on iced mocha and starving for information I could actually use, I packed up my laptop and hurried past tattoo parlors, sex boutiques, and sushi bars, toward the one person who could tell me what I needed to know. Unpleasant as the prospect was, I needed to talk to Hence.

When I got to The Underground, the front door was propped open. Men in tight black T-shirts were noisily unloading amps and other gear from the back of a truck. I squeezed past them into the building. Cooper was so busy positioning guitars on the stage that he didn't even notice as I breezed past.

I found Hence in his office, standing at the desk, arms crossed, glaring down at a ledger like it had done him some kind of personal insult. Maybe it wasn't a good time to bother him, but from what I'd seen so far, I doubted there would ever be a good time. I'd have to be careful not to say anything to tick him off—a tall order, since ticked off seemed to be his more or less permanent state.

I took a deep breath and tried to sound confident. "So," I said. "That's my mother's apartment I'm sleeping in?" I might as well start with the obvious.

"It was her bedroom. She had that whole floor to herself." His tone implied something about my mother—maybe that she was some kind of princess. "Anyway, don't get used to it. You're not moving in." He went back to scowling down at the desk.

"No, of course not." I edged a little closer. A folding chair leaned against the wall nearest me. I grabbed it and plopped myself down. "But I'd like to stay a little longer...just till I figure out where to look for her next." When he didn't respond, I kept going. "We could find her if we worked together. I have some clues, and you have some clues. Maybe if we helped each other—"

He broke in. "Are you delusional? I told you last night that she can't possibly be alive."

"How can you be so sure?" I asked. "Maybe she wanted to get in touch with me but couldn't. Maybe she was afraid...."

"Catherine was never afraid of anything in her life," he said, with a certainty that was starting to get on my nerves. He sank down into the chair behind the desk, still glowering.

A question occurred to me. "You say she got here and you weren't around. After she left my dad and me. Where were you?"

Hence winced. "Trying to get out of England. First there was a railroad strike. I had to hitchhike to Heathrow. Then they kept canceling flights due to bad weather."

"Well, maybe she got here and was mad to find you gone," I said. "Maybe that's why she didn't stay."

"Don't you think I've considered that possibility?" He still sounded scornful, but he did look interested in what I was saying.

I figured if I sucked up a little, I might get somewhere. "I guess you knew her a lot better than I did. Which is why I need your help. Something happened to her. She didn't just vanish. And if you let me stay here awhile, maybe we can figure it out."

"I hired a private detective when she went missing," he said. "He got nowhere. Just like the cops."

"So if they couldn't find her, nobody can? Not even you?"

He rubbed his eyes as if he was thinking I must be something out of a bad dream. But I'd appealed to his pride, and it worked. "I tried everything," he said finally. "I looked for her everywhere she might possibly have gone."

Something in his voice told me I'd found a little opening, and I knew I'd better squeeze through it fast. "Everywhere in the world? Maybe there's someplace you didn't think of. Maybe if we work together we can look for clues."

"Clues?" His tone was scornful. "Like that letter you showed me? It was a whole lot of nothing."

"Wrong," I said. "There's useful information in there. For one thing, she mentions going to visit her friend Jackie. We have to track down this Jackie person and find out if she knows anything about where Mom went after she left town."

72

"Jackie Gray. She was Catherine's friend in high school. I could have told you that."

"And?" I crossed my arms.

"And what? Don't you think I've already tried to get information out of Jackie? She said Catherine never came to see her."

"Because it's the truth?" I asked. "Or because she didn't want *you* to know my mom visited her?"

Hence was silent.

"See, that's why you need me," I said. "This Jackie Gray person might want to be nice to her best friend's poor motherless daughter."

He slammed his ledger shut.

Behind me, someone cleared his throat. It was Cooper, his cheeks flushed and his hair disheveled. "The band's done unloading. They're going out for dinner. They'll be back by six thirty for sound check."

"Okay, okay." Hence waved Cooper off, but he stood there a moment, looking questioningly at me. The vertical line between Hence's eyebrows deepened again. "Go upstairs and make dinner," he ordered. "I'll be up in a half hour."

Cooper hurried off. I still hadn't worked out exactly what his relationship to Hence was. Cooper had said Hence was his friend, but to me it looked more like they were boss and lackey, or cranky father and eager-to-please son. I decided I'd better talk fast, before Hence shooed me off, too. "Of course, I'd be a much better detective if I knew more about my mother's life before she had me." I watched for a reaction, but didn't get one. "You could fill me in."

"Fill you in?"

73

"It sounds like you knew her better than anyone," I said, thinking that might flatter him. And then I really pushed my luck. "You were her boyfriend, right?"

If Hence were like most normal people, he might have enjoyed the opportunity to talk about someone he'd been in love with. But no. He slammed his fist into his desk and stomped off, out the door and down the hallway. Just then, Cooper made a reappearance, still giving me that wary look.

"What's his problem, anyway?" I gestured to the spot where Hence had been standing. "All I did was ask him a simple question."

Cooper said nothing for a long moment. Then, leaning in a bit closer, he whispered, "Hence will help you. Don't make him so angry, and he'll give you what you want."

"What makes you so sure?"

"He wants to find out what happened to your mother as much as you do. Maybe more."

This piqued my interest. "How long till he stops sulking?"

"It depends." Then, after a pause: "I can tell you things."

"Things?"

"About Hence," he said. I waited for him to say more, but he didn't.

"What do you mean by *things?*"

Cooper glanced around the room. "I have to go buy eggs."

I followed him to the supermarket. He was a fast walker, the kind who crosses the street when the DON'T WALK sign is flashing; I had to struggle not to lose him. He didn't say much until we got to the store, and by then I was completely out of breath. He pulled out a shopping cart and started filling it with raw meat—steaks and pork chops and ribs.

"I thought all you needed was eggs?"

Cooper swerved the cart into the next aisle and didn't answer.

"So what do I need to know about Hence? Besides that he likes red meat."

"You should cut him a little slack. He may not be the easiest person in the world, but he's earned the right to be a little moody."

A *little* moody? For a moment or two, I couldn't speak. "Why?"

"He's a genius, for one thing. Riptide was one of the most important bands of the whole post-post-punk New York music scene. No—one of the most important bands in the history of rock music." The passion in his voice startled me.

I struggled for a comeback. "If they were so great, why did they only have one hit?"

"They were visionaries. Commercial radio didn't appreciate them, but that doesn't mean they weren't groundbreakers. They didn't fit into a convenient slot. Besides, Hence left the band right at their peak...."

"So I've heard."

"Who knows what they would have done if they hadn't split up."

I shrugged, then reached for a package of frosted strawberry Pop-Tarts and tucked it under my arm.

"Besides all that, he's a good person." Cooper tossed a couple of boxes of cornflakes into his cart. "He took me in when I had nowhere else to go. I didn't have money or any place to sleep, and

Hence gave me work and a bed." Speech over, he clammed up. Splotches of red blossomed on his cheeks from the effort.

Hence, a good person? I knew I should say something polite to show Cooper I'd heard him and would try to give Hence another chance, but my mind was blank. While I regrouped, I stood on tiptoe, failing to reach a bottle of chocolate syrup on the top shelf. With one swift motion Cooper palmed it and slipped it into his cart.

"You should say thank you," he told me.

So I did.

"Not to me. To Hence. For letting you stay in The Underground."

"I will," I said, not sure I really meant it. "If he ever stops barking and glowering at me."

Cooper gave the shopping cart a shove, and I hurried down the aisle after him.

"Do you know anything about a Jackie Gray?" I asked his back. "She was a friend of my mom's. Hence knows her. He said so."

Cooper slowed his pace. "Sorry," he said over his shoulder.

"Meaning you don't know her? Or you won't tell me about her?"

"I've never even heard her name before." He paused in the international aisle, watching me through the lock of light brown hair that had fallen into his eyes.

Emboldened, I tried another approach. "What about Hence's ex-wife? Nina Bevilaqua."

A storm cloud crossed Cooper's face. "I wouldn't mention her to Hence. Unless you really want to rub him the wrong way."

"Well, sure. But *you* could tell me about her."

"Tell you what?" He started loading up on refried beans and taco shells.

"Where she lives," I said. "Her phone number."

"So you can track her down, and she can complain to Hence? I don't feel like losing my job, thanks. Not to mention my home." He grabbed a jar of salsa from the shelf, scowled absently at it, then replaced it.

"You said you could tell me things," I mumbled in the direction of Cooper's back. Feeling discouraged, I followed him to the checkout aisle and dug in my pockets for cash.

Coop unloaded the cart in silence and we waited for the cashier to ring up the old guy in front of us. Finally he sighed. "Please don't look like that."

"Like what?"

"Like I just kicked your dog."

"But you *did* just kick my dog."

"Nina won't know anything recent about your mother. She and Hence are barely on speaking terms. The only contact they have is once a month, when he writes her an alimony check, and every six months or so when she calls to scream at him. *You selfish bastard.*" Cooper spoke that last bit in a whiny falsetto. "*I wasted the best part of my life on you.* She's so loud I can hear her from across the room."

"Sounds like they deserve each other."

Groceries paid for, we trudged toward The Underground. The wheels in my head spun without getting traction. So Hence's ex-wife couldn't tell me anything, and all I knew about Jackie Gray was her name—a name so common a Google search would probably give me thousands of hits. Hence wouldn't help me and Cooper couldn't tell me anything without losing his job, and God only knew how long I had before my dad guessed my whereabouts and showed up on the doorstep of The Underground. Maybe I should beat him to the punch and just go home and accept whatever punishment was waiting for me. Dad could only ground me until my eighteenth birthday, I figured.

As if he were reading my mind, Cooper interrupted my thoughts. "Your dad called."

I froze, thinking I must not have heard him right. I'd only been gone for a little over a day, and he'd found the missing letter already?

"He sounded really worried about you," Cooper added.

My mouth had trouble forming words. "What? When?"

Cooper's reply seemed to come in slow motion. "This morning. You're lucky I was the one who answered the phone. He said he was calling every possible place you might have thought to go, and he knew it was a long shot, but had we seen you?"

"What did you say?"

"I lied for you." The pink splotches returned to Cooper's cheeks. "I said I'd let him know if someone who fit your description showed up. He seemed to believe me...."

Cooper had covered for me? I threw my arms around him, completely forgetting the grocery bag slung from my wrist and accidentally whacking him with its contents.

"Sorry. I can't believe you lied for me."

"I didn't like doing it," Coop said. "He sounded really worried."

I pushed aside the image of my frantic dad making phone

calls to everyone he could think of. "You won't tell Hence my dad called?"

Coop looked pained. "I probably should, but I won't."

"I don't think he'd mind my dad suffering. He seems to really have it in for my father. I can't imagine why."

"You can't?" We reached the back door of the club. Cooper set his bags down and fumbled in his pocket for the keys. Once we were in, he grabbed a notebook and pen from a countertop, ripped off a square of paper, wrote something on it, folded it in half, and handed it to me.

"What's this?"

"You need the WiFi password, right? So you can do your sleuthing?'

I thanked him and slipped the paper into my pocket. We rode the elevator together and Cooper lugged all his bags off at the second floor. As the elevator made its slow way up to my mother's apppartment, I unfolded the little square of paper and took a look.

The password was CATHERINE.

Catherine

A few days after the Splendid Weather show, I crept up to Hence while he was mopping the floor of the main room. Though he'd basically saved my life, we hadn't spoken of it since that night; in fact, we'd hardly spoken at all, which just seemed wrong. Hence froze when I walked into the room. Without a word, I slipped something into his hand.

"What's this?"

"A guitar pick."

"Right." He leaned his mop against the wall. "I mean, why are you giving it to me?"

I took the pick from his hand and turned it over. "You see that?" The white plastic was embossed with a guitar in shades of black, pink, and purple. "It belonged to Joe Strummer. Dad took me to see The Clash when I was maybe ten. Joe tossed it to me at the end of the show." Was I boasting? I hoped it didn't come across that way.

Hence looked down at it with something like wonder. "Joe Strummer? Are you serious?"

"It's my prized possession," I said. "Or one of them, anyway. I want you to have it."

His smile disappeared. "You don't have to do that, just because..." His voice trailed off, but I knew what he meant. "Anyone would have helped you. It was nothing."

"Anyone wouldn't," I said. "Anyone didn't. It was more than nothing. That guy was about to..." I paused, unnerved by the memory. "I don't think I could have stopped him without your help. But that's not why." I pressed the pick back into his palm and closed his fingers around it. "I knew you'd appreciate it. Maybe more than I do."

Hence looked at me for a moment. He moved his lips like he was about to say something, but he didn't speak. Then he slipped the pick into the pocket at his hip bone. The gesture seemed oddly intimate, as if he'd put a small sliver of me in there. "Thank you," he said. "I'll take good care of it."

A moment later he was back to mopping the floor like the whole exchange hadn't even happened. Even so, for days after, my pulse sped up each time I thought of him carrying my pick, pulling it from his pocket, looking at it with wonder, and maybe thinking of me.

From that moment on, it felt like Hence and I had an understanding. Every day I'd pop into the club at least once to say hi. And while he still wouldn't say much about himself, I could get him to talk about the bands he admired. X, Bad Religion, The Shaggs, The Del-Lords, The Ramones. The list was long and varied. And he would listen to my tales of woe—my angst over calculus, whatever humiliation had happened that day in gym, the ins and outs of coediting the Idlewild Prep literary magazine with a peppy sophomore whose taste favored syrupy verse about butterflies and rainbows. I'm sure my problems seemed bourgeois and boring compared to whatever Hence had known before he arrived on our doorstep, but he never made me feel fluffy or overprivileged. He listened as though he really heard me, and I wanted to do the same for him, if only he would let me.

"Where do you go on your days off?" As secretive as Hence was about his past, I wasn't at all sure how he'd feel about the question, but I was dying to know. "I've seen you heading out with your guitar." We were sitting side by side on the stage, our legs dangling. There wasn't a show that night, so the club was relatively quiet, and Hence had more time than usual to chat.

To my surprise, he answered eagerly. "I've been jamming with some guys I met at Sweet Daddy's Music."

"You're in a band?"

He shook his head. "They're great guys, and decent musicians, but they just play for fun." And though we had the main room all to ourselves, he lowered his voice and leaned in closer, and I caught the green-apple scent of his shampoo and another, fainter scent— like baking bread. "I've been looking for something more serious. In fact, I just lined up my first audition."

"That's fantastic! Who with?"

It turned out to be a band I hadn't heard of, but Hence had done his research. "The Pickup Sticks are feel-good pop—heavy on the synth. They mostly play covers. They're kind of light-weight."

"But trying out will be good practice," I said. "So when the right band does come along..."

"Exactly. I've never auditioned before. Even though the stakes are low, I'm all keyed up. I don't want to look like an idiot."

"You'll be fine," I said. "Just ask ahead of time what they want you to play and what equipment you'll need. The equipment is key; if you don't have your own, they won't take you seriously. When you're warming up, play the kind of stuff they play, because they'll be listening even if it seems like they aren't. Oh, and see if you can get the scoop on who you'll be replacing, and act as much *un*like that guy as possible."

Hence's eyes grew progressively wider as I spoke.

"What? I may not be a musician, but I've been hanging around in their world my whole life." A harebrained idea occurred to me, but I quickly dismissed it. "Too bad I can't come along to the audi-tion and give you feedback afterward."

"You can't?" Was it my imagination, or did he actually sound disappointed?

"I mean, I could. I'd love to. But I've heard stories...a guy brings his girlfriend along and she makes suggestions, or talks a lot, and it drives the band crazy." Had I just implied I wanted to be Hence's girlfriend? I rambled on faster to distract him from my slip. "Even if she sits in the corner and says nothing, most bands assume there's something wrong with a guy who brings a girl to an audition. Come to think of it, the whole thing's kind of sexist."

Hence leaned back on his elbows and looked up at the ceiling. "But since I don't really want the job..." he said, letting the thought hang in the air above our heads.

I waited for the rest of it.

"I want the music part of the audition to go well," he continued. "I'd be embarrassed if it didn't. But I don't care if they like me as a person."

I leaned back on my own elbows, and we both scrutinized the ceiling's track lighting and pockmarks.

"I want you to come with me," he concluded. It was exactly what I'd been hoping he'd say. He scooched a hair closer, his arm brushing mine, but only for a second. "That is, if you don't mind."

If I didn't *mind?*

Over the next few days, Hence and I talked strategy. He would introduce me to the band as his girlfriend—his idea, not mine. I wouldn't say much, but I'd watch closely and take notes. I'd be able to help him prep for bigger auditions in the future.

I coached Hence on what to wear—a black-and-white checkerboard T-shirt we picked out together at Unique Clothing Warehouse and regulation skinny black jeans. That Thursday, I put on a slinky leopard-skin dress I'd stumbled on at Vintage Threads. I did my hair up in a high ponytail, and even put on lipstick. Though I normally wasn't all that into fashion, I couldn't resist the chance to dress up for Hence, if only to see what his reaction would be.

By the look on his face when I met him in front of The Underground, I could tell he hadn't expected me to dress the part of a rocker's girlfriend. "You look…" He seemed to struggle for the right word. "Convincing." The expression in his eyes was as appreciative as I could have hoped.

"I'll take that as a compliment," I said, trying to sound flippant. "I'd offer to help you carry your equipment, but in these heels it will be all I can do to stay upright."

There wasn't time to bask in the moment; we had to get to Chelsea. We caught the A train at Canal Street and found two side-by-side seats, but he seemed too preoccupied to talk, so we fell silent. We arrived early, just as we'd planned, with time for Hence to set up. The guitarist before him—a big-haired glam-metal guy who apparently hadn't gotten the memo about dressing the part—was finishing up his audition as we arrived.

When Hence introduced me to the guys in The Pickup Sticks, saying, "She's going to sit in—I hope that's not a problem," the bassist and the drummer rolled their eyes at each other. But any annoyance I felt was wiped away by the thrill I got from watching Hence play. The drummer had pulled up a folding chair for me to sit on, and I perched as far from the stage as I could get in that shoebox of a room, trying to look blasé and probably failing spectacularly.

Hence had taken my advice and asked what songs the band wanted him to play at the audition, and he'd practiced them for hours; all week I'd been able to pick out bits of "Come On Eileen" and "Blister in the Sun" wafting from behind the basement door. Now he played them like a pro, and it was easy to see he could have outplayed the others if he let himself. Instead, he was focused on blending in, the way I'd suggested . . . but not so focused that he didn't look over at me from time to time, as if making sure I was still there.

After the audition, we walked to a diner up the street. Hence was oddly quiet, considering he'd just had such a great audition. "You were awesome," I said once we'd placed our orders. "I wouldn't be surprised if they called you back, even if you did bring your 'girlfriend.'" I surrounded the word with air quotes.

"If I get called back, it will be because the keyboard player wants to get your phone number." Hence had been tapping his fingers rhythmically against the Formica tabletop, as if he couldn't stop making music once he'd started. Now he slapped both palms down on the table and looked at me with an expression I couldn't quite read. There was a coldness in his dark eyes that took me by surprise.

"Ha," I said breezily, though I, too, had caught the ultraskinny keyboard player watching me more than once.

"I'm serious," Hence said, his voice very still. "I didn't like how he was looking at you."

This was a side of Hence I'd never seen before. Was he jealous? A thrill ran through me—equal parts excitement and fear, though of what, I couldn't say. "He's not my type at all," I said.

Hence's expression softened, but I still detected doubt in his eyes. How had I hurt him? That was the last thing I'd intended to do.

"I wouldn't go out with him on a bet," I continued. *He's not you*, I thought, the words echoing in my head so loudly that for a moment I worried I'd actually said them aloud. As soon as they took shape I realized how true they were. I didn't want anyone but Hence.

"If The Pickup Sticks call, it won't have anything to do with me." I chose my words with care. "It'll be because you rocked the audition."

This seemed to do the trick. Hence's jaw muscles relaxed. "You really think so?"

I smiled, resisting the urge to grab his hands and hold on tight. "I totally do."

The Pickup Sticks did call Hence back, and he told them he wasn't interested. "They couldn't believe their ears," he reported. "They couldn't imagine me not jumping at the offer."

"There will be other bands," I told him. "Better ones."

Hence nodded, and his smile made my heart do a little flip in my chest. In the few days since the audition, I hadn't been able to stop thinking about what had passed between us, obsessing over what would—or wouldn't—happen next. If Hence liked me enough to be jealous when another guy looked at me, why didn't he just ask me out? But I was his boss's daughter. Maybe he thought that made me off-limits?

I'd worked out a little speech, and now I took a deep breath and tried to sound breezy. "Do you have anything lined up for this coming Thursday?" I happened to know that was his next day off. "I know you like to get together with your friends from the guitar store and jam, but I was thinking maybe we could go to the Angelika for cappuccino and a movie. Or check out the Strand bookstore."

The reluctance on Hence's face made me wish I hadn't asked.

"I'm saving up for a better guitar," he said. "I've got my eye on a starburst Telecaster I saw at Sweet Daddy's."

Of course: Money was an issue for Hence. Why hadn't I thought of that? I could offer to pay for us both, but would that be rubbing his lack of money in his face? "It doesn't cost anything to window-shop," I ventured.

But still he looked doubtful, so I tried another tack. "Is there something you've always wanted to do in the city but haven't had a chance?"

To my relief, Hence snapped to attention. He told me that ever since he'd started reading about the seventies punk scene he'd imagined himself living someday in the Hotel Chelsea. "You know—where all those musicians and writers lived. Patti Smith. Leonard Cohen. Iggy Pop..."

"Where Sid Vicious stabbed his girlfriend?" I asked. "We could pay it a visit. I've never been inside, but I've passed it. It's not that far from here."

"Seriously?"

So that Thursday we made a trek uptown. Like me, Hence was a fast walker, and I loved keeping pace with him, the brisk wind blowing our hair back as we walked. When we reached the Chelsea, we stood across the street and stared at the hulking red-

88

brick exterior, the ornate black balconies, and the familiar hotel sign. Nobody went in or came out for a long time.

"Look." I pointed at Chelsea Guitars, a narrow storefront tucked into the hotel's ground floor. "We'll have to check it out." I turned my attention to El Quijote, the funky-looking restaurant beside it. "And maybe that place, too."

Hence nodded. "People still stay at the Chelsea?"

Just then, a couple stepped out through the hotel's glass doors, he in a black trench coat and with slicked-back hair, she in red heels and a black miniskirt. We watched them disappear into the sidewalk crowd.

"Let's get closer." I grabbed his arm. Across the street, we could read the bronze plaques dedicated in memory of Dylan Thomas, Thomas Wolfe, and Arthur Miller.

"I wish I had a camera," Hence said, still sounding awed.

I released him. "We're going in, right?"

"They'll let us in?"

"It's a hotel. People come and go all the time. Just act like you know where you're going, and they'll think we're staying here."

Hence looked doubtful.

"The worst they can do is kick us out."

The hotel lobby was dark and grungy, not at all glamorous, but its walls were hung with colorful paintings. We hurried past the front desk, where the burly clerk was absorbed in a phone conversation and seemed not to notice us at all.

"Over here." I slipped around a corner, out of sight of the few hotel guests in the lobby, and Hence followed. "Shhh. Close your eyes."

"What are we doing?"

"Take a deep breath."

He complied.

"We're breathing in the air all those poets and musicians exhaled," I told him. "We're taking them into us... and adding our breath to theirs."

There in the dim corridor, I could swear an electrical current charged the air between us. I was *almost* sure he felt that charge, too. But almost wasn't enough. We stood there a moment, just breathing, until someone behind us cleared his throat. We opened our eyes and an older man in a worn tweed suit slipped around us to get down the hall, breaking the spell.

Chelsea

In the privacy of my mother's room, I toasted some Pop-Tarts and settled down in front of my computer. As it turned out, a search for *Jackie Gray* turned up a mere thirty-two thousand hits. I scrolled through the list, looking for clues to which one was my mom's Jackie—a New York address, maybe? That narrowed it down to about five hundred. It was all so frustrating. Hence could have told me which one was my mom's friend, but I wasn't ready to face him again just yet. Coward that I was, I munched my Pop-Tarts and scrutinized the faces of Jackie Gray the biology professor, Jackie Gray the screenplay writer, and Jackie Gray the financial strategist, willing them to come to life and give up their secrets.

The music started around eight. I'd given up on the Internet and had taken down a stack of my mother's books to browse through when the bass started thumping from downstairs. So far I hadn't found much of anything new—just some doodles of men with curlicue mustaches and women with elaborate beehives.

Close to giving up hope, I paged listlessly through another book, then another, and finally found something on the first page of Edna St. Vincent Millay's collected sonnets: my mom's name doodled many different ways—curly script, balloon letters, zigzag letters. *Catherine Eversole* for a quarter page, and then, over and over, *Catherine Hence*, filling the rest of the flyleaf. So my mother had daydreamed about marrying him. It wasn't terribly useful information, but it was one more tiny piece of evidence that Catherine Eversole had once existed, had been about my age, and had lived in this bright little apartment with her lace curtains and books. Had she been kept awake by the endless pounding bass guitar, and by drums I hadn't noticed before but that seemed to have gotten louder? Had she been tempted to dress in her best clothes, make herself up to look older, and slip downstairs to blend in with the crowd, just to see what all the fuss was about?

Because, come to think of it, I was tempted.

Not that I had brought much in the way of clothes. I did have my best pair of jeans with me, a pair of boots, a purple T-shirt, and some dangly earrings. I had lip balm, and some smoky eyeshadow that might make me look a bit older. I dressed slowly, unsure if I was really going to go through with the plan blossoming in my mind. I bent over at the waist and brushed my hair upside down so it would look fuller. I took a deep breath and stepped out into the hall, locking the apartment door behind me.

The elevator's creaking was, luckily enough, drowned out by

music that grew louder as I drew closer. When the door slid open into the gray hall at the rear of the building, I looked both ways, then hurried down the hallway and into the main room, which was almost full and buzzing with conversation. The blue neon cast its otherworldly spell on the room, and bartenders in black vests waited on the gathering crowd.

An audience pressed in close to the stage. On the room's fringes, people were gathered around high tables. I found a spot in a dark corner off toward the side and watched the band, a trio of skinny dudes in matching snakeskin boots. The music was jittery, full of jagged edges—not my usual taste, but catchy. From the edge of the room I could watch the bassist joke around with the rhythm guitarist, and take in every emotion on the lead singer's face; I could even catch his eye from time to time. Did my mother get to do this when she was my age? And how had she not missed living over The Underground after she married my dad and moved to suburbia?

Once the song ended, I thought to check the room for Hence. When I didn't see him, I slipped closer to the stage. Just then, Cooper passed by carrying a bin of empty bottles and glasses. He looked shocked to see me there and shouted something in my direction. I couldn't hear what he was saying, so he shouted it louder: "You're not twenty-one."

"Neither are you," I yelled, fairly certain it was true.

He shook his head and started to go. I tapped his shoulder before he got away.

"Don't tell," I begged, mouthing the words exaggeratedly so he wouldn't miss them. "Please?"

He frowned and stalked off. Still, I didn't think he would rat me out to Hence, so I stayed where I was, wishing I was daring enough to slip up to the bar and order a soda. Instead, I retreated to my shadowy place on the sidelines. After a while, the spotlight flashed on to bathe the stage in red light. The crowd started milling around, jockeying for a position near the band. As tempted as I was to squeeze through the crowd for a better view, I stayed put.

Eventually, a new band took the stage. "Hey, everybody. We're the Charmed Particles," a man's voice shouted. Around me, the crowd went berserk. Yellow and white lights flooded the stage, and there, front and center, stood a guy with longish hair and a triangle-shaped soul patch that made his grin seem devilish. Soul Patch grabbed the mike and started to sing, stalking the stage in his tight black jeans and motorcycle boots. A thrill ran through my body, from my feet right to the roots of my hair.

It wasn't just that he was gorgeous, though he was. The rest of the band was gorgeous, too, in a super-skinny, cooler-than-thou kind of way. The guitarist, a tall man whose white-blond Afro contrasted with his dark skin, pogoed up and down as he played; the shirtless drummer's long, straight hair flew in and out of his high-cheekboned face. A sleek woman with flame-red hair stalked the stage in a crushed-velvet catsuit, playing her bass guitar almost as an afterthought. I couldn't help envying her—so confident and in charge, holding a whole room full of people at attention just by doing something she obviously loved.

"What are you doing down here?" Hence growled in my ear, picking that moment to find and humiliate me. He grabbed me by the arm and yanked me out of the room, the crowd parting to let us through, and pulled me down the long hall toward the elevator.

"Stop it!" I struggled to free my arm. "I can walk on my own."

"What do you think you're doing? This isn't some teen hangout."

"I know that."

"Do you know what kind of trouble a girl like you could get into in a nightclub?" He was screaming at me now. "For one thing, you can attract the wrong kind of attention. You could get . . ." His voice trailed off.

"I could get what?"

No answer. He glowered down at me.

"You don't need to worry. I can take care of myself."

Hence's voice got quieter, but if anything, he sounded even angrier. "It's not you I'm worried about. I could get busted for having an underage *child* in my club. Fined. Or even shut down."

"I wasn't planning to drink. I was just watching the show." I started to explain that the noise had kept me awake and that I'd been curious, but he cut me off with a wave of his hand.

"No excuses. I'm letting you stay in my house, and if you give me any reason—the tiniest reason—to regret it, I'll kick you out faster than you can say 'boo.'" His eyes narrowed and his glare froze my tongue.

What choice did I have? I got into the elevator. Up in my mother's apartment, I changed into my pajamas and lay in bed seething. If only I could at least make out the words and music— but, like a cruel taunt, all I could hear was that thumping bassline.

Catherine

Just when it felt like I was on the verge of really getting to know Hence, fate touched down like a tornado to spin me off track. Early the next week, I was making chicken salad, hacking the last of the white meat from the previous night's bird, when Dad came into the kitchen and kissed me on the cheek. "Have I told you lately how proud I am of you?"

"Once or twice."

"Your creative writing teacher couldn't stop raving about you." He'd gone to parent-teacher conferences the night before. "She says you're one of the most promising writers she's ever taught. She wants to submit one of your poems to a real literary magazine. And here I've got you slaving over the stove when you should be off at a writer's colony, working on your magnum opus."

"Somebody's got to make dinner." Dad's cooking repertoire

consisted of instant mac and cheese and frozen peas. As for Q, he lived on Big Macs, potato chips, and Gatorade. The two of them would have been perfectly happy eating takeout every night, but I couldn't go without home-cooked food very long without starting to feel sad and motherless. Which of course I was, but that didn't mean I had to eat pork fried rice every single night of the week.

"You won't forget your old man when you go off to Harvard, will you?"

"I can't go off to Harvard. Who would feed you?"

"Peking Road misses me. I'll go back to being their best customer." Dad picked a chunk of chicken out of the bowl with his fingers. I pretended to wave my chef's knife at him, and he pretended to cower in fear. "You win! I'll wait till dinner."

"You'd better."

Dad got a glass out of the cupboard and poured himself some cabernet, his dinnertime ritual. "Of course you'll go to Harvard. You'll make all sorts of snooty friends, and be ashamed of your lowbrow old man."

"*You* went to Harvard," I reminded him, as if he needed reminding.

"And got gentleman's Cs. I wasted my college years screwing around." That's my dad: Even when I was a little kid, he talked to me like I was a grown-up, swearing, making embarrassing revelations about his past, and generally saying whatever popped into his head.

"Mom went to Harvard," I said, and immediately wished I hadn't. Though eleven years had passed since we lost her, the

97

mention of her could still send Dad into his sad and wistful mode, and that night was no exception.

"Your mother kicked Harvard's ass," he said after a pause. "She had this amazing swagger. And determination: That woman knew her own mind. She wanted to write for *Rolling Stone*, and she never let anything get in her way. God knows what she saw in a dilettante like me. I had no idea what I wanted out of life." I'd heard this story before, but it never got old for Dad. "I wasted all my time at college partying with musicians, painters, writers, wishing I had some kind of talent. Did I ever tell you I played drums in a punk band for a while?"

"The Bloody Crusades," I offered, filling in the blanks.

Dad smiled absently. "I even had my retro-beatnik phase— smoked clove cigarettes and wore a beret, if you can picture that."

I smiled, washing the mess off my hands.

"All I ever wanted was to be some kind of great artist, but all I turned out good at was business, like my old fart of a father, and . . . well, you know the rest. Look at me now."

"Yeah, you're a real failure, Dad." I rolled my eyes. "I don't know how you live with yourself."

He kissed me on the cheek. "I'm relieved you got your mother's brains." Then he grabbed the rolled-up newspaper from the kitchen table and bonked me on the head with it. "I know what we should do: Let's take a family vacation. You deserve a break, and come to think of it, so do I."

So, less than a week later, we were headed for Mykonos, Greece. Sebastian Clegg, one of Dad's rock-star friends, had a

98

villa there, and Dad pulled some strings. "But I'll miss school," I said when he showed me the plane tickets.

"You'll make it up."

"But what about Q? Can he afford to skip a whole week of classes?"

"Your brother can fend for himself. He'll charm his professors into giving him extensions." Dad grinned. "You and Q will learn more about the world from going places than from sitting in some stuffy classroom, daughter of mine. So no more worrying. Just sit back and enjoy."

For about a minute and a half, I was thrilled. I'd always loved our family trips. And Dad had taken us lots of places, but never to Greece. But then I thought about Hence. Did I really want to leave him behind, even for just ten days? Our time together wandering through Chelsea had been so much fun. After the Hotel Chelsea I'd even lured him into a few record stores, and while we browsed through used albums, he told me about the first time he'd picked up a guitar at a friend's house, how right it had felt in his hands, and how he'd hated to give it back.

"As soon as I could, I got one of my own," he told me. "A supercheap acoustic, but I loved that thing. I taught myself by ear." He talked about going to the public library to read and reread the one book they'd had on the punk-rock scene, and how he'd hatched his plan to come to New York. "New York or London, but London seemed out of reach, so here I am." He had finally started talking about his past, and I listened eagerly, hoping he would reveal more about himself, but all I could piece together from his stories was that he hadn't had a lot of money, and that music had meant more to him than school, or his friends, or even his family.

Now, as Dad showed off our tickets to Greece, a crazy thought popped into my head. Why not ask Dad if we could bring Hence along with us? It would only be one more plane ticket, and Sebastian Clegg's villa must have at least one extra bedroom. Hence had probably never been to Europe. Was it fair that I was getting to go there again, and he'd be stuck holding down the fort at The Underground?

As I looked into Dad's glowing face, I realized how irrational I was being. The tickets were already bought. And, anyway, as nice as Dad was to his employees, he'd never bring one along on a family vacation.

"What's wrong, Cupcake? Aren't you excited?" Dad took a closer look at me. "I thought you loved our family adventures."

I shut the dishwasher and punched its buttons, not knowing what to say.

"Are you thinking of Mom?" he asked, in a quieter voice. "She'd want you to be happy. You know that, don't you?"

After that I felt bad, because I hadn't been thinking of Mom at all. I threw my arms around Dad's shoulders and hid my face in his shirt. A wave of sadness swept through me, as though I were absorbing it from him. My father needed this vacation. I would go to keep him company and try to have the best time possible, for his sake.

Dad kissed my forehead. Before I could stop him, he started rummaging in his wallet. "You'll need clothes, right? A bathing suit? Or maybe a sundress? Don't say no—what's money for if I can't treat my only daughter to something nice once in a while?"

As hard as I protested, he kept insisting, until, feeling even guiltier, I pocketed his money.

Mykonos was every bit as gorgeous as I'd imagined, its houses and hotels blindingly white against the cloudless sky; by day I stretched out and read beside the deep blue Aegean or wandered through the winding streets, popping into boutique after boutique to shop for souvenirs. Dad, Q, and I went out every night to hear live music in little seaside clubs, and for two glorious days, we chartered a sailboat and took an overnight trip to Vernon Hale's villa on Naxos. Vernon was one of Dad's oldest friends and one of my musical heroes; I had every album he'd ever recorded. He and his band jammed until three AM under a delicate crescent moon. His wife, Riki, made me virgin piña coladas, and all her party guests danced barefoot on the patio under Japanese paper lanterns. I was blissfully happy until I thought of Hence, a whole ocean away, mopping the floor and hauling crates while I was having the time of my life.

The very next day, I stopped at a kiosk, bought myself a phone card, and called The Underground from a pay phone beside a seaside taverna. When Hence picked up the phone, the sound of his voice made me sad and happy all at once.

"It's Catherine." Should I pretend I was checking up on the club? No, that would be ridiculous. Why hadn't I planned this better?

Finally, I thought of something to say: "What's new?" It wasn't exactly snappy repartee, but it was better than nothing.

"You won't believe this," Hence said, excitement in his voice, almost like he'd been waiting for me to call, storing up some important piece of information. "I have an audition lined up with Riptide. You know who they are, right?"

"Of course I do." Riptide had played The Underground a few months earlier—*A white-hot band on the verge of a breakthrough,* Dad had called them. "They're hiring a guitarist?"

"Bill Dierks quit. Out of the blue. He had a nervous breakdown, or at least that's what people are saying. The crazy thing is, they were about to get signed. So they're desperate for a front man."

"Wow." There had been a few other auditions since the one with The Pickup Sticks, but so far nothing had clicked. "Riptide. They're brilliant."

"I'm worried they'll think I'm too inexperienced."

"What does it matter, if you can play?"

"They need a lead singer, too. Dierks was their vocalist. Stan—the drummer—says none of the rest of them has a strong enough voice to carry the lead."

"You can sing," I told him. "I've heard you. And you've got range."

"You really think so?"

"I know so."

There was a long, awkward pause.

"I had this feeling I should call you today," I added.

He laughed. "I'm glad you did."

Before long we said our good-byes. In Hence's presence, the silences that sometimes fell between us never felt uncomfortable, but over the phone was another story. The minute I hung up, I wished I hadn't, but calling back would have been even weirder than having phoned in the first place, so I made myself trudge uphill to Vernon's villa. Four and a half days until our flight home. How would I stand the wait?

The trip home from Greece felt like it took a million years. When we finally pulled up beside the club, I burst out of the car and let myself in the front door. Hence was exactly where we'd left him, strumming his guitar at the edge of the stage and scribbling lyrics in a nearby notebook. He jumped to his feet as if I'd caught him slacking off. Dad was still outside, trying to find a better parking spot for the Jeep, but Q was right behind me, so I didn't dare greet Hence the way I wanted to, by throwing my arms around him.

Q dumped his duffel bag at Hence's feet. "This goes upstairs," he said, then turned away, headed for the elevator up to our apartment.

Hence's eyes met mine, and instead of the happiness I expected to see in them, I saw anger. Before I could do or say anything, Hence bent to hoist my brother's duffel and reach for my suitcase.

"I'll carry mine," I said, feeling my cheeks grow hot. This wasn't how I'd imagined our reunion. We lugged the bags to the elevator and waited for it to return to the first floor. "I'm sorry my brother's such a jerk."

"It's not your fault," Hence said, not meeting my eyes. We

rode up to the second floor, and I held the door while he deposited Q's dusty duffel bag in the vestibule. Only after the door slid shut again did he venture a look at me, and I saw that his expression had softened.

"So, what happened with the audition?" It had been killing me, not knowing how things had gone with Riptide. Though I'd known there was no way Hence would contact me at Sebastian's villa, every time the phone rang I jumped, hoping it might be him, calling with good news.

He allowed himself a small smile. "I'm in," he said. "We had our first rehearsal—"

But I cut off his air supply with an enormous hug of congratulations. "I knew it! I knew they'd pick you!" Hence was stiff at first. We'd never hugged before, and I'm sure he wasn't expecting it. But then he hugged me back, and electricity crackled between us again. For once, the stupid elevator moved too quickly, lurching to a halt at my floor, and Hence released me.

Despite my protests, he lugged my suitcase to my room. I fumbled with the keys. "I want to hear all about how it went, and what the band is like," I said as soon as we were through the door.

"They just signed a contract with Plasma Records. I mean *we* did. We're going to be recording." He said that last part quietly, as if he hardly dared believe his good luck.

"Don't forget me when you're famous, okay?" I let myself give his arm a playful squeeze.

"Like I could forget you," he said, looking into my eyes, then away. We stood awhile in the middle of my bedroom, not saying anything. "I'd better get downstairs," he finally said.

"We'll talk soon, okay?" I gave a casual little wave, trying to look like my heart wasn't pounding a thousand times a second. As soon as he shut the door behind him, I dropped down to my bed and stared up at the ceiling. Had Hence really said *Like I could forget you?* Could I have imagined those words? And what did they mean, exactly? That hug, though. I knew that part had really happened. The scent of him—green-apple shampoo and a faint whiff of baking bread—clung to me, and I could still feel the hug itself, warm and lingering, like neither of us wanted it to end.

Chelsea

~∞~

Despite the noise and my fury at Hence, I managed to fall asleep, but my dreams were anything but restful. I tossed and turned in the brass bed that used to be my mother's, until a sound startled me awake—the scratch of branches against the window. Eyes shut, I pulled the covers tighter around me, trying to get back to sleep, until I remembered: There were no branches outside my mother's window.

I bolted upright, surprised to find the room bright with moonlight—or maybe light from the street. I turned to the window to find out where the scratching sound was coming from. Even as I moved I knew I didn't really want to know, that the sound could only mean bad news. What I saw at the window chilled me all the way through. White twigs. No, not twigs at all. Fingers—long and thin, with stubby fingernails like mine, clawing at the window. Just then a face pressed itself to the glass, so close that its features were distorted and its breath began to form a cloud.

I started, the sound of my own screaming filling my head. I wanted to leap out of bed and run from the room, but I was frozen in place, too shocked to move, even as the fingers clawed at the pane, trying to part the glass like water.

This has to be a dream, I told myself. *It can't be real.* But knowing that didn't make me feel any less petrified. She wanted something—the girl at the window. Somehow I knew it was a she. The face drew back so that I could see her large desperate eyes, her untamed hair, and her moving lips, enunciating three syllables I couldn't make out at first. But she repeated them over and over until I got it and said them along with her: *Let. Me. In.*

Just then, I heard the elevator outside the door creaking to a stop. A second later, the apartment door opened, and a man strode into the room—a half-familiar, black-haired, glowering man jangling a key ring. I had that densely foggy confusion that comes with being woken up in the middle of a dream, and for a moment I couldn't remember his name. I turned back to the window—only a second or two had passed since I'd looked away—and the face was gone.

"What's going on up here?" the man demanded. "You woke me out of a sound sleep. Didn't I tell you I'd kick you out if you caused me any more trouble?"

Hence. Slowly the night before came back to me. I nodded.

"Why were you screaming?"

"I had a dream," I said. "A nightmare. I couldn't help it."

He exhaled as though he was completely exasperated. "A

nightmare? I'm an idiot for letting you stay here. Do you always scream in your sleep?"

"I've never done it before," I said. "There was a face outside the window."

"What do you mean, a face?"

I struggled for words to convey what I had seen. "A girl. In my dream. With sad eyes and long hair."

Hence said nothing, but his eyes widened.

"She scratched at the window and told me to let her in. It felt so real." Come to think of it, I didn't remember waking up, exactly. Could I still be dreaming? Or had it not been a dream at all? I gestured at the window. "Could somebody have climbed the fire escape?"

To my surprise and amazement, Hence took a single long stride—a leap, really—and, leaning over me, tore the window open in one swift motion. He threw a leg over the sill, climbed outside, and started down the fire escape, its metal groaning under his weight. Still shaky, I drew my legs to my chest and hugged them. Minutes passed. A cool wind blew in through the open window; the temperature must have dropped outside. I wrapped the blanket around myself and got out of bed to pace awhile, wondering where on earth Hence had gone and if he was coming back. I was fairly certain I wasn't dreaming anymore. No, I was positive. This was real. And the girl scratching at my window...could she have been real, too? Hence must think so, or else why would he be running around barefoot on the street below?

Just as I'd started to consider closing the window, the fire escape creaked and I heard him climbing back up. He clambered over the sill, his hair crazy and his eyes wide.

"What was that all about?" I asked, but he didn't answer. He stood there a moment, looking at me as though I were a figment of his imagination. "Did you find her?"

His face crumpled. For a moment, he looked like he was about to cry. "I thought she'd come home." His voice was softer than I'd ever heard it, wondering and sad. "I thought maybe..."

He didn't have to say any more. I knew right away who he meant.

"That couldn't have been my mother," I told him. "I told you, it was a girl... she was around my age."

He didn't answer, but I could read what he was thinking on his face.

"I don't believe in ghosts." Just saying the words freaked me out. "You don't—do you?" He didn't seem like someone who believed in much of anything.

He stood there awhile longer, staring wild-eyed at the window, making no move to shut it, as though he hoped my mother's ghost would fly in.

"She's not dead," I told him. "I know she isn't." I closed the window myself, snapping the lock shut. "That couldn't have been her. It was just a dream."

We stared at each other for a long moment.

"If she comes back, scream your lungs out," he said. He left, locking the apartment door behind him.

After that, I tried getting into bed, but my pulse was pounding, and I knew there was no way I could sleep. *If only I had someone to talk to*, I thought. According to the clock radio, it was 3:12. It was going to be a long night. When I shut my eyes, I could still see that frantic face, white as the moon and weirdly familiar, pressing up against the glass.

Maybe I would never sleep again. Hence's parting words stuck with me: What if the girl came back? What if Hence was right and she hadn't been a figment of my imagination? What I'd said was true: I didn't believe in ghosts. Still, the girl's fingers clawing at the glass had seemed every bit as real as the hand I now held up to my face.

Finally, I switched on the bedside light. Maybe a book would settle my nerves. I would find a boring one to help me fall asleep. I assessed the collection, looking among the ones I hadn't gotten to yet. On the bottom shelf, near the corner of the room, I noticed a volume I hadn't seen before. Twice as thick as any of the others, it bore an unlikely title: *A Compendium of Anatomy and Physiology*. All of the other books in the room were novels. Why had my mom kept such a thick, dull-looking textbook? I knelt on the floor for a closer look. It was heavy in my hands, old-looking and -smelling.

I sat on the edge of the bed, opened the cover, and almost shrieked again. What I held in my hand was no ordinary book. Someone had hollowed out the pages, making it into a secret hiding place. Inside was a second, smaller book, its cream cover peppered with little pink flowers. A journal.

Fingers trembling, I dug it out. I had to work to pry it loose; the journal fit snugly into its carved-out hole, like she'd measured the size of the space she'd need before cutting. I opened the cover, and what I found was better than anything I could have hoped for—page after page of journal entries written in my mother's loopy, extravagant handwriting. I riffled through, then pressed the open book to my chest, hugging it as if it were her. Once I'd blinked back my tears of happiness, I opened to the first page and saw the date. She would have been seventeen when she began the journal—the same age I was now.

Book in hand, I slipped under the covers. Reading my mother's words—hearing her voice—was exciting but painful. She wrote about school, about her dad and her brother, Quentin, about her friend Jackie and a trip she'd taken to Greece, but most of all she wrote about Hence—pages and pages about how intriguing he was and how much she hoped he liked her back. As I read, I was torn between feelings of love for her (right away, she seemed like somebody I would *like*) and sadness that I never really got to know her. I even felt jealous of her, growing up in a nightclub, getting to watch all the shows and hang around with famous and soon-to-be-famous rockers. Plus, she seemed every bit as smart, focused, and talented as my dad had always said she was. Mixed in with her journal entries were poems she had written, and more of her elaborate doodles—faces, birds, a tiara, flowers; all sorts of ordinary things made beautiful by her pen.

When my eyes got heavy, I closed the pink-and-cream cover and tucked the book within a book into its place on the shelf, but my mind still buzzed with questions. Had my mother ever wanted my father anywhere near as much as she wanted Hence? Had her life with Dad and me been a disappointment? Was that why she ran away? Somewhere in the journal there must be a clue to where she had gone, and why, and I planned to keep reading until I found it.

Catherine

A few days later, to my utter surprise, Hence turned up at Idlewild Prep just as school was letting out. I was walking out the door with Jackie when I caught sight of him waiting at the front gate, looking windblown and determined. For a moment I thought he might offer to carry my books home from school, the way boys did in old movies, but instead he just stood there, looking first at me, then at Jackie, then at me again, a question mark in his dark eyes.

"It's okay," Jackie said finally. "I need to hurry home, anyway. I promised my mom I would let her take me shopping this afternoon." She shot me a funny look and raced off across the street.

So I stood there, waiting for Hence to explain his presence, and he stared back at me, not explaining. Meanwhile, I could see Francesca Pasquale and Bonnie Day whispering to each other about this new piece of hot gossip unfolding in front of their eyes.

Francesca had hated me since fourth grade, when I stopped her from picking on Jackie, who was the new girl in school, and Bonnie had the biggest mouth in the whole senior class. I knew they were looking for something about Hence they could turn into a joke at my expense: his scruffy hair, the holes in his jeans, his army surplus jacket—all the things that set him apart from the clean-cut jocks they liked so much. But Hence himself—his deep eyes, his way of standing there not even noticing that everyone around us was watching—well, there was no put-down they could manage about *him*.

So I stood my ground and let them watch, waiting for Hence to say something, feeling braver by the second.

"Hi," he said finally.

"You came to see me?" Of course he did. Why else would he be waiting at the gates of my school? But I wanted to hear him say it.

"Looks that way." And he allowed himself that cautious smile that always made me think somebody used to slap the grin right off his face. Every time I saw that smile, I wanted to throw my whole self between Hence and the memories of whatever made him afraid to cut loose and be truly happy.

But that day, Francesca, Bonnie, and everyone else who watched us with calculating eyes were the ones I wanted to protect Hence from. Before I could think too hard about what I was doing, I stood on tiptoe and kissed him on the lips—hard at first, defiantly. Once he got over his surprise and started to respond, our kiss softened into something gentle and lingering. I heard gasps and giggles at first, but after a moment or two, I heard nothing but the blood rushing in my ears.

113

When I pulled back, finally, all I saw were Hence's startled eyes and his parted lips. The school and everyone in front of it had vanished from my mind. "Let's go home," I said, taking his hand. But we didn't make it home—at least not at first. We stopped to kiss in front of Gristedes, and again by China Yearnings. By the time we started walking for real, the sky had turned a deep twilight blue and a cold wind had whipped up. My lips were chapped, and I had a crick in my neck from tilting my face up to his, but I was happier than I could ever remember being. We held hands almost all the way to The Underground, but half a block away we let go because it still felt too soon to let Dad know about any of this.

When we got to the door, Q was there waiting for us, and from the look in his eyes, I knew Bad Quentin had come out to play.

"Go around the back," he snarled at Hence. "You were supposed to be on the clock over an hour ago."

Without a glance at me, Hence did as he'd been ordered, while I stood there fuming. Q wasn't Hence's boss. He didn't even officially work at The Underground, except when Dad was short of help, and then he would stomp around looking all put out, as though it were beneath him to change lightbulbs or stock napkin holders.

For a moment I thought Dad had run out somewhere and left Quentin in charge. I thought Hence's lateness for work was the whole problem. I tried to slip past Q and through the front door.

"Not so fast," he said, his voice ominously still, and right away I knew what was wrong: One of those bitchy girls from school had told him about Hence showing up there, and about how we had kissed in front of everyone—a serious kiss, and not a mere peck on the lips. A lot of the girls at school had their eyes on Q, and would welcome a chance to score points with him.

But even if we'd been told on, it still didn't strike me as such a big deal. So Hence was my boyfriend. Why should Q care? I waited there, hands on my hips, for whatever he would say next.

He sputtered for a moment, as if he didn't know how to begin. "Not in front of the whole world," he said finally. "Get inside."

"I *was* going inside. Until you stopped me."

The moment we were through the door, he laid into me. His first question was shocking enough: What kind of slut was I, making out in public, in front of the whole school? But what came after was even worse: Was I sleeping with Hence? Or planning to? (I didn't answer either question; my love life was none of Q's business.) And things went downhill from there. How could I stoop so low as to involve myself with "some bottom-dweller busboy who had come out of nowhere to work for minimum wage and sleep in our basement"? Those were his exact words, and they shocked me. I'd had no idea until that very moment how much of a snob my brother was.

As much as that last question stunned me, it was nothing compared to what came out of Q's mouth next: "He's not even white."

My jaw dropped. "What does that mean, Quentin?"

"Look at him. No way he's white. He's part black or Indian or Mexican or something."

I'd never given a second's thought to Hence's race. "So what?"

115

I said. "Jackie's been my friend forever, and she's black. You never cared about that. What does it matter?"

But Q didn't respond, probably because he knew there could be no good answer. "He doesn't even have a last name. You're the daughter of Jim Eversole, owner of one of the biggest nightclubs in Manhattan. You've got this bright future ahead of you. You still want to go to Harvard, right?"

I didn't answer.

"So why would you get involved with some nobody who's only going to drag you down? A *musician*." The expression on Q's face could only be described as a sneer.

"Who *are* you? Seriously, Q, how long have you been such a racist snob?"

He ignored my questions. "What do you think Dad will say when he finds out you've been sneaking around with Hence?"

My laughter came out as a snort. "This is our dad you're talking about? The guy who lets me go clubbing?"

Quentin's frown deepened. "Dad's only a pushover because he thinks he can trust you. You think he'll keep Hence on here if he knows you two are up to whatever it is you're up to?"

"You're going to tell on me?" This was yet another shock. Hadn't Q and I always been on the same side? "Hence and I are *not* sneaking around. If we'd been sneaky, you wouldn't know about any of this."

"Is there anything else you want to tell me? Because Dad will definitely want to know if you've been screwing the help."

I froze. Dad wasn't a bigot; I couldn't imagine he would care about Hence's race, or what kind of family he came from. But the ugly way Q made his last point gave me pause. The more I thought about it, the more I knew Quentin was right about one thing: Dad might care whether or not I had sex. Not that he'd ever told me I shouldn't, not in so many words. But he still thought of me as his little Cupcake. He'd always trusted me, and I'd never given him any reason not to. And if Dad thought there was a chance Hence and I were heading in that direction, he might fire Hence and kick him out of the building. I couldn't let that happen.

"I'm not sleeping with Hence," I told Q. "I'm not sleeping with anyone." I adjusted my tone, trying for something more conciliatory. "Please don't say anything. Please, Q? We've always looked out for each other."

"I'm looking out for you now," he said.

"What if I promise to stay out of trouble? Not to . . ." I couldn't even bring myself to say it. "You know."

Q looked at me closely, his eyes that steely shade they took on whenever his mood turned sour. "That's not good enough," he said. "It's him I don't trust, not you."

I thought for a moment. What could I say that would keep Q out of my hair? There seemed to be only one answer. "What if I stop seeing Hence? I'll stay away from him. I swear."

Q's expression softened, but only slightly. "Give me a reason to think you're lying and I'll go straight to Dad. Don't think I won't. And your boyfriend will be out on the street . . . or worse."

While I hated letting Q have the last word, I knew from long experience that there was no winning an argument with Bad Quentin. I punched the elevator button, but the car was off on another floor, and there was no way I was going to stand around waiting for it in Q's presence. Instead, I stomped up the stairs to my bedroom and slammed the door behind me. It was a kind of hell, being trapped in my room when I knew Hence was downstairs somewhere, probably being further abused by Q. I wanted so badly to throw myself between them, to stand up for Hence, but how could I get involved without making Q even angrier and more suspicious than he already was? While I didn't know what he had meant by "or worse," I didn't want to find out.

One thing was clear: Hence and I would have to stay apart at The Underground and avoid doing anything to cause suspicion. Of course I had lied to Quentin. Nothing would keep me away from Hence now that I was sure he felt the same way about me that I did about him. Because I *was* sure. I lay on my bed a long while, replaying the events of that afternoon, remembering how we'd held each other in front of China Yearnings, how Hence had taken my face in his hands, and how, into the tent made by my hair, he'd whispered that he had loved me almost from the moment we met.

Chelsea

That night while I slept, my mind whirred along without me. When I woke up, two words I'd read the night before were pin-balling through my mind, lighting up bumpers and bouncing off of each other: *Jackie* and *sculpture*. So I flew out of bed, grabbed my mom's journal, and paged through it to find the place where she mentioned Jackie's after-school sculpture class at the 92nd Street Y. It was a long shot, but it was something.

Back at my laptop, I typed the words *Jackie Gray* and *sculptor*, but not much came up. So I tried *Jacqueline Gray*, hoping I was spelling the first name right, and sure enough, there she was: *Jacqueline Gray—American Sculptor*. Finally, I was getting somewhere.

I scrolled through photographs of her work: marble statues of women, their forms blooming from—or maybe melting into—backgrounds of chunky rock or glossy polished walls. Dad used to drag me to museums to "civilize" me (his word, not mine), but as soon as I got old enough to have some say, I put a stop to that. I don't get most art, but Jackie Gray's statues were cool—scary and beautiful all at once.

I clicked on a link that read "Biography" and arrived at a page titled "About Jacqueline Gray," complete with a photo of a woman about my mother's age. Jackie's multicolored scarf held back a thick cascade of dreadlocks, and she wore a floaty tangerine blouse over a black tank top. I skimmed her biography. She had grown up in Manhattan and earned a degree from Tisch School of the Arts at NYU. I breezed through a ton of information about all the awards she'd won and the galleries she'd shown at, hoping to find clues. Near the bottom of the page, my attention snagged on a single sentence: *Jacqueline's work has been exhibited internationally, and a statue from her groundbreaking sequence, Missing Person, was acquired by the Miami Institute of Contemporary Art for its permanent collection.*

The words *Missing Person* caught my attention. I followed the link to a photograph that stole my breath—a woman cut from black marble, her arms flung wide before her, her loose dress billowing. Her straight hair spread out into the air behind her as though blasted by a powerful wind. Her face—the narrow nose, the big eyes, the full lower lip—was my mother's. From the hips up, the statue looked like any normal portrait, but below that her body morphed into a gnarled tree trunk, as if she had been caught in the middle of a transformation. Was my mother turning into a tree? Or was she a tree turning human? The statue's mouth gaped with horror or sorrow.

Jackie's phone number wasn't listed, but a link on her web page led me to an address in the East Williamsburg section of Brooklyn—close enough to get to by public transportation, if I could navigate the spaghetti tangle of the New York City subway map. Or if I could enlist a local to help me.

I found Cooper downstairs, lugging a dolly loaded with cases of beer. "Whoa. Where are you running to?" he asked. It was hard to tell if he was still annoyed with me for the previous night's adventures.

"Looking for you," I said. "Is there a show tonight?"

Cooper jutted his chin at me. "Don't even think about sneaking into the club again. Hence has been in a terrible mood all day, thanks to you."

I thought of the girl scratching on the window and Hence's off-the-charts bizarre reaction. Had Hence told Cooper about that?

"I won't," I promised, crossing my heart. "Anyway, I've got more urgent things to take care of. I figured out where my mother's best friend lives."

Cooper leaned against the beer dolly, waiting.

"In East Williamsburg, Brooklyn. I'm going to go knock on her door. Want to come along?"

He gave me a look I couldn't quite read.

"The subway lines are confusing. I could really use your help."

Cooper let out a sigh that ruffled his bangs. "Right," he said. "I'm on the clock. There isn't a show tonight, but that doesn't mean I don't have work to do." And with one monumental push, he and the dolly vanished around a corner.

"Whatever," I said to the empty hallway. Had I done something to make Cooper dislike me? How did I manage to rub everyone I met the wrong way? I was still standing there, frozen, wondering what to do next, when I heard footsteps coming toward me.

It was Cooper again. "Okay," he said, sounding grumpy and reluctant. "I'll take you there."

"You will? Tonight?"

"You heard me say I had to work, right?" He inclined his head toward Hence's office. "Tomorrow morning." Cooper lowered his voice to a whisper. "Until then, would you please get upstairs before Hence sees you? He'll come up with even more busywork to torture me with, and then I might not be able to get away tomorrow at all."

Stupid Hence. Why did he have to make things so difficult? Without another word, I ducked off toward the elevator and punched the button.

While it annoyed me to have to hide out in my room, a lot of my mother's journal still needed to be read. I spent the rest of the day stretched across her bed, reading much more slowly than usual so I wouldn't miss the one crucial bit of information that would make everything fall into place. I was puzzling through one of her poems, trying to figure out what it meant, when I noticed the smell of food—something hot and delicious rising from somewhere in the building. All at once I was starving, not to mention a little loopy from spending so much time alone. Beyond the window, the sky had darkened to an electric blue. How long had it been since I'd spoken to a human being, or eaten anything that wasn't a Pop-Tart?

As I was tucking the journal into its hiding place, someone knocked on the apartment door. I pressed my eye to the peephole and saw Cooper on the other side, looking less exasperated than I'd seen him in a while. "Coming," I said as I undid the locks.

"Want some dinner?" he asked. This was a surprise. A few hours earlier, I could have sworn I'd exhausted the last of Cooper's patience. Now he was inviting me for a home-cooked meal?

"I'm starving." I followed him onto the elevator. He hit the button for the second floor—Hence's apartment, I guessed. "Is His Majesty going to be eating with us?"

I was relieved when Coop shook his head, his bangs falling into his eyes. I had to restrain myself from brushing them back. His eyes—an unusual blue-green and fringed with long lashes— deserved not to be hidden. "Hence is out somewhere," Coop said.

This was welcome news. Coop undid what seemed like seventeen locks and swept into the apartment ahead of me. I didn't know what I'd been expecting—a dungeon full of cob- webs and spiders?—but I found myself in a stylish living room done up in earth tones and leather, with a faded Persian rug on the gleaming wood floor. Glaring from the far wall was an Andy Warhol–style portrait of a punk rocker with spiky red hair and bugged-out eyes.

"Who's that?" I pointed.

"Johnny Rotten. Front man for the Sex Pistols. A seminal punk-rock band of the seventies."

123

"I *know* who the Sex Pistols are."

"And do you know this band?" Cooper pointed to the wall behind us, which bore a large, silver-framed professional shot of four now-familiar skinny dudes in black, the most familiar one brandishing a V-shaped guitar.

"That's Riptide."

"Very good. Now you should try listening to their music."

"How do you know I haven't?" I asked, though of course he was more or less right.

"Just a wild guess." Coop led me through a dining room—also surprisingly posh—into a kitchen full of shiny appliances and black granite countertops. A cookbook was splayed open on the counter, and the sink was full of dirty pots and pans. "I hope you eat meat."

Dinner turned out to be lasagna with sausage. Sitting side by side at the kitchen island, we wolfed down our first helping, not even talking, and when he asked if I wanted seconds, I nodded and held out my plate. "This is surprisingly not bad," I told him.

"I'll take that as a compliment." He fished a couple of Cokes out of the enormous refrigerator.

"You cook like this when Hence isn't here? It looks like a lot of work."

"He'll eat it when he gets home."

"That's not going to be soon, is it?"

"You're that scared of him?"

"I'm not scared. I just can't figure out why he doesn't want to help me find my mother."

"You really don't get why you bother him?" Coop got to his

124

feet and beckoned for me to follow. "Put that plate down. I've got something to show you."

Intrigued, I complied. Hence's bedroom was huge, decorated in shades of tobacco and cream, with a Bose stereo system and a heavy king-size bed. The sight of it brought a new and distressing thought into my head: Did Hence have a girlfriend? Did he bring her here? I had an uneasy feeling I was about to see something I wouldn't want to.

Coop hit a switch, illuminating track lights trained on the wall beyond the enormous bed, and I got the answer to my question. From waist height to the ceiling, the wall was covered with framed photographs. I looked from one to the next until it became clear: Every single one contained my mother. In the center hung a large photo I recognized—my mother's high school graduation portrait, her black hair gleaming against the white gown, a gold honors tassel draped over her shoulder, a mischievous smile on her lips. To its right hung a grainier, more candid shot of her in front of an ice-cream store, smiling over a triple-decker strawberry cone. In the photo beneath, she wore braids, a navy-and-white-plaid school uniform, and knee socks, and her arms were flung around a young version of Jackie Gray, both of them laughing. I let my gaze travel to the next photo and the next and the next: my mother in a tank top and cutoffs; my mother sitting on the edge of a fountain; my mother in front of CBGB in a belted trench coat and a pink beret. The come-hither look in her dark blue eyes told me all I needed to know about who had taken that picture—who had probably taken most of the shots on the wall.

My gaze landed on a strip of black-and-white photo-booth

125

shots—matted, framed, and under glass—of my mother kissing a young Hence, his hands on her waist and her arms wrapped around his shoulders. In the last of the four frames they had pulled apart and were looking sideways at each other, their expressions identically naughty, as if they were getting away with something unspeakably delicious but forbidden. They certainly looked like they were in love—or very seriously in lust. Had she ever looked at my father that way? I took a giant step back from the wall and was surprised to find Coop watching me. I'd forgotten he was in the room. He seemed to be waiting for me to say something, but I couldn't think what it might be.

"Did you see this one?" He pointed at the photograph farthest to the left, one I had missed. I walked over to it and recognized a portrait of my mother on her wedding day, clutching daisies, a wreath of baby's breath in her simply done hair. I had always loved that photo; we had a copy of it on a shelf in our living room. Though my mother's dress was nothing special—just a simple white sundress—in it she looked supremely confident and regal. Beside her my father looked proud, and a little afraid, in his navy-blue suit. But unlike the version at home, this one had been scissored down the middle so it contained only my mother, like those snapshots I'd found at home with Hence cut out. An ornate silver frame surrounded the portrait as though it were an ordinary, unvandalized wedding photo.

"That's creepy," I said. "Like something a stalker would hang on his wall. I feel dirty just looking at these."

Coop snapped off the light, and I followed him into the kitchen. My appetite had disappeared, but he went back to eating.

"You know why I showed you those pictures," he said after a while, not looking up from his plate.

He was right. Suddenly it all made sense: why the very sight of me seemed to make Hence angry. Before tonight I would have guessed that Hence hadn't completely gotten over my mother. But now I knew it was more than that: He was positively obsessed with her. Even if he did have a girlfriend, he certainly couldn't bring her to his bedroom, where she would be faced with his shrine to Catherine Eversole Price. How had he even gotten that copy of her wedding photo? Had she sent it to him to make him jealous? And why had she married my father if she still cared enough about Hence to bother? I was so preoccupied I barely heard what Cooper said next.

"Maybe you understand now why he's convinced your mother is dead. If he believed she was alive, he'd have to admit she chose not to come back to him all these years."

I snapped to attention. "So you think she could be alive?" I didn't wait for an answer. "What else do you know about my mother?"

Coop helped himself to yet another slice of lasagna. "Hence talks sometimes. He tells me things."

"What things?" I could hear my voice rising with impatience. It hurt to think Cooper might know things about my own mother that I didn't.

"All kinds of things. Some would maybe be more useful to you than others. . . ."

"It's all useful. You've got to tell me everything. You don't understand." I could hear that I sounded a little bit unhinged, but

I kept going. "Until I got here, I hardly knew anything about my own mother. My father kept everything important from me." Barely realizing what I was doing, I reached over to squeeze Coop's arm, as if to keep him from running away. He looked up from his plate, and I let go.

For a long moment, we sat in silence, until Coop finally got up to rinse his plate. "I don't know what time Hence is coming home. I don't want him walking in on us while we're having this conversation."

So I held back my questions until we were finally up in my mother's apartment, sitting on her blue plaid love seat. "Now tell me everything you know."

"First you have to swear not to let Hence know I've told you any of this."

"I swear."

So Coop told me about how sometimes Hence would wake him up when he couldn't sleep and needed someone to talk to. The conversation always went pretty much the same: Hence would start out lamenting how my mother had betrayed him, how she'd bought into society's expectations that a rich girl had to go to an Ivy League school and marry into wealth. He'd thought she was above all that conventional bullshit, but he'd been wrong.

"That's seriously messed up," I said. "She wasn't a snob. My dad isn't remotely rich."

"The way Hence sees it, that's what must have happened. Why else would she marry your father?"

"Because *he's* not insane." I grabbed a throw pillow and squashed it against my stomach. "Keep going."

Hence would drink as he talked, getting angrier and angrier. Once he'd lost it completely and punched a hole in the apartment wall. Most nights, though, his rage would give way to sadness, and he'd talk about how beautiful and brave my mother had been, how fiercely she'd protected the people she loved. How she was brilliant and talented, how blue her eyes were, and how she'd saved his life by taking him into her father's club. (Was that the corniest thing I'd ever heard or the most beautiful? I wasn't sure.) Once, after a lot of whiskey, he'd even said he didn't understand how my mother could have married some eggheaded college professor when she and Hence shared a single soul.

"Whoa," I interrupted. "He said that?"

"Maybe not those exact words. But something that over-the-top. I know he comes off as a cynic. But after hearing him go on and on about your mother, I think the Hence most of the world knows is really made out of…I don't know…scar tissue. All tough and gnarly to cover up the hurt."

I made a face. "He's gnarly, all right. Oh, God—am I going to have to like Hence now? I'm not sure I can." I gave my mother's throw pillow a punch. "So I'm guessing he doesn't have a girlfriend?"

Coop grabbed the pillow from me and tossed it onto the bed. "He has girlfriends. Or maybe you'd call them groupies. Women who hang around him at the club. He never brings them up here, and I don't think it ever gets serious. I imagine it's pretty much just sex."

I couldn't help grimacing in the face of too much information.

"You want the whole story, right?"

"I'm pretty creeped out right now. But don't stop. I need to

129

know everything. Please." *You're the only person I've got on my side,* I thought.

Coop went on with the story, telling me about Hence's marriage to Nina Bevilaqua, the woman I'd seen on the Infamous Groupies website. Despite the fact that Hence barely even liked her, they'd eloped after Mom had sent him her wedding picture to show him she'd moved on.

"Are you serious? He married her for revenge?"

Coop's cheeks glowed red. "He's made some mistakes."

"Um, yeah. Why do you stand up for him?" I could feel myself on the verge of getting carried away with my own argument the way I sometimes do, but I kept going, trying to wrestle Coop's loyalty out of Hence's hands and into mine. "I know he was a great rock star once upon a time...."

"Not exactly a rock star. Riptide only had the one hit."

"And now all he is is some guy who owns a nightclub."

"Who completely shapes the New York music scene. Hence has broken more acts than you can imagine. And he's serious about the music. He's a genius."

"He's a stalker."

Coop winced. "Not technically."

"I don't get it. You're just his employee. He doesn't even treat you all that well."

"He's been good to me. When I got to the city, I didn't have a place to stay, and I was running out of money fast. He took me in. Gave me work. He's been teaching me about the music industry...."

130

"Oh! You're hoping he'll help make you a star?" I recalled the guitar leaning against Coop's cot.

"He's mentoring me. He's always doing that—finding promising musicians, helping them develop their talent."

"You're a promising musician?" Why did everyone seem to have a special talent but me?

"Hence seems to think so," Coop said, blushing again. "I just know I have to try."

"What does it feel like?" I asked. "Knowing what you want?"

He laughed. "You're the most determined person I've ever met. You tell me."

"I'm not. This thing with my mother is different." But I couldn't help wondering if Coop was seeing some part of me that I couldn't see. "It doesn't count."

"Of course it counts," he insisted.

After that, we shared an awkward moment, with him wiping his hands on his jeans and me not knowing what to say.

"Would you play your guitar for me?" I asked, in part to break the silence and in part because I was curious.

But something in his eyes stopped me short. He looked startled, even shocked. It took me a few seconds to realize he wasn't reacting to my question, but to something he'd heard: the elevator creaking up to the fifth floor and coming to a stop outside the apartment door.

It could only be Hence. He knocked on the door once, twice. I froze, not sure what to do next. The look on Coop's face told me he'd been caught doing something that would displease his boss.

Would Hence realize Cooper had been giving his secrets away? Would Coop lose his job over me?

"I know you're home," Hence growled on the other side of the door. "I'm looking for Cooper. Open up or I'll break the door in."

I looked at Coop for a sense of what he wanted me to do.

"Open it," he said in a resigned voice.

I unlocked the door, and Hence looked past me into the room. His gaze came to rest on the love seat, where Cooper sat upright, his position oddly stiff. "What is this?"

"We were talking," Cooper said quietly.

"He was telling me about the New York club scene," I lied.

But Hence wasn't worried about his secrets. "In her bedroom?" he demanded of Cooper. "You know how this looks, the two of you alone up here at midnight? I don't pay you to sneak around with girls, and especially not with her." He pointed at me like I was Exhibit A.

"I'm not on the clock. This is my free time," Cooper said, which struck me as way beside the point.

"We weren't sneaking around," I protested. "Hooking up with him is the last thing on my mind." I gestured toward Cooper and saw the expression on his face, like he'd been slapped. Too late, I realized how mean that last part must have sounded, even though it was the truth: I hadn't been thinking about hooking up with Cooper. We'd only just met. And I did have other things on my mind.

But Hence had barged in on our conversation, sneering down at us, acting morally superior. Once again I was struck by the strangeness of it all. How had my mother ever loved someone so

132

horrible? With his pathetic wall of ancient photos, who was he to judge me, anyway?

So many thoughts were colliding in my head that all I could do was sputter and fume as Cooper stomped off past me and Hence hurried behind him out the door. I heard yelling from the floor below mine, and a slamming door. Then, for a long time, silence.

Catherine

After Hence and I kissed, the world seemed to stand between us, keeping us apart. As usual, I would hang around the club after school, pretending to do homework but completely unable to concentrate, and sometimes our eyes would meet, but with Dad or Q or the bartenders around, that would be it. I was starting to think I'd imagined the other day, that I'd invented the current in the air between us ever since. Then, one afternoon when nobody was looking, Hence passed me in the hallway and pressed a tightly folded note into my hand. I waited until I was alone in the elevator to read it, my heart fluttering: CHRISTOPHER PARK, 4:15 PM TOMORROW.

As a meet-up spot, Christopher Park wasn't foolproof. As far as I knew, none of Q's friends lived near there, so he was unlikely to be passing through, but anybody from Idlewild Prep could wander by and see me. I disguised myself in sunglasses and a trench coat and stood as deep in the park as I could get, leaning against the wrought-iron fence near the garden. At 4:17 he showed up, coatless, rumpled, and breathless, and we stood there for a moment, shy and unsure of what to do next.

He broke the silence. "I'm so glad you're here. I wanted to be alone with you again...but I didn't know where or how." Then, before I could think or speak, he wrapped his arms around me and pulled me close. A heartbeat later he was kissing me, the park around us—the people walking their dogs, two shrieking toddlers chasing a red rubber ball—all evaporating into mist.

We didn't have long together. Hence was on his break, and if he was late getting back Q would hear about it and get suspicious. "Tomorrow?" he asked. "Same time, same place?"

I nodded. After he'd hurried off toward the subway, I lingered on a park bench, savoring the tingle on my lips—the only sign that our kisses had really happened, that I hadn't simply imagined them.

A few days later, I took Jackie aside in homeroom. "I need your help. Hence and I have been meeting at Christopher Park, and yesterday two of Q's friends from high school passed right by us. If they had seen us, it would've been the end." I had told Jackie about the promise Q had extracted from me, but I'd left out his comment about Hence not being white because I knew how much it would hurt her feelings, and because I was embarrassed my brother was such a cretin.

"But Christopher Park is so public. Why are you meeting there?"

"Where else could we meet? Q *will* catch us. It's just a matter of time. One of his friends, or one of these people"—I made a sweeping gesture at the room full of our classmates—"will see us and start gossiping. Hence could lose his job and his home, and it would be all my fault."

Jackie jiggled her foot like she knew there must be more to my request.

"But if I could meet him at your house, it would be so much safer. Your mom will be at work, and—"

"At my house?" Jackie sounded exasperated. "You mean you want the three of us to sit around together and do what? Watch TV? You, your boyfriend, and Jackie the third wheel? Are you going to make out in front of me?"

I inhaled sharply for courage. "You wouldn't have to watch us." When Jackie started to protest, I grabbed her hand in both of mine. "Shhh! People will hear."

Jackie lowered her voice to a hiss. "They'll hear that you want to use my bedroom—"

"Your guest room."

"Wherever. To *make out* with your boyfriend." A moment later, almost in disbelief, she added, "You're going to have sex with him."

"Since when are you so judgmental? We're in love, Jack. This is totally it."

"What if you get pregnant?"

"We'll be careful."

"What if my mom comes home early? She does that sometimes, you know."

136

"We'll climb down the fire escape. Listen, Jack. I'd do it for you."

"I wouldn't ask you to." Jackie straightened in her seat and stared at the blackboard. I knew she was thinking of all the things I'd done for her. Helping her spy on Q when we were little and he was still her Prince Charming. Standing up for her when the girls at school made fun of her less-than-stylish shoes. Not to mention being her best friend when she was the new girl at school.

Just then, Mrs. Farley started taking attendance.

"Think about it," I whispered. "That's all I ask. I promise I won't change." I added the last part because I knew Jackie. She wasn't worried about my getting pregnant or her mother coming home early. Or maybe she was, but she was more worried because I was moving ahead, starting a new phase of my life, and she wasn't there yet. She was worried my feelings for Hence would change our friendship.

Jackie shot me a narrow-eyed look and folded her hands in the perfect imitation of a prim schoolmarm. We didn't talk to each other again until lunch, when I was relieved to see her sitting at our usual table. I slipped in beside her. "Want my cookie?"

"You can't buy me with oatmeal raisin," Jackie grumbled, but something in her voice told me she was about to give in.

"It's chocolate chip," I said, giving her side a gentle you-can't-stay-mad-at-me poke.

"Sometimes I hate you."

"But mostly you love me." I threw my arms around her and squeezed. "Is that the new perfume your mom bought you? *Très, très chic.* I like it."

"Quit buttering me up." But Jackie was hugging me back. That's how I knew for certain she was on our side.

When I reached the front steps of Jackie's town house, Hence was already there, wearing a shirt I'd never seen before, a crisp white button-down that looked gorgeous against his skin. He still didn't have a jacket on, and when he took my hand, his touch, usually so warm, was ice cold. Without a word—not even a hello to Hence— Jackie unlocked her front door and flung it open for us to go in first. "Why do I feel like a pimp?" she muttered under her breath as I passed her.

"Shhh," I whispered in her ear. "You're Cupid."

I led Hence up two flights of stairs to the sunny guest room, with its itchy plaid bedspread. It smelled like potpourri and lemon Pledge.

Hence stood in the middle of the room, looking to me to make the first move, I guess. I clicked the door gently shut behind us.

"It's okay," I told him. "Jackie will warn us if her mother comes home early, but she hardly ever does." I went over to him and took both his hands in mine. "You're so cold," I said. "Were you waiting long?"

Hence nodded. We'd both been waiting—whole agonizing days—for a chance to be alone together. Still, we hesitated, unsure how to begin. In Jackie's room, just under ours, the stereo switched on, playing death metal—a kind of music Jackie didn't even like. Well, if she thought she could ruin the mood for us, she was wrong. I smiled up at Hence apologetically, and that was the moment he chose to kiss me, his lips softer than soft and tasting of the cold afternoon air.

"You don't have to feel like a pimp," I reported to Jackie after Hence had left for The Underground. "All we did was kiss. He didn't even try to touch me." I sat beside Jackie on the bottom bunk of her bed, where we'd once built pillow forts and I'd helped her write love letters to my brother, where she'd made me laugh so hard I'd fallen off the top bunk and needed stitches in my head.

"Humph." Jackie scooted over to make room. The heavy metal had been replaced with the Fine Young Cannibals' "She Drives Me Crazy"—probably a commentary on me, come to think of it.

"Nice music," I said. "Much better than before."

Jackie humphed again.

I sang softly in her ear. "I drive you crazy, ooh, ooh, like no one else, ooh, ooh." Then I sprang to my feet and did a little dance to make her laugh, which it did. I yanked her to her feet, and we did the moves we'd perfected in middle school, and that's how Mrs. Gray found us, giggling and doing the Safety Dance and the Electric Boogaloo till our sides were sore.

For the next few days, Hence and I met at Jackie's guest room hideaway. Hence had only an hour-long break each afternoon, and he had to get back and forth from The Underground, which left us with forty minutes alone together. Even so, he was late getting back to work once, and Dad gave him a friendly talking-to and a warning that it had better not happen again.

At night, as I tried to fall asleep, I swear I felt actual pain at being away from Hence, especially knowing he was just five floors away, missing me, too. But being alone together for that little chunk of time each weekday was like heaven, even if the guest room door didn't lock and we could hear Jackie's clever musical commentary wafting up from the floor below. "Like a Virgin." "Keep Your Hands to Yourself." "Another One Bites the Dust." When Jackie fired up that last one, I couldn't help myself; I burst into giggles, and couldn't bring myself to explain to Hence why I was laughing.

The moment his lips touched mine, though, everything else faded away and it was like we were in a suite at the Empire Hotel, on a plush bed with violins playing and sunshine streaming in to bathe us in liquid gold. All we did was kiss—a full forty minutes of nothing but lip-lock, until I thought I would explode if we didn't go any further.

I'd done my share of making out before, but the guys I'd been with had always been in much more of a hurry than I was. I would break up with them when they got too pushy. Unlike some of the girls at school, I was never in a big rush to lose my virginity; I'd always figured I would know when the time was right.

As it turned out, I did know. After a few afternoon make-out sessions with Hence, I *absolutely* knew. The tingling I'd never felt before with any other boy had become an actual ache, and still his hands hadn't once left my hips.

I spent the weekend in a state of restlessness. On Saturday, Dad kept Hence so busy he didn't even get a break, and on Sunday he had rehearsal with Riptide all afternoon and most of the night. By Monday morning, I didn't think I could stand the wait until we were alone together again.

That afternoon, in the guest room, we kissed and kissed and kissed. When I couldn't stand it for another second, I pulled away.

"What's wrong?" Hence asked, his lips as puffy and cherry-red as mine felt. He looked worried as I got to my feet and took a step back from the bed.

In reply, I unbuttoned the top of my school uniform. Underneath it, I'd worn my nicest lacy pink bra. "Don't you want to go further?"

Hence closed his eyes. "Of course I do." When his eyes opened again, they seemed bigger and darker than ever—like bottomless pools. "I didn't want to rush you."

I unzipped my skirt. Beneath it, I was wearing matching underwear. I let the skirt fall and climbed back onto the bed, leaning over Hence so my hair fell around his face like a curtain. "You're not rushing me."

This time when we kissed, his hands explored me, then unhooked my bra. His lips on my skin were softer than I could have imagined. Because my hands were trembling, Hence helped me unzip his pants. Without his clothes, he was even more amazing than I had imagined, his skin smooth and mocha sweet. Seeing him like that—leaning back on his elbows, eager and exposed—made my heart inflate.

I wasn't exactly sure what to do next, but he took charge. To my surprise, he'd come prepared—he had a condom in his pocket. He was careful not to hurt me, but even so, it did hurt. I couldn't imagine wanting to feel that pain with anyone else.

Afterward, we held each other for a while longer, though we knew he was taking a chance on being late for work again. I kissed his chin. "That was my first time."

He nodded.

"Was it yours?"

He shook his head no.

"Never mind," I said. "I don't want to know." For once, I didn't mind his reticence. I couldn't bear to think of Hence with anyone else, no matter how casual the encounter had been. As long as I didn't know the details, I could pretend I was the only one he'd ever touched with that look of wonder on his face.

One day a distributor didn't make his delivery when he was supposed to, and Frank the assistant manager called in sick, so Hence didn't get his usual break. I went straight from school to Jackie's only to find he wasn't there. So I talked Jackie into putting off her homework and renting a video—one of those romantic comedies she loved so much. We microwaved popcorn and settled in, but of course we had so much to talk about that we hardly watched the movie at all.

"You're going to tell me everything, right?" she asked. "What it's like?"

It was a relief to talk about Hence to the only person who knew he and I were together. Sometimes it seemed like I'd stepped into an alternate universe where people walked around on the ceiling and nobody around me even noticed anything was strange. Pretending I wasn't in love hadn't been easy. The week before, David Hasmith had asked me to the winter formal and I hadn't been able to come up with a reason for saying no, but of course I couldn't say yes. He looked hurt, and soon everybody was looking at me like I was a freak because David was popular and lots of girls would jump at the chance to go *anywhere* with him. My turning him down confirmed everything they already thought about what a weirdo I was.

Like I cared.

In another life, I might have said yes to David. He was cute enough, and less of a self-involved jerk than the rest of the popular guys. I probably would have been thrilled to go shopping with Jackie and her mom for the right dress. But I was glad to be in my life, exactly as it was. No—more than glad. I felt like I had been born for that exact moment, my life opening up the way crocuses do, popping out of the snow just when you can't stand another minute of winter.

I struggled to find the words to answer Jackie's question. Even when I wrote in my journal, where I'd always done my best thinking, it was hard to find the right words. I wanted to get down every detail so I'd never forget a single one: Jackie's footsteps in the room below ours; Hence's warm, smooth skin; the muscles of his legs and the heat of his lips. How even though we wanted to shout, we had to whisper.

Afterward, we held each other, my hands wound in his damp hair. The afternoon sun rippled on the blanket and he smelled deliciously like himself, and also like the outdoors, the scent of wind and fresh-cut grass clinging to his skin even though he'd walked through exhaust-choked city streets to get to me.

"We fit so perfectly," I said, and Jackie hid her face in her hands and screeched with laughter. "No, not like that! Or not *just* like that. Even when we're standing up, the top of my head comes to just below his chin, so he can rest his chin on my head. And sometimes he knows what I'm thinking without my having to say anything."

"You're so lucky," Jackie said. "I don't think I'm ever going to fall in love like that." Over the last week or so, she had mellowed out about my whole situation, and had cut out the musical commentary. It seemed like she'd come to accept my love for Hence as the inevitability it was.

"Of course you will," I assured her.

"There's no 'of course' about it. I've never seen anything like the two of you. The way you look at each other." She picked at the pilling on her bedspread, making a little pile of fluffballs. "It's so intense it's almost scary."

I couldn't honestly disagree. Though I was sure Jackie would fall in love someday with someone who would adore her, I doubted any other couple had ever felt the way Hence and I did about each other.

"Besides"—Jackie added a few more pills to her pile—"I don't even want to think about guys. I'm still recovering from your brother."

I sighed. Hadn't Jackie resigned herself to Q's taste in giraffe-thin exchange students? "He's not worth your time."

144

She looked puzzled, and I realized that as far as she knew, Q was still the handsome, athletic big brother who had protected us from the mean kids in elementary school. Sure, she knew about Bad Quentin, but she'd never seen him in action, and I'd always downplayed that side of him, not wanting to share my brother's weirdness, even with my very best friend.

I chose my words carefully. "If he can't see how fabulous you are, he's an idiot."

Jackie waved me off, embarrassed. After that, we tried to watch the movie, but before long Jackie's mom came home from work and started asking about homework, so I figured that was my cue to leave.

I hurried home in the dark, frustrated at not having had my alone time with Hence. It seemed so stupid and unfair that we had to sneak around like our being together was some kind of crime, when it was really the most natural, beautiful thing in our lives. Besides, it was scary being at Q's mercy, knowing he could rat us out at any moment. Lately he'd been putting in a lot of hours at the club. He said he was saving up for spring break in Cancun, but I couldn't help thinking he had other motivations. When I did my homework downstairs, I'd overhear him ordering Hence around in a way that got nastier when Dad wasn't within earshot. But Hence couldn't complain without risking the loss of the job he so desperately wanted to hang on to.

To him The Underground was still the Promised Land, and Dad was a hero. A few days earlier I'd gone downstairs to find the two of them immersed in another of their impromptu jam sessions, Dad encouraging Hence to take a solo. From the way Dad smiled, I could tell he was impressed with Hence's guitarwork. I hid out in the shadows, not wanting to ruin the moment. When the song was over, they laughed together. They played a few more songs before Dad noticed I was listening.

"Why are you lurking in the shadows, Cath?" Dad took a swig from the beer bottle at his feet.

"Just enjoying the music," I said. "Don't stop."

But Dad got to his feet. "I have places to be," he said. "Thought I'd check out that guitar shop over on Bleecker. Have you ever been there?" That last question was directed at Hence, and for a second I hoped Dad might invite him along. But Dad clapped a hand on Hence's shoulder and said, "Maybe we'll check it out together when you're not on the clock."

If Hence was disappointed the moment had passed, he didn't let it show. Minutes after Dad left the building, Q barged into the room and ordered Hence to scrub out the dishwasher. Hence gave me a quick, meaningful look. Then he was gone.

Chelsea

As it turned out, I didn't need Cooper's help—or anyone else's—to find Jackie's studio. And that was a good thing, because when the elevator deposited me on the first floor of The Underground the next morning, the lights were out and the club was silent. I called Coop's name a couple of times, and when there was no answer, I went down the creaky stairs into the basement, where light trickled in through the high windows. Coop's cot was made and he was gone; there was no way of knowing when he might come back. Something about the echoing quiet of the building felt like a reproach. It was easy to believe he'd gone out early to teach me a lesson.

The thought of navigating the subway alone made me sick to my stomach, but it also made me queasy to know I'd said something to hurt Cooper's feelings. I felt a twinge when the words came back to me: *Hooking up with him is the last thing on my mind.*

Okay, it hadn't been a nice thing to say. But he didn't seem interested in *me* in that way, either. So why had he stormed out and deserted me?

I considered my options. I could leave a note on Cooper's nightstand, but what would it say? You'd think I'd be better at apologizing, considering this wasn't the first time I'd lost a friend by blurting out the first thing that popped into my head. As I searched for a scrap of paper and a pen, I struggled with the right wording. I tried *I'm sorry you took what I said the wrong way*, but I could hear my dad's voice in my head, calling that a non-apology. But if I wrote that I hadn't meant what I'd said, would he take it to mean that I *did* want to hook up with him? That would make things even more complicated.

I'm sorry, I finally scrawled on a scrap of paper ripped out of the previous day's *Times*. I left it on Cooper's pillow. Not much— but the best I could manage.

Before I could lose my resolve, I let myself out of The Underground and headed for the subway, arms swinging, chin up, trying to look like someone who knew where she was going. Someone who shouldn't be messed with. And it worked: Nobody messed with me. I followed the directions I'd gotten from the Internet, and it didn't even take me all that long to get to East Williamsburg.

I rang the buzzer to Jackie Gray's redbrick warehouse-style building, thinking how depressing it would be if I'd traveled all this way only to find she wasn't in. To my relief, a woman's voice came over the intercom. "Hello?"

I hadn't given any thought to how I would introduce myself. "Chelsea Price. Catherine Eversole's daughter." I blurted the

148

words out. There was a long silence, then a buzz. Before Jackie could change her mind, I slipped inside and climbed the narrow staircase to the third floor.

Shorter than she looked in her photo and dressed in a turquoise tunic over a floaty black skirt, Jackie Gray waited in the hallway, her back pressed to the door of apartment 5E. "I don't believe it," she said when she saw me. And again, "I don't believe it." She threw her arms around me. "You don't mind if I hug you? I know I'm a stranger...."

"You're not," I said, because after reading about her in my mom's journal, I felt like she was a long-lost friend. We clung to each other for a moment, and then I followed her into a huge loft with shimmering swaths of cloth hung from the ceiling to mark out rooms. Sunshine fell in wide bars through the tall glass windows and onto the gleaming wood floor. I noticed a scattering of children's toys in the corner of the room—a city built out of blocks and Matchbox cars.

"My husband's at work, and my kids are at kindergarten," Jackie explained. "Twins, Zach and Zoe. I wish Cathy could have met them." She invited me to sit on a long mauve couch and started bombarding me with questions: Where was I living? How was my father? What was I doing in New York? I filled her in, leaving out the part about my being a runaway, trying—without actually lying—to make it sound like my dad knew I was on a solo jaunt to Manhattan. It seemed to work, though when I mentioned Hence, and how I was staying above The Underground, I saw her eyes narrow. She didn't say anything, so I continued my tale, ending with the purpose for my visit to her loft.

"Oh, Chelsea." Jackie put a hand on my arm. "I've been trying to figure out for years what could have happened to your mom." Then she started talking. She had a deep, actressy voice and long hands that fluttered as she spoke. I struggled to burn each detail into my memory.

Mom and Jackie had met in fourth grade. Jackie had come to Idlewild Prep on scholarship, and when Francesca Pasquale, the school's queen bee, had picked on her, my mom had threatened to punch Francesca out. "Not that Cathy knew the first thing about fighting, but she wouldn't have let a little detail like that stop her." Jackie told me how *normal* Mom had been for the daughter of someone rich and important, how eagerly she'd lent Jackie her nice clothes—even the diamond earrings she'd been given for her thirteenth birthday. How when Mom left to tour Italy the summer she was fifteen she'd sent Jackie daily postcards, promising that the two of them would travel together someday.

"Where did she go?" I prodded her. "What were her favorite places?"

The list was dauntingly long: Florence, Venice, Siena, Sorrento. It wasn't as though I could track her all over Italy. Absently fingering the beads of her orange necklace, Jackie reminisced about high school, and before long she got around to talking about Hence, and how his appearance on Mom's doorstep had changed everything.

"After that, we weren't as close. Cathy and Hence were attached at the lips most of the time. It wasn't the two of us anymore; it was the three of us, with me tagging along, feeling resentful. It's an old story, I guess."

"You didn't like Hence?"

"I was jealous. I wanted a boyfriend of my own, for one thing. But mostly I missed having Cathy's undivided attention." Jackie's cat, an elegant Siamese, had been watching me warily from the doorway; now it rubbed against her legs, and she reached down to scratch between its ears. "Hence was okay. He was very earnest— about his music, and about Cathy."

"Did she break up with him?" After seeing Hence's bedroom shrine, I figured my mom must have dumped him, but I was eager for the details.

"It was complicated," Jackie said.

"Complicated?" I stretched out a hand toward the cat, but it hissed at me and bolted from her lap and out of sight.

"Oh, you know. They grew up. Figured out they wanted different things. Had a few misunderstandings. I don't recall the details, to tell the truth. It was so long ago." She sighed. "She wanted to go to college, and he wanted to go on tour with that band of his, and neither of them would back down. Then he got involved with some woman he met at a club. I don't remember her name."

"Nina Bevilaqua?" I guessed.

"That sounds about right. If you ask me, I think he started seeing her to make your mother jealous. And she did the same to him." Jackie hesitated. "I don't mean to imply she didn't love your father, Chelsea."

"I wouldn't call it love. She ditched him. And me."

She leaned in like she might hug me again. "I'm so sorry."

"It doesn't matter." If she started going all kind and motherly

151

on me, I might lose it. "Did she tell you why she left us when she did? I mean, she'd been apart from Hence for years, and then all of a sudden she couldn't stand her life with us for another minute?"

"She called me when she got into town. She said Hence was flying in from England and she had to be at The Underground when he got there." Jackie looked down into her cupped hands. "I can't tell you how many times I've wished I'd told her to go home to you and your father. No—I *did* tell her that. I wish I'd worded it more strongly."

"Would she have listened?"

"Probably not. But I still should have spoken my mind. Her thing with Hence...it wasn't healthy. Too intense, the pair of them. Cathy needed somebody like your dad—steady and mild-tempered."

"I guess *she* didn't think so."

"Your mom...she was pretty impulsive. It got her in trouble sometimes."

So maybe I did inherit some of my mother's personality after all. Figures it would be her worst trait. "So she wasn't perfect," I said, more to myself than to Jackie.

Jackie chuckled. "No, honey," she said gently. "She wasn't. Who is?"

I wanted to let those words sink in, to hear about the ways in which my mom had been an ordinary girl, like me. But my first priority had to be tracking her down. "Where do you think she went?" I asked. "After she came to New York that last time. She came to see you, right?"

"We talked on the phone. She wanted to get together, but she never got back in touch. She mentioned having some business to attend to while she waited for Hence. I've wondered a thousand times what she meant by 'business.'" Jackie jumped to her feet. "I have something to show you."

At the back of her apartment, she held aside a gauzy curtain to let me into her studio. Statues have always creeped me out, and hers were no exception: life-size stone figures lurking in the dark, like storybook characters frozen by an evil curse. I maneuvered through the room, careful not to brush against them.

In the room's darkest corner, Jackie flipped a switch. There under the floodlights gleamed my mother in black marble, her arms raised in alarm, her blank eyes wide with what looked like fright, her long hair whipping behind her as though she were caught in a hurricane. At the knees, she melted into a black mass, like she was being swallowed by the earth or by a rising flood. It was more creepy than cool.

I caught Jackie's eye. "You think something terrible happened to her."

"I have no way of knowing," she said. "I might be wrong. After she disappeared, she was the only thing I could sculpt for months. I had this recurring dream—she was banging on my door, asking for help. I would try to run to her, but I couldn't get my legs to move." Her tone of voice changed. "Nobody just disappears for fourteen years, Chelsea."

"They do if they don't want to be found. Maybe she wanted to start a completely new life. Maybe she got sick of waiting for Hence." I touched the cold marble of my mother's bare arm. I'd been wondering which was worse, a dead mother or a still-living one who had abandoned me without a backward glance, but Jackie's stories had given me the answer. If she was alive somewhere, I would find a way to forgive her. "One of the detectives said Mom could still be hiding out in New York." I explained about the letter she'd sent me when she'd been staying at The Underground.

But Jackie shook her head. "The place was all boarded up. She couldn't have been staying there. I assumed she'd checked into a hotel. She called me from a pay phone on a street corner in Midtown."

"But what if she found a way into The Underground?" The suspicion I'd dismissed two days ago was returning. "What if Hence met her there? Could he have..." I couldn't bring myself to say the word *murdered*. "He had a motive, right? Jealousy. And he has such a nasty temper...."

"The police investigated him, but they cleared him pretty quickly," Jackie said. "He was still in England, stranded at Heathrow, when Cathy got here. Some kind of bad weather had grounded all the flights for a few days. Also, a transit strike slowed him down, if memory serves. As soon as he got into town he called me, looking for her."

"Could the police have gotten it wrong?" I asked. "Could Hence have—"

"He's not my favorite person in the world, but I can't imagine him hurting a hair on Catherine's head." Jackie shut her eyes, as if she was trying to look into the past. "He worshipped her."

At least I could still stay at the club without having to fear for my life. "Were there other suspects?"

Jackie looked like she'd bitten into something sour. "Your father."

"That's insane." My father was a lot of things—bumbling, hypocritical, distracted—but there was no way he was a murderer.

"He was cleared, of course," Jackie assured me. "A lot of missing women turn out to be victims of domestic abuse, so the husband usually comes under suspicion. Especially if the marriage was rocky."

Had the marriage been rocky? I suppose it must have been, given that my mother was in love with another man. Still, my dad didn't have it in him to hurt anyone, much less kill them. "If he finds a stinkbug in the bathroom, he carries it out the front door."

"Nobody who knew your father thought he was responsible for her disappearance," Jackie said. "Maybe I shouldn't have told you...."

"I asked you to tell me everything. I meant it."

She threw her arms around me again. "You're a brave girl," she said. "Just like your mom."

Her words—maybe the nicest thing anyone had ever said to me—sent a wave of warmth through my body. For a long time neither of us spoke, until an image popped into my head: the girl I'd seen, or maybe dreamed, scratching at the bedroom window, trying to get in. "What if she climbed up the fire escape and let herself in through the window in her bedroom? She could have been waiting in The Underground for Hence."

Jackie let go. "Of course! That window of hers. She used to leave it unlocked so Hence could climb in. She kept a two-by-four hidden behind the club so he could trip the ladder."

"So when she came back, she could have let herself into her bedroom." The idea exhilarated me; at last I'd made a breakthrough, however small: I'd found a piece of information I could offer to Hence in exchange for his help.

But that was as far as we got before Jackie's phone rang. "My gallery's calling; I have to take this," she told me, her hand over the receiver.

"I'll go," I said.

Before I left, Jackie scrawled her phone number on a piece of scrap paper. *Call me if you need anything,* she mouthed, her ear still pressed to her phone.

Oddly, when I let myself into The Underground, it was quiet and empty. I crept back downstairs to Cooper's bedroom, and he was still gone. My note lay on his pillow, exactly where I'd left it.

Catherine

For a while, Hence and I met up at Jackie's every day after school. Then, one afternoon, as he was slipping back into his jeans, he gave me a sheepish look. "I won't be able to meet up tomorrow. Riptide's rehearsing."

I bent to kiss his forehead. "That's okay."

"This won't be the only time. We'll need to rehearse at least a few times a week from now on."

"Got it," I said. "I understand."

Hence wrapped his arms around me and gave me a squeeze. "You're amazing," he said, and then he was gone.

I dressed slowly, giving myself a pep talk. *Being in Riptide is a great thing for Hence. I'll get more writing done now, and missing him will make my poems deeper, because poets are supposed to suffer. Aren't they?*

Dad was really excited for Hence and gladly cut back his hours at the club, but rehearsal time with the band quickly expanded to take up most of Hence's new free time. *Suck it up, I told myself whenever I felt a pang of longing. You don't need to hang around your boyfriend constantly. Besides, this will make the time we do get to spend together even more special.*

Still, on the afternoons when Hence was rehearsing, I couldn't help wishing I could be there, too. I wasn't about to suggest it, though; I knew from experience that guys in bands don't like girlfriends at practice any more than they like them at auditions.

I'd heard Dad's musician friends grouse endlessly on the subject. "Paulie insists on bringing his old lady to every rehearsal, and she's a colossal pain," I remembered Dave D'Amato saying about his bassist's girlfriend at one of Dad's late-night drinking-and-bullshit sessions. "She thinks she can *make suggestions.*" There had been true horror in his voice.

And Dave's weaselly drummer, whose name I could never remember, actually chimed in, "I don't mind if a guy brings his girl along, provided she's hot and she brings us beers."

Dave laughed. "We need a new rule. Hot girls welcome...but no Yokos."

"They're sexist pigs," I told my dad the next day as we were clearing away the empties from the living room. "Why don't you say something?"

"Dave's an old friend. Besides, he's essentially right. Bringing a girlfriend to practice is unprofessional."

"Or a boyfriend." I sniffed. "Girls are in bands, too."

Dad chuckled. "Or a boyfriend."

158

So I knew better than to ask Hence if I could sit in, which was why I was floored when he brought up the idea himself. "The guys said you could come watch us rehearse tomorrow if you want." We were cuddling under a blanket, and I was so happy to be in his arms that I hadn't even been thinking about rehearsals.

"You asked them?" I was thrilled. "And they really don't mind?"

"Stan and Andy weren't so into the idea at first," he admitted. "They had some bad experiences with the last lead guitarist's girlfriend. But I said you'd be totally cool."

I snuggled my face into his neck and inhaled deeply, breathing him in. "You're the best boyfriend ever." But then I pulled back. "They're not going to want me to fetch their beers, are they? Because there's no way."

Hence laughed, a sound I heard so rarely that it never failed to bring me joy. "Nobody expects you to fetch beer. Or make sandwiches." He cupped my face in his hands so I was looking straight into that gaze that melted me every time. "I want you there with me. And they want me to be happy, so they said yes."

So that's how I came to be curled up in an armchair in a bone-cold warehouse in the Meatpacking District. Though I wore my warmest down coat, I was still freezing; if there was a next time, I thought, I'd really have to sneak a quilt out in my backpack, and maybe a thermos of hot coffee. With fingers that felt brittle as icicles, I scribbled nonstop in my journal. Just being there, listening to Riptide practice, made me hungry to create something. Though I'd considered myself a writer ever since I could hold a pencil, I couldn't help wishing I knew how to dance or play an instrument—anything that would let me use my whole body to express myself, the way Hence was doing. He was a more physical guitar player than I had expected, pogoing, windmilling, sliding across the floor on his knees. The quiet, hesitant Hence I knew was nothing like this wildman swinging his prized Telecaster around like he might smash it, Pete Townshend–style, just for the thrill.

Of course I'd seen more than my share of rehearsals and sound checks at the club, to the point where even when a band was good I could feel pretty blasé about it. But it was different with Riptide, and not just because I was biased (though, admittedly, I was). Plenty of bands spoiled catchy hooks with lyrics so dumb they made my teeth ache. Others coupled lyrics that were clever or deep with music that moped along, monotonous and grating. But Riptide had the music *and* the lyrics. Not to mention the most gorgeous and talented front man in the history of rock and roll. In my humble opinion.

And while I was pretty sure Hence's bandmates would consider it an intrusion or a distraction, I couldn't help wishing I'd brought my camera so I could capture them in action. They weren't bad guys, as musicians go. I decided right away that I liked Ruben—the bassist—the best. He was the friendliest, with a smile that took up his whole face, and he won points for his fearless fashion sense; that day he had on a purple crushed-velvet jumpsuit and a furry red top hat. He was the one who ran upstairs to bring down an armchair for me to sit in, a comfy but musty one the guys had found by the side of the road on trash day. I felt bad making him go to all that trouble, but he brushed away my protests.

160

Stan, the drummer, was skinny, with a black pompadour and a crooked nose. Andy, the rhythm guitarist, had curly, sandy-colored hair; a round, impish face; and a to-die-for Cockney accent. At first I couldn't help wondering if maybe they'd agreed to let me sit in because of who my dad is, but after observing them in action, I finally decided that Hence had been right: They honestly were delighted to have him in the band, and he'd made them see that we were a package deal. "Your boyfriend's got pipes," Andy said to me before the band got down to business. "It's a huge relief to have somebody in Riptide who can actually sing."

It was true: Hence's voice could flow like silk one minute and rasp like sandpaper the next—whatever a song called for. That afternoon he was wearing a shirt I'd bought for him, a crisp, electric-blue button-down, the sleeves rolled up to his elbows, untucked over jeans. Each time I looked up from my journal and caught sight of him—slender, dark, and intense—the blood rushed to my head and I reeled with the pleasure of it all. Riptide's front man. My secret boyfriend.

One night in November, when Quentin was out with his friends and Dad was preoccupied with that night's show, Hence climbed the fire escape to my window. We'd talked the plan out for days and decided the elevator was too noisy. Even the stairs at the rear of the building were out, because Dad and the workers used them. Not that our plan wasn't still risky, since any passerby could look up to see Hence climbing through the window.

"I'll be careful," he'd promised. "I'll wait till the music's loud and nobody's looking." We agreed that the risk was worth it, especially now that Hence's free afternoons were so few. Besides, this way I could fall asleep in his arms, his breath warm in my hair, his scent seeping into my pillowcase. Best of all, we would wake up together, albeit not in that luxurious way I imagined us someday being able to. I was careful to set my alarm for four AM, when I knew Dad would be sound asleep, and Hence slipped back out the window and down the fire escape without a hitch. It was so easy we wondered why we hadn't tried it sooner.

After Hence reached the street safely, I snuggled under the covers, reliving how it had felt to fall asleep beside him, my head tucked under his chin while he absently drummed out a rhythm on my hip and hummed in my ear. It was the song he had started writing last week, the one about me. He hadn't worked out all of the lyrics yet, but there was a line about being tangled in my midnight hair, and a bit about how he wanted to kidnap me from school and take me to St. Mark's Place and walk through the streets holding hands. My favorite part was about how he wanted us to kiss in a rainstorm, daring lightning to strike.

The last verse was giving him trouble, though. I wanted to offer to help him, but it would have been supremely weird to cowrite a song about myself. Instead, I would wait and see what he came up with on his own. By then, I'd showed him all of my poems—not just the recent ones about him, but the old ones, too—and he really liked them. In fact, more than once he said he wanted to pick one out and write music for it—a plan that completely thrilled me. If he had been anyone else, I might have suspected he was just being polite, but I don't think Hence ever said a word to me that he didn't truly mean. Which is why I was so pleased by what he whispered just before he fell asleep: "I've been thinking about us living together. After you graduate. Getting a little apartment of our own."

How could I sleep after that? I could imagine precisely what our apartment would look like: cozy and just big enough for two, with sunshine streaming in the windows, lace curtains, and a cat—I'd always wanted a Siamese, but Q was allergic—curled in the middle of our bed. We'd have cut flowers—daffodils or wild irises—and stacks and stacks of books in every room, and there would be music on the stereo every hour of the day, and maybe even at night while we slept.

I could picture it all so clearly. Even so, I knew I might have to be flexible. If lace curtains and daffodils sounded too girly to Hence, I would adjust. I wouldn't mind living in a more masculine apartment, either, with black walls and graffiti art and a pinball machine against the wall, with floor pillows instead of furniture—something as bohemian and original as Hence himself—as long as I got the cat and a desk to write and study at and we were close to the T so I could get to my classes at Harvard. Maybe we could even live right in Cambridge, with its shady trees, quirky book-stores and restaurants, and the Brattle Theatre, where they showed the best independent films and sold cappuccino in the lobby. Of all the places Dad had ever taken me, Cambridge—his alma mater and my future college town—was the only place I'd ever wanted to move to.

I could have cuddled in bed dreaming about the future all the next day, if I didn't have to go to school. It was too soon for senior-itis to kick in, since I hadn't yet started on my college applications. Apart from Harvard, I would apply to Yale and Brown, and maybe Smith and Bryn Mawr, with SUNY Binghamton as my safety school. My guidance counselor had scolded me when I'd told her I planned to apply only to Harvard. "Even a straight-A student needs safety schools," she'd said, and as annoyed as I'd been, I realized she was probably right.

Though I hadn't mentioned any of this to Hence yet, as I inhaled his scent on my pillow, a new and thrilling idea occurred to me: Maybe he could apply to Harvard, too? Or, failing that, some other nearby school—Emerson, or Berklee College of Music. Maybe I could even talk Dad into helping out with his tuition. That last part would be tricky; I wouldn't want my father to suspect that Hence and I were a couple—at least not while we were still living under his roof. Even so, I felt pretty certain I could pull it off without arousing Dad's suspicion. The best way to get Dad to do anything was to plant an idea in his head and let it grow there for a while, until he thought it was his own. Some night after dinner, when Dad was in a good mood, I would ask him whether he thought Hence would ever go to college. That would get him started on his own Harvard memories, and on how these days everyone needs a college education—a speech I'd heard a thou-sand times before. And I would mention how smart Hence was, and how he had next to nothing—no money, no family, and no chance at going to college.

The tricky part would be convincing Dad that I was casually interested in Hence's well-being, that he had become a cause, like some little kid in Zambia or Appalachia who needed money for shoes or dental care. The last thing I wanted to do was let on how much Hence's future mattered to *me*.

As certain as I was that Hence would be psyched about my plan to get him into college, something kept me from mentioning it to him, until the day I couldn't help myself. We were headed home from rehearsal. The subway car was crowded, but we'd managed to score the last two seats, and even though a few passengers had groused about Hence's amp and guitar case being in the way, he was in a great mood. Practice had gone well, and he was building a rapport with Andy, Stan, and Ruben. A gig at the Big Bang—Hence's first as lead singer—had been scheduled for the following month. As clubs go, the Big Bang wasn't quite as big a deal as The Underground, but almost.

Hence was as talkative as I'd ever seen him. "I like how serious the guys are," he was saying. "Riptide isn't a hobby to them—it's their lives. Besides, they're good guys. That will be key when we go on tour together. Once the album's done, we may even get to do an international tour. The U.S. *and* Western Europe."

"You'll love Europe," I said, a little absently. "It's magical—all the villages and castles." Somewhere around the edges of my consciousness, an unpleasant new thought was creeping in, one I hadn't let myself entertain until now.

"I'll love seeing it with you," he responded. "Between gigs, you can take me around to places you've been."

But by then the unpleasant thought had formed and taken hold. "When would this be, this tour of Europe?"

"It would probably start next summer. Does it matter? I'll have to quit The Underground, but your dad will understand."

"Um." I barely knew where to start. It wasn't like I hadn't mentioned my college plans to Hence. More than once, I'd gone on and on about the trip to Cambridge my family took when I was ten, about how much I'd loved it there—the redbrick buildings and the cool, leafy courtyards. It was true that I hadn't said much about the applications I was starting to fill out. I hadn't mentioned the plans I'd been working on for Hence's education, and how I was going to convince Dad to help out with tuition. "How long would the tour be?" Maybe it would just be a summer thing. That would be fine.

Hence laughed. "Oh, I don't know, Catherine. It's all hypothetical right now. Our manager is still working out the details."

"Hypothetical." That sounded better. I rested my hand on Hence's knee. It wasn't his fault he couldn't read my mind. I made my voice as light as I possibly could. "You know, I've been thinking, these last few weeks. About what comes after graduation." I bit the bullet. "Have you ever thought about college?"

Hence snorted, and the woman across the aisle looked up from her *Daily News* to give him a disapproving look. "What would I need college for?"

"Everyone needs college. To get in the door anywhere, you need a bachelor's degree." It was my father's speech, coming through my lips. "Even creative people. Especially creative people."

"Get in what door?" Hence said. "I've already got a job. Riptide's the only door I need to get into...." His expression changed. "We passed our stop. Now we're going to have to walk ten blocks."

"Big deal."

"You're not the one hauling an amp." This was the first time Hence had ever gotten angry at me, and I didn't like the edge to his voice. At the next stop, we carried his stuff out onto the platform, and our conversation stalled while we climbed up into daylight.

"Musicians go to college," I told him once we'd reached the top of the stairs. "Lots of bands meet at college."

"I've already got a band," he said. "What are you saying?"

"*I'm* going to Harvard." I said it straight out, just like that. "If they accept me. I've been planning it for years."

"Harvard." Hence's frown deepened. "It doesn't get any snootier than that, does it?"

"Snooty?" We were blocking the sidewalk. Annoyed commuters were dodging us, some of them swearing, but I couldn't have cared less. "I've wanted this all my life. I've worked hard for it, too."

"So what am I supposed to do? While you're up there in... wherever it is."

"Cambridge, Massachusetts. Everybody knows that."

Hence raised a single eyebrow at me. "Everybody? Maybe in *your* world."

"What's that supposed to mean?" The words came out louder than I'd intended. This wasn't at all how I had imagined this conversation going. Asking him to move with me to Cambridge should have been a romantic gesture. Instead, we were yelling at each other, putting on a show for smirking passersby.

"Not everyone lives in *your* world. Believe it or not, not everyone wants to." With a sour look on his face, Hence picked up his amp and plunged into the crowd. I struggled to keep up, not wanting him to have the last word.

"If you don't want to live in *my* world, why did you even come here?" I waved my arms. "In *this* world, Harvard is the best school—the most prestigious."

"*Prestigious?*" Now he was mocking me, and I didn't like it one bit. I let go of his guitar case. Actually, I threw it down to the pavement. "Carry your own damn guitar." I stomped off through the crowd.

"Hey!" I heard him shout behind me, but I was running, bumping into people, leaving a trail of pissed-off pedestrians in my wake. I didn't stop till I reached The Underground. I let myself in, locked the door behind me, and tore up the stairs, too angry to wait for the elevator. Up in my room, I flung myself facedown on the bed. Hadn't I tried my best to help Hence, to support him, to *be* with him, even when it meant distancing myself from my own brother? And had he ever so much as asked me what *my* plans were, what *I* wanted out of life? Did he expect me to trail along behind him from show to show, watching adoringly while he had all the fun?

"Selfish jerk," I growled into my pillow. Would I have to choose between Hence and my future? That hardly seemed fair.

Just then, someone knocked on the door.

It was Hence, his hair damp with sweat. He didn't look as angry as he had before.

"What are you doing up here? What if Q hears you?" I took a step out into the hallway.

"I don't care what he thinks," Hence said grimly. "I only care about you."

After that, I couldn't be angry with him anymore, though I still sort of wanted to be. I clasped my hands behind my back to keep from reaching out to brush the damp bangs from his eyes.

"The thing is, I can't go to Harvard with you," Hence continued, but at least he didn't sound scornful when he said it.

"It wouldn't have to be Harvard. There are tons of colleges up in Boston—all different kinds. You're the smartest and most creative person I know. You'd get in somewhere, and maybe I could talk Dad into helping with tuition, and—"

"Catherine." He scuffed one lime-green Chuck Taylor against the other. "When I left home, I dropped out of high school. I didn't even finish my junior year."

"Oh." Now it was my turn to look down at my own sneakers, ashamed. "I didn't realize...."

"That's okay," he said. "But you see why college is a problem."

"You can get your GED. I'd help you. You'd breeze right through it."

"But there's no point," Hence said. "I came to New York to break into the music business. And now I'm in a band...a really good band, with a future."

"There are bands in Boston."

"Riptide is here." His voice was starting to take on that unpleasant tone again. He inhaled sharply, and for a moment I thought he was going to break up with me. Instead, he gave me a pleading look. "Isn't New York City the capital of the world? Aren't there colleges here?"

"Yes," I admitted.

"Aren't some of them as good as Harvard?" He tipped my face gently up toward his, and I felt myself thaw.

"Columbia, maybe. Or Fordham." After all, Harvard without Hence didn't sound like the glorious college experience I'd been imagining.

"If you went to one of those, we could live together here, get an apartment of our own, once I get home from my tour. Maybe you could come with me for the summer part of it? You'd like that, wouldn't you?"

"Yes," I told him. "I'd like that." Wasn't Hence more important to me than anything else?

After that, I urged him to get downstairs before Q could catch us together and complicate our lives further. I sat on my bed for a long time, revising my plans. So what if I'd lived in New York City all my life? I'd already traveled to plenty of other places. Hence was right—New York was at least as cool and exciting as anyplace else. And it was easier to imagine a life without Harvard than a life without Hence. So I made up my mind: I would apply to Columbia, NYU, and Fordham—all good schools.

Still, I couldn't help wanting to apply to Harvard, too—just to see if I would get in. What would it hurt? Maybe it would be enough to know they wanted me. I could go somewhere else, secure in the knowledge that I had been accepted into my first-choice school. And, besides, who was I kidding? A million people must apply to Harvard every year. They probably wouldn't accept me, anyway.

Catherine

A few nights later, at three in the morning, the ringing of the phone beside my bed woke me. Over the pounding of my heart I could barely make out what the voice on the other end was saying—something about an emergency room at Lenox Hill Hospital. "Are you related to James Eversole?"

"He's my father."

"Can you get here? Right away?"

I moved in what felt like slow motion, out the door and down the stairs. Q's bedroom door was locked, so I pounded on it, screaming his name. When he opened it, I flew into his arms. "Dad's had a heart attack." I sobbed the words into his rumpled T-shirt.

We took a cab to the hospital. Q urged the cabdriver to run each of the million red lights we hit, but he refused. In the painfully bright light of the waiting room, the nurse wouldn't let us in to see Dad, saying he was in surgery. "I don't care," I kept insisting. "He would want us there. I could hold his hand so he would know I was with him."

But she kept shaking her head. "Wait right over there." She pointed to a bank of empty chairs. "I promise, I'll come get you the second you can see him."

What could we do but comply? The wait seemed to take hours. I rested my head on Q's shoulder, all our differences forgotten, and I could feel him clenching his fists, then releasing. Clenching, releasing.

Then the doctor came out—a black-haired woman in a white coat—and she was moving her mouth, trying to tell us something, and I was screaming so I wouldn't have to hear her.

We didn't even get to say good-bye.

Chelsea

Alone in The Underground, I couldn't seem to relax. I kept glancing up at the window, remembering the girl whose face I'd seen there, only now when I imagined her face it wore the panicked look I'd seen on Jackie's statue. Though I knew it was crazy, I checked the window's lock to make sure it was still fastened. Of course it was. But even that didn't make me feel less jumpy.

There was still so much of my mother's journal left, but getting through it had become harder. At first reading each entry had been like tasting a delicious little piece of her. The more I read, though, the more scared I was that when I reached the end, that would be it—I'd have uncovered all of her that was left. When I got to the part about my grandfather's death, I had to put the book down, to take a break from all the sadness. Even reading the happier parts gave me this dizzying feeling of forgetting who I was, of losing track of my own life and getting caught up in hers.

The whole thing made me confused. While I was reading, I found myself liking Hence. *Her* Hence, that is—the young, vulnerable, romantic one. And it got harder to hate the Hence I knew—older, crankier, in need of a shave. Weirder still, as I read I found myself rooting for her and Hence to get together in the end, stupidly hoping the Catherine in the journal would find a way to get everything she wanted—Harvard and Hence at the same time. It was disturbing to catch myself rooting against my own father. Against my very existence.

I couldn't help wondering: If she was alive, would I rather see her reunited with Hence than with my dad? If I found her, would I help make that happen? I wasn't sure of the answers to those questions anymore, and that made me feel uncomfortable. Disloyal. Confused.

Then there were the poems, each one a puzzle waiting for me to unlock its secrets. Like this one:

Riptide

*The crash of waves like an invitation
wakes me from my nap,
calling me into the drama
of high winds and foamy surf.
So I strip down to my suit
and dip my toes in ice water.*

Once I'm in up to my hips,
I know I won't be turning back. I dive
and slice through gray saltwater.
In love with the unreachable horizon,
I lose track of myself—too far
out of the lifeguard's sight,
when a riptide washes back from shore
to tug me under and fling me like driftwood
farther and farther away
from everything I know. I flail
and tread water, wanting nothing
but dry sand beneath my feet,
nothing but the warm, familiar beach.
Too late. To my friends on their blankets
who shield their eyes and squint at the sea
I'm nothing but a speck—
going, going, gone.

Given the title, it had to be about Hence and his band. Of course my mom would have been thrilled that her boyfriend was becoming a rock star. Who wouldn't be? But all that business about being tugged away from shore and flung around like driftwood sounded sad, or maybe scared. Then again, what did I know about poetry? My mom's creative-writing genes had completely skipped me. Lately my language arts grades had been *profoundly disappointing*, according to Dad. Maybe the poem was all about being swept away by happiness, and I just wasn't getting it. I reread it over and over, waiting for light to dawn.

Finally, the sounds of unloading on the street below broke into my reading. There was a show that night—which meant Cooper must be back. I tucked the journal into its hiding place and cursed the pokey old elevator all the way down to the first floor.

Sure enough, I found Cooper out front, instructing the roadies about what went where. He kept going about his business, helping to lug a drum kit onto the stage while I watched, waiting for the right moment. But the suspense was killing me. I shifted from foot to foot.

Finally, drums in place, he looked up to find me there. "Oh," was all he said.

"You got my note?" I asked. "About what I said last night? I was just mad at Hence for jumping to conclusions."

But instead of replying, Cooper scanned the room, looking for the next task to turn his attention to, as if I weren't standing there, right in front of him, practically begging for his forgiveness.

"Please don't stay angry," I said. "You're the only actual friend I have right now. Nobody else knows where I am and what I'm going through. Besides, I can't help what comes out of my mouth when I get mad. It's, like, my tragic flaw."

Cooper's lips twitched in what might have been a smile. "It's tragic, all right."

"It doesn't have to be," I said.

But the smile disappeared. "You know what really would be tragic? If I lost my job. I took a real risk last night. It's pretty clear Hence doesn't want me anywhere near you."

"But that's ridiculous! He's crazy and paranoid. He's..." I

could feel myself starting to sputter. Knowing I might be about to veer into saying the wrong thing again, I bit my lip so hard I actually drew blood.

I inhaled and began again. "You said you and he are friends, right? Maybe if you tried explaining to him…"

"Explaining what? The truth is, Hence wouldn't like the fact that I showed you those pictures of your mother. He wouldn't like…" Unable or unwilling to finish, he dug his hands into his pockets and looked off into the distance, his blue-green eyes full of some kind of distress.

"Wouldn't like what?" I asked.

"Us being friends," he whispered.

"Oh," I said. That was when my lower lip started to tremble, because although I hadn't given it too much thought, it was true: Coop and I had become friends. And now suddenly we weren't, and I was back to being completely on my own.

"I'm not here to make friends." I whirled around so he wouldn't see me blinking back tears, and stomped off in the direction of Hence's office. Like it or not, I needed to talk to him. I had to find my mother so I could get out of this place where nobody liked me and never come back.

When Hence looked up from the papers on his desk, his jaw dropped at the sight of me in his doorway, but I spoke before he could start yelling.

"Calm down," I said, in no mood to take any more crap from him. "I promise to leave before the club opens. I won't get you in trouble with the NYPD or the FBI, or whoever it is that cares about underage drinking."

Hence gave me a funny look, like he was searching for something scathing to say but couldn't find it.

"I went to see Jackie this morning," I said. "My mom's friend."

To my utter surprise, his expression softened. Without saying a word, he beckoned me to sit down in a spare chair on the other side of his desk, so I did. It was a pretty ordinary office—just some file cabinets and a gray metal desk—except that the walls were plastered with eight-by-ten glossies of bands that had played The Underground.

"Did you find out anything useful?"

I ran through the memory of all that Jackie had told me, hardly knowing where to start. It had all been interesting, but was any of it *useful*? Then I remembered. "She might have been in the building," I told him. "This building. In fact, I'm sure she was, even though the front was boarded up. She could have climbed up the fire escape and in through the window."

Hence made a teepee with his fingers. Above it, his eyes twinkled unpleasantly. "Did you find out anything I didn't already know?"

His words stung as though he'd slapped me. "*You* could tell me things," I said. "But you don't. You just sit there smirking at me."

As soon as I said the words, I regretted them. I thought he'd blow up at me again, but to my surprise, that didn't happen. Instead, he unlocked his desk and pulled something out. It looked like a postcard. "How much do you know about your mother and me?" he asked, his voice neutral, like he was working not to betray any emotion.

"Everything," I said. "Well, not *everything*." I struggled for an unembarrassing way to say it. "I know you were *together*." Saying the words, I felt a flood of relief. Now he knew I knew, and maybe we could talk for real. "I know she left us to be with you."

His eyes narrowed, taking me in more closely, and handed me the postcard. On one side was a glossy picture of some nightclub, with a little Union Jack embossed in the corner. Just as I was turning it over, a band started playing in the next room, the heavy bass and drums thundering through the walls. Hence leaped from his seat.

"I'll be right back," he said over his shoulder. "Don't go anywhere with that."

Glad to be unobserved, I read the postcard.

Catherine,

Don't you think it's time we stop playing games? Riptide's success, my farce of a marriage—nothing I've done since you left means anything. I wanted to hurt you, but I'm over all that. Come to The Underground. I only bought it so you would have a home to come back to. As soon as I can get out of England, I'll meet you there. The window's open.

All my love, always,
Hence

The postmark was blurry, with a date I couldn't make out. The card had been addressed to our old house in Danvers. So this was the trigger for my mother's running away from home. I turned it over and over in my hands, hardly knowing how I felt about this new information.

"Cooper's got everything under control," Hence said as he reentered the room. "We have some time."

I handed back the postcard. "But how do you have this if you sent it to her? Did you...did the two of you...?" I was trying to ask if he'd come home and found her here after all, if they'd had time together before she disappeared. But what about the alibi that supposedly put him in England at the time of her disappearance? I wanted to ask, but the look on his face—a terrible sadness—made me fall silent.

"I found it here, up in her bedroom, lying on the rug. She'd left the window open. The downstairs was boarded up; there was no other way in or out. There were no signs of forced entry, or of any kind of a scuffle. She left the way she came—of her own free will."

"Why would she leave before you got here?" Could he be lying? Somehow I didn't think so. "If she left us to be with you, why wouldn't she wait till you got here?"

Hence frowned. "Isn't that what you're supposed to be finding out?"

"Jackie said something about her having business to attend to."

"I know that," Hence snapped.

His tone of voice set me on edge. But a new thought occurred to me. "Do the police know about that postcard? Do they know my mother was here before she disappeared?"

"It doesn't change anything," Hence said. "It wouldn't have helped them find her."

"You can't know that for sure," I said. "You withheld evidence that might have made you look guilty. That's got to be some kind of crime...." The words popped out of my mouth before I could think about what I was saying. I'd just gotten a tiny bit comfortable with Hence, had decided I could maybe trust him, and he seemed to have decided the same thing about me. But the look that crossed his face now frightened me.

"It's nobody's business," he said. "Not the police's. Not even yours."

"Then why did you show it to me?"

I thought my question was innocent enough, but it seemed to enrage him. He jumped to his feet and glowered down at me. For a moment I wondered who would hear me if I screamed. Nobody, not with the racket being made by the band one room over. "So you can go home and tell that egghead father of yours his marriage was a lie. Catherine could never love somebody like him. She spent their whole marriage waiting for a chance to come back to me."

This made me so angry I forgot to be scared. I sputtered, unable to speak.

"She was only trying to hurt me, like I was trying to hurt her. Everything I did—buying the club, marrying my sorry excuse of a...I never loved that bitch, never even liked her. I couldn't hear her voice without wanting to slap her. Not that I ever hit her, but I was tempted. I came close, more than once. I could have...." He turned and, without warning, smashed his fist through the wall, the plaster crumbling under his hand.

Maybe I should have jumped to my feet and raced out of the room, but all I could do was stare.

181

"And that's what I'll do to the skull of the son of a bitch who killed Catherine, when I find out who he is."

"She's alive," I heard myself say. "Just because she didn't wait here for you to come back doesn't mean she's dead."

He spun around and looked at me like he'd forgotten I was in the room. What was I saying? Did I really want to make him angrier than he already was? He took a step toward me, his arm still raised.

"You're seriously going to hit a girl?" It was the only thing I could think of to say that might stop him.

To my surprise, it worked. He laughed. It wasn't a nice laugh, but at least he wasn't putting his hand through my skull.

"You do have some of your mother's courage," he said grudgingly.

Coming from him, this was a compliment. For one weird moment, it made me almost happy.

But then he frowned, and his tone turned poisonous again. "Even so, if there was any justice in this universe, you would never have been born."

What was I supposed to say to that?

"You'd better get out of here. I'll give you half an hour to pack." He looked at his watch. "Starting now." He turned his back to me, so I left the room.

It's a good thing Cooper wasn't in sight; I was way too upset to explain what had happened. I punched the button for the elevator over and over, as if that would get me upstairs faster. There was no way I wanted to spend another minute in the same building with that madman Hence.

182

But where would I go? I wasn't ready to give up my search and crawl home to Massachusetts. I couldn't face my father, knowing what I knew about his marriage to my mom. I'd have to explain where I'd been and what I'd learned, and how could I do that without breaking his heart?

As I stuffed clothes and my mother's journal into my backpack, I tried to think who in all of New York City would be willing to give me a bed for the night. That's how I wound up on Jackie Gray's front stoop.

Catherine

A thousand strangers lined up for Dad's wake, waiting for more than an hour to see that waxy-looking, made-up body I could barely believe had ever been him. I knew I should be grateful for how beloved Dad was, for how many people knew him and how important some of those people were. Sal Battaglia, Dad's best friend, stepped in to handle the arrangements, organizing the wake and booking the space for the memorial service. TV crews came, and the room filled up.

"Standing room only," Sal whispered in my ear during the service. "Jim always did like a full house."

I tried to smile, but all I wanted was to be left alone so I could have a nervous breakdown in peace.

On my other side, Q looked grim and pale in one of the Italian suits Dad liked to buy for himself but never seemed to wear. That whole afternoon, he didn't so much as speak a word. It was nothing like when Mom died and the two of us held on to each other and cried. Sitting beside this silent version of Q in his oversize Armani suit was almost worse than being next to a stranger.

So many of Dad's friends and business contacts wanted to speak at the funeral that it seemed endless. Guy Snarker—Dad's least favorite of all the acts he broke—showed up in leather pants and gave a long talk about how Jim Eversole was a visionary, and a rebel against conformity, a John the Baptist who cleared the way in the wilderness of commercial radio for prophets to come. It wasn't lost on anyone that Guy Snarker was Jesus Christ in that scenario.

Guy's speech was the first of many. I'd known Dad was important in the music world, but I hadn't realized *how* important. I should have been proud of all the photographers and news networks straining to get footage, and impressed by the people who'd never even met Dad who showed up wearing black and sobbing audibly. But the man they all were talking about sounded like some distant celebrity—not the generous, spontaneous, funny, loving father I had known. It was hard not to feel that Q and I had wandered into some ghoulish three-ring media circus. I kept wishing we'd told Sal to make the funeral private so I wouldn't have to keep endlessly shaking hands and comforting acquaintances who struggled to come up with the right words.

Hence came to the service. He sat near the back, with Jackie and her mother. He should have been beside me, but we'd fallen into the habit of secrecy for Dad's sake, and, now that he was gone, we hadn't yet worked through how important it was to maintain the secret. All through the funeral, I had to fight the urge to run to the back of the church, to grab Hence by the hand and drag him up to the front of the room with me, where he belonged. I was really, truly sorry I'd never told Dad about me and Hence. As he died, did he worry that he was leaving me alone in the world?

Of course, as far as Dad knew, Q and I were as close as we'd ever been. He wouldn't have wanted to know otherwise. Dad had been an only child and thought his life would have been so much better if only he'd had a brother or sister.

As we rode in the back of Sal's car to the funeral home, I put my head on Q's shoulder and he didn't pull away, even when my tears spilled down Dad's charcoal-gray jacket. For a moment it felt the way it used to between us. We'd both lost Dad, but at least we still had each other. But when we got home, Quentin ran straight upstairs, locked himself in his room, and stayed there all night, leaving me to wander through an apartment that felt too large and full of echoes, too emptied of my father's booming laugh.

A few days after the funeral, Q and I went uptown to Dad's lawyer's office, Harmon, Federman and Gluck, for the reading of his will, one more official sign that our lives had changed forever. I didn't want to go, but I had no choice. I needed to find out what would happen next, to us and to the club. I only wished Hence could have come along to hold my hand in the fancy waiting room, a warm and steady friend to keep me from falling apart.

Q's presence was the opposite of calming; he paced, jingling keys in the pocket of the pin-striped trousers he had taken from

Dad's closet as if he was now the man in the family and had to dress the part. He seemed more anxious than sad, and I couldn't help feeling he was worried about what Dad had left him. But maybe the truth wasn't that ugly; maybe he was concerned with how he would look after me from then on. As for me, I didn't care what stuff Dad had left us. I didn't want his money or his property—I only wanted what I couldn't have: him.

Danny Gluck had been Dad's roommate in college. The two of them used to play together in that band Dad always talked about, and when he walked into the room, he clasped first Quentin's hand, then mine, moisture in his hooded blue eyes. "Your father was a good man," he said. "The best of the best."

Tears sprang to my eyes in response. After that, it was hard to sit up straight in his gold-and-blue-striped office chairs and listen, but I caught the most important parts. Q would be getting the club itself. And Dad left me money—enough to put me through any college I got into. But college felt a million years away. I could barely imagine how we would get through the next few minutes, hours, days.

For most of the taxi ride home, Q didn't say a word. I watched him out of the corner of my eye, trying to get a sense of how he felt about the will. It wasn't a huge surprise that Dad had left him the club; Dad had always said that someday Q would take over the family business. But Q had never been interested in running The Underground. Instead of studying business, the way Dad wanted him to, he was majoring in criminal justice at CUNY, and before Dad died Q had been talking about transferring to some school in Miami where he could windsurf and jet-ski year-round.

187

But somebody had to run the club, and I wasn't old enough. It would have been scarily easy to imagine Q unloading the club and taking off for parts unknown, but Dad's will stipulated that Quentin couldn't sell the building until I graduated college, so I would have a place to live if I needed it. When Danny Gluck had read that part, I'd dared a quick look over at Q. He had looked pained. Now, in the cab, he still looked like he had a massive headache.

"Are you okay?"

No answer.

"What happens next, Q?"

Still no answer.

I stared out the window, at the first snow of the season falling to the earth in soft, fluffy flakes. The festive snowfall and the Christmas lights in all the store windows felt ludicrous. It should have been pouring icy rain on the streets of Manhattan.

The wheels in my head kept spinning. Dad's will made Quentin my legal guardian until I turned eighteen, in nine months. And of course Q was Hence's boss now, too. How much would it matter to Q that Dad had cared for Hence and wanted to look out for him?

"What about The Underground?" I asked Q, even though I barely dared hope for an answer.

The question shook him out of his silence. "What about it?"

"When are you going to open it back up?" What I really wanted to ask—but didn't dare—was *if* he was going to reopen the club.

His answer wasn't exactly reassuring. "Hell if I know."

"But what about the shows Dad scheduled?"

"I'll cancel them."

"All of them?" Q knew perfectly well that Dad booked shows a year in advance.

But Q had fallen back into silence, his jaw muscles visibly flexing, and I couldn't bring myself to say what I was thinking: Q had to reopen the club. It would break Dad's heart if The Underground died along with him. I had to believe Dad's soul was somewhere, watching over us. Heaven, maybe, or some version of it where they had loud music, Harleys, and Jack Daniel's.

When the cab pulled up to The Underground, I got out, but Q didn't move. "Take me to Sutton Place," I heard him tell the driver, and I realized that he was planning to disappear wherever it was he went for another night.

"When will you be home?"

Q shrugged. "Don't worry about me." If he was the least bit worried about me—about whether I was feeling lonely or depressed or scared—he certainly didn't let it show. The cab pulled away while I was still on the sidewalk.

Inside the club, Hence was leaning against the stage, waiting. When he saw that I was alone, he ran to throw his arms around me, and I buried my head in his chest and sobbed; though I'd known him for just four months, he'd become the only real family I had left.

Hence didn't ask about what happened at the lawyer's office, and I didn't tell him my worst fear—that The Underground would go out of business and Q would kick him out on the street. I couldn't think how to begin saying the words. Together, in silence, we rode the elevator up to my bedroom, where he held me—nothing more—as the snow thickened and erased the streets around us.

Catherine

Everything in my life felt heavy that winter. It was all I could do to put on clean clothes and drag myself to school in the mornings, much less do my homework—all the term papers and pop quizzes so meaningless to me now. It was good I'd sent my college applications in early; I would never have been able to make myself do them that long, dreadful December. College—the future I had been so worried over—now seemed a million years away, with each of the days in between long and empty.

As soon as I started functioning like my normal self, when I managed to think about something besides Dad, some random object would remind me of him—his lucky shoes where he'd left them in the parlor, or his winter coat in the hall closet—and I would fall back into grief, as though a trapdoor had opened under my feet. Once in a while, when I was off somewhere with Hence, shopping for groceries or walking aimlessly around the neighborhood, I would forget to think of Dad. Then I would remember and guilt would slap me across the face.

Christmas was the worst. Quentin had said he'd be around for the holiday, but when I woke up that morning, he was gone to who knows where, the way he was most of the time. Hence and I spent the day alone together, eating mu shu pork and watching old movies on TV. Neither of us felt like exchanging presents.

On those rare occasions when he was actually home, Q would spend hours locked in his room, refusing to come out for meals, sometimes not even answering when I knocked on the door. When I would come home from school and find his parka in the hall closet and the door to his bedroom shut and locked, it felt worse to have Q there than it did to have him away.

One day I finally couldn't stand it anymore. Instead of knocking, I banged on the door for about five minutes straight, until he opened it and stared at me like I was a lamp that had come to life and started speaking.

"What's wrong?"

"Nothing. Everything." I sighed, not knowing how to begin answering that question. I started over. "I'm making grilled cheese and cream of tomato soup. Do you want some?"

"What?" It was like we spoke two different languages.

"You know. Dinner. Food on a plate? That you sit down and eat?"

And he looked blankly at me, shook his head, and shut the door without so much as a thank-you. I thought about banging again, demanding that he talk to me, but I was scared I'd find the

191

Q I used to know had been completely replaced by the expression-less, almost wordless guy I'd just seen in the doorway. Even Bad Quentin, with his temper tantrums and steely eyes, would be better than this new, scary, silent Quentin.

Less than an hour after that non-conversation, he emerged from his room, grabbed his parka, and hurried out of the apartment without even saying good-bye, locking his bedroom door behind him. I pressed my forehead to the window to watch him disappear down the street and around a corner.

The questions I longed to ask him crowded my brain: *What's wrong with you? What are you doing in there? Where do you go when you're out of the house? When are you going to reopen the club? What happens next?*

Meanwhile, The Underground stayed closed. I had more than enough money for food and subway fare, and it seemed Q was paying the bills for the phone, heat, and electricity because so far at least we still had all three. One thing was certain: Q had stopped paying Hence's salary. In fact, he hadn't so much as mentioned Hence, hadn't said a word about whether he expected him to stay on in case we reopened the club.

Before we lost Dad, Hence's presence in the house was a constant annoyance to Q. Afterward, it was like he had completely forgotten Hence was living in our basement. And, in fact, he wasn't. With Q away for days at a time, Hence started spending every night up in my room. I would fall asleep in his arms and wake up beside him, and he was the only good thing in my sorry life.

*   *   *

Around that time, Hence's portion of Riptide's record advance came in, and he threw himself into his music with a vengeance. In late January, the band went into the studio and rarely came out. We had even less time together than before, and I couldn't help feeling lonely those long winter evenings when night fell early and I ate dinner by myself in front of the TV, waiting for him to come home.

But it was all for the best, of course; Hence had important work to do. Two of his songs were slated for inclusion on the album, and, in my opinion, they were the best material Riptide had. Meanwhile, the band had been booking stray gigs here and there, and I'd been going with Hence to the shows. Because I was with the band it hardly ever mattered that I was underage, and I didn't drink, anyway. I was there to pay attention, to hang on to the side of the stage as Hence sang his heart out or played a blistering solo on his new Telecaster.

And I wasn't the only one gaping adoringly up at him. There were always groupies—sometimes new ones, but always a familiar few that showed up wherever Riptide played. One in particular drove me crazy because she was so fixated on Hence, screaming his name whenever he did anything, flipping her straggly fuchsia hair if he looked in her direction, and bouncing around to the beat. And I do mean bouncing. No matter that it was the dead of winter; she showed up every night in a teensy tube top and a short skirt over ripped tights. She'd seen Hence and me together after the shows, so she must have known he had a girlfriend, but it didn't seem to matter to her. I guess she hoped one day he would take a good long look at her and realize how sexy and available she was, and go home with her instead.

Not that I was worried. One night after a show, I asked Hence if he'd noticed her. She'd retreated to the bar but was still watching him from across the room, her eyes burning like cigarettes through the smoky air.

"Who? Oh, that one with the pink hair? She's a trip, isn't she?" He slid his guitar into its case and snapped it shut. "She slipped me her phone number. More than once. She's persistent."

"What? Why didn't you tell me?"

Hence shrugged. "What does it matter? She's nothing to me. Less than nothing." He grabbed my hands, pulled me close, and wrapped my arms around his waist. "I don't even see anyone who isn't you."

I laughed. "Oh, please. Like anyone could not notice her jiggling and shrieking."

"I notice. I just don't care."

"Well, maybe you should care." It was a strange argument to be making, but I didn't seem to be able to stop myself. "After all, she's your biggest fan."

"We'll have plenty of fans soon enough. We can stand to lose one here and there."

"Maybe you should tell her to quit stalking you. Tell her you've got a girlfriend, and that you're not interested."

"I could do that," he said. "But I'd rather do this." He tipped my face up toward his and kissed me deeply, lingeringly, his hands tangled in my hair, for so long that I almost forgot about the pink-haired girl and the rest of the groupies. But when we finally pulled apart, I did remember to check and see if she was still watching. I was happy to find her gone.

*   *   *

With every passing day, Hence's dreams came a little more true. When school let out, we would meet on the corner, and he would tell me how that day's recording had gone. He was always excited and happy, full of news—the band was about to meet with its new publicist, or they'd decided what "look" they wanted for an upcoming photo shoot, or that day's recording session had gone better than usual. On weekends, I would tag along with him to the studio and sit in a corner, watching and listening. Sitting in was exciting at first, but the sessions got repetitive after a while. Sometimes, when I'd been listening to an hour's worth of solemn debate about how far forward the voices should be in the mix, I was tempted to plug my ears and scream.

But screaming was out: I had to be every inch the supportive girlfriend. Eventually I began bringing along a book to distract myself. Sometimes I would be deep in my reading and get the feeling that I was being watched. I'd look up to find Hence's eyes on me as he played a solo or sang, and when our eyes met, no matter what he was doing, he would smile, giving off the happy vibe of someone on the brink of having everything he'd ever wished for. I'd remember how rare his smiles were when we first met, how he'd almost seemed incapable of smiling, and my heart would twist in my chest. It was as if he'd been running up a hill, struggling like mad, and was about to reach the crest, and everything from there would be a wild downhill plunge. And of course I was happy for him. More than happy. Thrilled. Just like anyone would expect me to be.

And yet.

I had news, too, and I'd been keeping it secret from him. When I'd thought I couldn't wait a second longer, the envelopes had started trickling in. The first to arrive was a rejection from Columbia, but the very next day, NYU sent me a fat acceptance letter. The day after that, I heard from Fordham—another yes. I knew I would have to tell Hence sometime soon, of course. And I planned to. But the memory of our big blowout made me cautious. I figured I might as well wait till I'd chosen my school. And though I spent most of every study hall agonizing over the college catalogs, I still couldn't seem to make up my mind.

In the meantime, there was one college I still hadn't heard from—the one I shouldn't even have applied to, given that I couldn't go there. When the rejection from Columbia arrived, I wasn't all that disappointed. My only thought was that if Columbia didn't take me, Harvard wouldn't, either, which actually was a good thing...wasn't it? As soon as the letter came, I told myself, I'd put all my Harvard fantasies behind me and take a giant step into the future. I would pick one of those other schools—Not-Harvard A or Not-Harvard B—and start imagining a future that wouldn't involve quaint redbrick buildings, leafy pathways, and the bustle of Harvard Square.

Whatever school I chose, it would work out all right. I was so lucky, really, to be going to college at all. That's what I kept telling myself whenever I started to feel sad about the whole Harvard thing. I would be fine wherever I went. What felt like the end of the world to me would be the kind of future most girls only dream of.

At least it would all be settled soon.

*   *   *

It was waiting for me in the mailbox on a Friday afternoon: the envelope with the Harvard seal. I had been expecting it to be thin—a rejection. When I saw that it was plump, full of information and documents to be filled out and sent in, my hands started shaking so badly I could hardly open it. *Dear Catherine Eversole,* the letter said, *We are pleased to inform you...*

I couldn't read any further. I felt on the verge of exploding. It felt like joy, but how could it be? It didn't matter that Harvard wanted me. I was going to turn them down, wasn't I? Tremors shook my legs so hard I had to sit down on the bottom step, the half-read letter in my lap. My applying, and the long, anxious wait—those things had been pointless. Hadn't they?

I sat on the step a long time, listening to the ticking of the hallway grandfather clock, willing myself to think clearly. Willing all that pointless joy and hope to fade away. After a while, I stopped trembling. I was able to pick the letter up and read the whole thing from start to finish.

When I got to the end, I burst into tears.

Catherine

Days passed, and I still hadn't thought of a way to bring up the dreaded subject of college. What's more, Hence hadn't so much as asked me if I'd heard from any schools. Annoyed that he was too preoccupied with his own future to have even a shred of curiosity about mine, I told myself, *I'll wait till he asks. Till then, he doesn't need to know.*

One night in late March, a hard rain swept in and rattled the windowpanes. Before I fell asleep that night, I spared a thought for Q. He hadn't been home for more than a week, and I still had no idea where he went when he wasn't at The Underground, whether he'd found a new girlfriend or was sleeping on the couch of one of his party-animal friends. For all I knew, he could be passed out on a park bench, soaked to the skin. Almost four months had passed since my dad died, I was nobody's kid anymore, and with Q gone, I felt like I was nobody's sister. I had all but forgotten there was anyone in the world who might care where I slept, and with whom. As I drifted off to sleep in Hence's arms, I thought of Q wandering alone through the dark and rainy streets, and felt only pity.

When the lights switched on, slicing into my dreams, I blinked awake. Over the bed loomed my brother, as though my thoughts had summoned him. "Q?" I mumbled, reaching in his direction. "Is that you?" Beside me, Hence stirred, then tensed.

"I knew you were up to something...." The edge to my brother's voice and his cast-iron expression put me on alert.

"What are you doing in here?"

"I guess I don't have to ask you what *you're* doing in here." His voice radiated scorn. "With our busboy."

"This is *my* room."

"So you'll bring whoever you want up here?" Quentin laughed unpleasantly. "I don't think so. I own this building. Dad left me in charge."

"He left you in charge of The Underground—not of me. If you care what I do, why are you never here?"

"I can see I should have been here, keeping you in line. I didn't know what a slut you were, spreading your legs for the first guy who came sniffing around."

Hence drew himself up in bed, clutching the sheet tight to his chest. "Are you insane, talking to her like that? She's your sister...."

That's when Quentin called Hence a word I'd never use myself, a word Dad would have been shocked to hear him say. He spat it into our faces, commanding Hence to shut up. A change came over his face. He fumbled in the pocket of his army surplus jacket, pulling out a handgun—small, silver, and deadly looking. He held it up in both hands and aimed it right into Hence's face. With that weapon in his hands, his voice came out different: cold and quiet. "You watch how you talk to me," he said. "Be respectful."

Before I could think, I was clambering out from under the covers, throwing myself between Quentin's gun and Hence. I needed to stop my brother's craziness before someone got hurt. In my panic, I forgot I didn't have much of anything on—just my underwear and a gauzy tank top. At the sight of me, a violent blush spread across Quentin's face and he looked away, the gun pointing askew—thank God—toward the corner of the room, and not into Hence's face. I exhaled.

"For God's sake, Cathy!" Q shouted, sounding more like his old self. "Put some clothes on."

"Not until you put that thing away," I said, seeing my chance. "I'm not moving while you're waving a gun around."

Quentin glared down at the carpet. "He has five minutes to get dressed and out of here. If he isn't gone by then, I'll shoot."

"I'm leaving, too," I told him.

"The hell you are. If you leave with him, I'll hunt the two of you down and blow his head off."

"You'll have to shoot me first."

"Don't think I won't." And he was gone, slamming the apartment door behind him. Hence and I barely had time to throw on our clothes. I packed a duffel bag with my journal, my bankbook, some clothes, and the jewelry Mom had left me, but most of

Hence's stuff was still in the basement, and neither of us wanted to pass Quentin in order to get it.

That's how we wound up homeless, me with everything I owned in a bag and Hence with nothing but the clothes he'd worn the night before and his guitar, which, luckily enough, he'd brought upstairs to serenade me with before we fell asleep. As we fled The Underground, Hence didn't say much. I know he must have been at least as angry as I was. Angrier. I thought of the look I'd seen on his face, how he'd been on his knees, naked except for a sheet, while Quentin pointed a gun at him and called him names, ordering him to be respectful. I thought how humiliated Hence must feel, and for a long time I couldn't think of anything to say. We rode the subway side by side, not speaking. I wasn't sure where we were going. Hence seemed to have some destination in mind, so I followed.

"That shithead." Hence spoke the words so quietly that at first I thought I'd imagined them. "Racist son of a bitch."

"He never used to be." That was true, wasn't it? He'd certainly liked Jackie well enough, teasing and flirting with her, sticking up for her, calling her pet names like Jackie-O and Jack O'Lantern. "Maybe that's part of it, but it's not the whole thing. Q hated you because Dad liked you so much. He hates you even more now that Dad's gone." I put a hand on his shoulder, but he shook it off.

"What do I care what his reasons are?" Hence spoke through clenched teeth. "Spoiled piece of shit. He had parents who loved him, and all the money in the world, and he couldn't stand to share his *daddy's* attention?" I felt a chill, because of course I was spoiled, too, compared to Hence. I knew he didn't mean to criticize me; it was Quentin he was angry with. Even so, feeling accused, I folded my hands in my lap, and we rode the rest of the way in silence.

While I waited in a coffee shop on Gansevoort Street, Hence ran over to the apartment his bandmates shared to see if they would be willing to make room for two more. We had money, of course; we could have gotten a hotel room if we'd wanted to. We could even have rented a place together, the way we'd dreamed of doing. But Hence's first thought was of his new friends in the band, and my first thought was of Hence, especially after what my brother had just put him through.

I was on my third cup of coffee by the time Hence returned, a relieved smile on his face, to lead me to the walk-up on West Thirteenth. It was nice of the guys to take us in, considering their place wasn't big enough for the three of them to begin with. Andy and Stan shared the bigger bedroom; Ruben could barely fit all of his stuff in the smaller one. That left the pull-out couch in the living room for me and Hence. It was a good thing we hadn't packed any more of our stuff; there would have been no place to put it. As shaken up as I'd been that morning, I would have liked a nice quiet evening alone with Hence instead of a long TV-watching session with the guys, but the living room was the TV room, so I had no choice.

The next morning, I made banana–chocolate chip pancakes, and they were a big hit. The boys consumed two enormous batches, and Ruben couldn't stop thanking me. It was kind of sweet, really; I felt like Peter Pan's Wendy, looking after her troop of Lost Boys. After that, the band went downstairs to the rehearsal space to practice for that night's show. Hence invited me to come along, but after a whole twenty-four hours spent breathing the same air as the Riptide guys, I needed space. Plus, it was the first day of my spring break, and I wanted to do something different, something to cheer myself up.

The trouble was, I didn't know what that would be. It had been a long time since I'd done something just because I felt like it, without worrying about what would make Hence happy. At first I thought I would hang around the apartment for the day, but I was sick of watching TV and, naturally, I didn't have any books with me. I thought with regret of the pile of library books beside my bed back home. There was no way Quentin would think to return them. As I washed the last of the breakfast dishes, I fantasized about sneaking into The Underground—maybe watching from down the street to catch Quentin on his way out, and then letting myself in to get more stuff, or even climbing in through the window, the way Hence used to. The thought was satisfying, but the memory of the gun in Quentin's twitching hand still made me queasy.

By the time I'd figured out where to stack the clean plates and coffee mugs, it was official: I was bored out of my skull. Plus, the whole apartment was seriously smelly and gross. I wasn't sure how I could stay there without picking up the dirty socks and putting things into piles, but it wasn't my job; after all, Hence and I would be chipping in on the rent while we looked for another place. I needed to find something else to do with myself before I started scrubbing the shower stall out of sheer boredom.

I would have gone over to Jackie's, but her mom had whisked her off to Washington, D.C., on a three-day trip to tour the Smithsonian museums and the White House, and to check out George Mason, one of the schools that had accepted Jackie. As dorky as that sounded, it was also kind of sweet. The last time I'd been to the Grays' house, Jackie's mom had been fretting about how it might be the last vacation they would take together as a family, her eyes bright and teary. Jackie told her she was being crazy, that of course they would still go places together once Jackie started college. "It's not like I have a terminal illness, Mom," she'd said, and the two of them hugged like they had forgotten I was in the room.

Even if Jackie had been in town, I wasn't at all sure I'd have felt like spending time with her. Jackie had been accepted by Columbia as well as George Mason, and when she'd broken the news, I could tell she was working hard to hide her excitement so I wouldn't get sad about having to turn down Harvard. I kept trying to get her to talk about which school she was leaning toward, because I honestly wanted her to relax and be her usual self. We were both trying so hard it was painful. It was even worse with the other girls from school, who were oblivious, always asking me where I'd be next year so they could boast about the fabulous schools that had accepted them.

As I paced Riptide's smelly crash pad, I couldn't stop obsessing about the one thing I should already have done. While I'd been frantically packing my things, I'd thought to shove my acceptance letters into the bottom of my duffel bag. Now I needed to pull them out and pick a New York school. But before I did that, I needed to make an X in the little box on the form that would tell Harvard I wasn't coming.

One little X. And yet I couldn't seem to make myself do it. The response deadlines were looming. If Harvard didn't hear from me, I supposed they would give my space away to someone else, so what was the big deal about sending in the form? Besides, it would give me something to do: take a walk to the nearest mailbox. Pretty pathetic when that's the day's big event.

Sitting cross-legged on the lumpy pullout bed, I spread the letters in front of me. Maybe if I chose a school, it would be easier to check off the *no* box on the Harvard form. I could spend the day wandering the campuses of NYU and Fordham, trying to make up my mind. I'd heard good things about both schools, and their glossy catalogs didn't make my decision any easier. Maybe actually going to each one would help me choose; maybe some sign from God would help me get over my stupid, pointless attachment to the idea of Harvard. Nothing could have been as perfect as my fantasy of strolling through Harvard Yard in October and engaging in long, deep conversations at Café Algiers. So why couldn't I get over it?

The more I thought about it, the sound of Riptide's guitars and drums rising up to me through the floorboards, the more I knew what I needed to do: catch a train to Boston and visit Cambridge again. The last time I'd been there, I'd seen it through a little girl's dreamy eyes. I needed to see it again so I could know— not just in my head, but in my heart—that it really wasn't superior to Fordham or NYU. Then I could get on with my life. There wasn't anything stopping me. I wouldn't even have to pack; everything I owned was already in my duffel bag.

205

But I couldn't miss Riptide's show that night. They would be headlining at the Trocadero, and I knew it was a big deal to Hence. He'd be hurt if I wasn't there. And how could I explain my absence when I hadn't told him I was applying to Harvard, much less that I was accepted? How could I make him understand that I needed to make one last trip, to say good-bye to my dream of what college should be? I knew he would think the opposite was true—that I was secretly thinking about saying yes to Harvard. But I wasn't. I really wasn't.

Was I?

I folded up my acceptance letters and tucked them into the duffel bag, putting off my big decision for another day. I couldn't go to Boston; I couldn't risk hurting Hence, as bruised and battered as he still was by his life before we met. It was a big responsibility knowing how broken he was, because what if I was the one who hurt him next?

When the rain finally petered out to a drizzle, I went prowling for bookstores and bought myself a stack of paperbacks to replace the books I'd abandoned. That should have put me in a better mood, but it didn't. When I met up with Hence and the guys at Gennaio's Pizza, they were all so giddy, joking and cracking up over the stupidest things, that it set my teeth on edge. Rehearsal had gone really well, and they were so excited about getting to play the Troc that none of them seemed to notice that I was quieter than usual. Andy and Stan were especially obnoxious, going on and on

206

about a pair of sisters they'd invited to the show. "You two had better stay out late," Andy warned Hence and me. "I'll be needing that pullout couch."

"Otherwise we'll be forced to have a foursome in our bedroom," Stan chimed in.

"Dude! Like I want to see your hairy ass in action!"

Stan, Ruben, and Hence laughed like that was the funniest thing they'd ever heard, but I could tell Andy really wanted us to give him the couch. It was only our second night in the apartment, and already the guys were letting us know how in the way we were. And where exactly were Hence and I supposed to go until morning?

The pizza at Gennaio's was cheap. Feeling queasy, I patted my slice with a paper napkin to mop up the extra grease. Until that moment, I hadn't given much thought to the way Andy and Stan treated the girls they went out with—like Kleenex to be used once and tossed into a corner.

"I'm spending the night at Drew's," Ruben offered, patting my hand. "So you don't need to worry, chica."

I mustered a smile in his direction. Ruben wasn't a playboy like the others. At least he had a steady boyfriend. Not all that long ago, he'd been almost as bad as Andy and Stan, with a new guy every weekend. As for Hence, he beamed all through dinner, squeezing my hand whenever he spoke, clearly pleased to be out with his band and me, one big jolly family.

That night was worse than usual, too. The pink-haired girl, Nina, and her bleached-blond friend were at the Troc, of course—did they ever miss a show?—in tube tops as tight as sausage casings.

As she always did, Nina hugged the stage right in front of Hence's microphone stand and shrieked whenever he came close to the edge. She was almost impossible to ignore, but Hence usually managed it. That night, though, when he was singing a ballad—not one of his, but one of Stan's—he was looking right at her the whole time. She certainly noticed; I could see it on her rapt, wide-eyed face, and in the way she grabbed and squeezed her friend's hand, as if to keep herself from swooning like some Victorian lady. If the Victorian lady was dressed like a skank.

You're being paranoid, I scolded myself. Usually Hence sang directly to me, but that night I was at the side of the stage, not directly in his sight line; I hadn't felt like standing in the thick of things, in part because I was feeling so cranky. So his eyes had to go somewhere, and why not to the girl right up front who had been killing herself to get his attention for a month's worth of gigs? She was there. And I wasn't. So what?

Still, it rankled. After the song ended, I saw Nina scream something into her girlfriend's ear, and the two of them ducked out of the crowd together—a highly unusual move. I don't think Nina had ever left the stage during a set before; what if she missed a chance to wave her breasts in Hence's face? I don't know what made me do it exactly, but I decided to follow them through the shifting crowd. They were most likely headed toward the ladies' room. For once, there wasn't a line; by the time I caught up, two of the three stalls were occupied. I ducked into the third and listened. I'd never heard Nina speak before, but I knew without a doubt the first voice I heard—husky and drunk-sounding—was hers.

"Oh my God oh my God oh my God oh my God. Tell me you

saw that. Tell me I wasn't imagining it." She was screaming to be heard over the band.

"You totally weren't imagining it. He was looking right at you. He didn't take his eyes off you for a second!"

"I know!"

"I guess that girlfriend of his isn't here tonight. Maybe they broke up?"

"Oh, she's here all right," Nina said. "I saw her off to the side of the stage, looking all pissed off about something. Maybe they had a fight?"

"Could be. You'd better get ready to pounce."

"Honey, I was born ready. You should have seen what she was wearing tonight. Baggy jeans and a flannel shirt. Who wears that to the Troc?"

I looked down at myself. I'd grabbed the first clothes I'd come across in my duffel bag. Not that it was any of their business.

"I'll bet she's still beautiful, even dressed like that. Some people have all the luck and don't even know it. I wish I had skin like hers. Not to mention that body..."

Nina made a hissing noise. "I know her type—taking everything for granted. So she's got nice skin and a good body. She doesn't have any idea how to work it. That hair of hers. Blow-dry it once in a while, right? She doesn't dress like she's trying to hang on to her ultrahot boyfriend...." The rest of whatever she was saying was drowned out by the sound of flushing, but when the noise died down the two of them were laughing.

"...Girl, you crack me up."

I thought about stepping out of my stall to confront Nina, or

209

at least to give her the evil eye and let her know I'd been listening, but what good would that do? Better to stay put, listen, and learn everything I could about the enemy, because that's what she had become.

"I'll get my chance. Sooner or later, she'll be out of the picture, and I'll swoop in."

"I know you will. Can I use some of your lipstick? I forgot mine. Thanks. I love this color. What's it called?"

"Mata Hari. And once I've got him, I'll make sure he's good and satisfied. I'll handcuff him to my bed and take him places that little girlfriend of his has never even heard of."

The blond whooped with laughter. "Nina, you are way, way too much."

After they left the bathroom, I just stood in the stall, sputtering, too mad to even move. I stayed there for the rest of the show, listening to women come and go, unready to face another human being.

When I finally got back to the main stage, I found Hence searching for me. He took one look at my face and knew something was wrong. "What is it? Are you okay?"

Over his shoulder, I could see Nina and her friend, pretending to be chatting with each other, not taking their eyes off us for a single moment.

"I'm fine," I told him. "It's nothing."

"Are you sure?" Hence's eyes were dark with worry. "When I didn't see you out in the audience..."

Was I crazy, or had Nina and her sidekick moved in for a better look? If they got any closer to us, they could eavesdrop on our conversation. A rush of anger flooded my brain, and before I could think better of it, I grabbed Hence's hands and wrapped them around my waist.

"You're amazing," I told him. And I kissed him, good and hard, as though no one was watching. He made a surprised sound, a happy little gasp, and I released him. "Let's get home before the guys so we can be alone together."

And we did. Going home with him should have made me happy. It was me with Hence, after all, and I'd make sure that it would always be me and never Nina. Still, as we kissed that night on the creaky pull-out couch, as I ran my lips down his throat and pulled the T-shirt over his head, I couldn't help feeling like I was making love to Hence not because I felt like it, but because I had something to prove. Even worse, he didn't seem to notice the difference.

Chelsea

A sleepy-eyed man in horn-rimmed glasses answered Jackie's door. "She's putting the twins to bed," he said. "I'm Craig, her husband." He took my backpack without a word, carried it into the living room, and slipped away. I'd phoned Jackie on my way to the subway, saying I needed a place to sleep, but I hadn't said why. Now she hurried into the room, a worried look in her eyes. "What happened? Oh, honey, you look exhausted." Her tone changed. "Hence kicked you out?"

"Something like that," I said. "He confused a wall with my head and punched a hole in *it*."

Jackie started making up the couch. "I shouldn't have let you go back there." Then she asked the exact question I'd been hoping she wouldn't. "After you left yesterday, I started wondering: Your dad doesn't really know where you are, does he?"

I didn't want to lie, so I didn't answer.

"The man must be frantic. You could use my phone. . . ."

What choice did I have but to make up a story on the spot? It came out all jumbled. "He knows I'm in New York. He thinks I'm staying with a friend of mine, whose family moved here." I scrambled for specifics. "Her name's Lisa. Her father works in television. Please don't tell Dad I was at The Underground. I'll only stay a few more days, then I'll take a bus right back to Marblehead." Then a chilling thought occurred to me. "He didn't try to get in touch with you, did he?"

"I never met your father," she said. "He and Cathy got married at city hall, and she didn't invite me. For all I know, he's never even heard my name."

Had my mother really shared so little of her past with my father? At least that meant Dad was unlikely to track me here. I sat down on the made-up couch, and Jackie joined me there. We sat awhile in silence.

"Please don't call my dad," I said finally. "He wouldn't want me to be looking for my mom, and I've got to. I can't stand it that she might be out there waiting for me to find her."

Jackie sighed.

I took that as a good sign. "I promise I'll get on a bus and head to Massachusetts the day my father expects me." I spoke fast, hoping she wouldn't ask when that day was.

"I can't even be around to look out for you," Jackie said. "I've got an all-day meeting tomorrow, and Craig has to be at the office."

"I don't need a babysitter." I tried not to sound as annoyed as I felt. "I'll stay away from Hence. I promise."

213

Jackie jumped to her feet and walked into the next room. "Since you're here…" she called, returning with a heavy photo album. She riffled through it and set it on my lap. "Look what I found."

I gazed down at a photograph I'd never seen before, of my mom and Jackie as teenagers, perched on the lip of a fountain, arms around each other's shoulders, heads thrown back in laughter. I turned the page and found myself confronted by the lazy smile of a guy with blond hair and eyes the same bright-blue shade as his polo shirt.

"Wasn't he gorgeous?" Jackie asked. "I used to stare at that photo every night before I went to sleep, hoping I would dream about him."

"Is that my uncle?" An electric tingle went through me; why hadn't I thought to ask Jackie about him?

"You've never met Q?" Jackie clucked her tongue. "I guess I shouldn't be surprised."

"Are you still in touch with him? Where does he live now?"

"The last I heard, he'd moved upstate, to some little town. It started with a C, I think." She shut her eyes. "Coxsackie. That was it."

"Do you have his phone number? Or maybe an e-mail address?"

"Heavens, no. I saw him just before he sold The Underground to Hence. In the days before e-mail, if you can imagine that. I dropped by to see how he was doing, but he'd changed."

I turned the page, but the next pictures were of strangers. "Changed? How?"

"The spark had gone out of him. He'd tried to turn the club

into an expensive steak house, and the whole thing had been a flop. All he could talk about was how badly he wanted to sell it and move upstate. He'd already bought himself a cabin in the mountains, and he had this fantasy of moving up there and spending all his time hunting."

"Do you at least have his address?" I asked.

Jackie's eyes narrowed. "Oh, Chelsea. I wouldn't want you to get in touch with him. That last time he seemed...I don't know. A little bit off. Not himself. Angry. He kept mentioning his gun collection. He said something about having enemies, and how they'd better watch out." She took the album from me, her expression suddenly sharp. "Promise me you won't go looking for him."

"I promise," I lied.

That night, after Jackie and Craig had gone to bed, I got out my laptop and searched for Quentin Eversole in Coxsackie, New York. I figured that if my mom had called Jackie when she came back to Manhattan, she might have gotten in touch with her brother as well; maybe she'd even told him where she was headed next. But I couldn't find a single Q. Eversole in upstate New York. Of course, he'd moved up there a long time ago; he might be living somewhere else by now. There had to be a way to track my Uncle Quentin down. Jackie's warnings aside, I needed to find him.

The next morning I woke up alone in Jackie's apartment. She'd left a note on the kitchen table: *We'll be back tonight. Help yourself to anything you can find in the fridge.* She'd even left a key to her apartment so I could come and go as I pleased. As soon as I knew for sure that she and Craig were out, I set to work. Jackie had said she didn't have my uncle's phone number, but she hadn't said anything about not having his address.

Okay, ransacking her drawers wasn't the most upstanding act of my life. But, honestly, I didn't have to look very hard; the address book was in almost the first place I looked, a writing desk in the master bedroom. I scribbled my uncle's address on a piece of scrap paper and tucked the book carefully back, covering my tracks. Then I called The Underground, hoping Hence wouldn't pick up. I got lucky; Cooper answered on the first ring, like he'd been waiting for my call.

"Where are you? I've been picturing you sleeping on a park bench, or riding the subway all night. And what did you do to put Hence in such a foul mood?"

"I didn't *do* anything." I could fill Cooper in on Hence's blowup later; for now I had more urgent business to take care of. I told him about my latest discovery. "So I'm thinking about going up to Coxsackie. What's the best way to get upstate? There's got to be a bus, right?"

Coop didn't sound all that excited for me. "I'm not sure that's the best idea, Chelsea," he said. "Seriously. I've heard a lot about your uncle...."

"From Hence," I said. "They hated each other. I wouldn't expect him to say nice things."

"But the guns..."

"I'm his niece. He's not going to shoot me. And it's not like I have any other way of tracking down my mom. Never mind, I can look up the bus information myself."

"Wait!" Coop was practically shouting into the phone. "Don't go alone." There was a long pause. "I'll take you."

"You'd do that?" I asked. "Really?" Did Coop care what happened to me after all?

"It can't be today. There's a show tonight, an important one. Rat Behavior. You know who that is, right?"

"Should I?"

"Stan Hodicek, the drummer from Riptide? It's his new band."

"Stan from Riptide?" This was an interesting twist. "Too bad I can't be there."

Coop fell silent a moment; then he surprised me again. "Take the train here."

"What about Hence?"

"You can hang out in the juice bar across the street. Wait there, and I'll slip over when things get quiet."

"I'll be right there," I said, scrounging under the sofa for my sneakers, more eager than I would have expected to get back to The Underground. "Thanks, Coop," I added, but he'd already hung up.

217

Catherine

The next afternoon I did something I'd never done before: I lied to Hence. We were at Unique Clothing Warehouse, rummaging through the bins, trying to replace the clothes we'd left behind at The Underground. He fished out a top in bright orange camo, held it up against his chest, and looked at me quizzically.

"Colorful," I said.

"Is that good or bad?"

I wrinkled my nose and he tossed the shirt back.

"Um, hey," I said, trying to sound casual. "I heard from Jackie. She wants me to meet up with her and her mom in D.C. I was thinking it might be fun."

"When would you leave?" It was a sign of how preoccupied Hence was that he didn't even notice the holes in my story. How would Jackie have known where to call me? I'd made up a convoluted backstory about how I'd left our new phone number on her answering machine, but I didn't even have to use it.

"Tonight. If I'm going, I should probably leave soon. I don't want to get in too late."

"How long will you be gone?'

"Not long." I handed him a shirt in olive. "Just overnight."

Hence held the shirt up to his chest and checked himself out in a nearby mirror. He looked at me, brows knit, and for a moment I thought he would challenge my lie. "You should go," he said finally. "It's hard on you, living with a bunch of guys." He smiled. "Don't stay away too long."

Guilt rose within me. "It's not like you'll be alone."

"I'm used to being alone." Now Hence sounded miffed, like I'd accused him of needing to sleep with a night-light on.

"I know." I sidled up closer. "But you don't have to be anymore." We kissed good-bye under the fluorescent Warehouse lights. He told me to have a good time and went back to digging through the bins.

Before I could think it through any harder, I hurried back to the apartment, grabbed my duffel, and headed off to Penn Station to catch the next train. *That was too easy*, I wrote in my journal. *Shouldn't it be harder to lie to the person you love?* My hands were shaking, and not just because of the moving train. *But I'm not doing anything wrong. Not really.*

In Boston, I grabbed the red line from South Station to Cambridge. I barely had to look at the map; I could still recall the route from when Dad took us to Boston. I climbed the steps of the T up into Harvard Square and was shocked by its instant familiarity. It was as though I'd never been away, like it was my soul's true home.

My first stop was the Grolier Poetry Book Shop, a cozy little hole in the wall, its high shelves crammed with narrow books. The fat gray shop cat rubbed against my ankles while I sat reading. As I paid for my purchase—eight books to load down my duffel bag like rocks—I was dying to tell the clerk that I was a poet and that someday my books would be on the shelves of her store, between Russell Edson and Lawrence Ferlinghetti. But I refrained.

From Plympton Street, I practically skipped across Massachusetts Avenue to Harvard Yard, where the kiosks were covered with fliers advertising upcoming events: a campus production of *Antigone*; a bake sale to benefit a local women's shelter; a choral society's annual spring concert; a reading by a visiting French novelist...and on and on. I stood in the sun-dappled square, arms crossed, while Harvard students passed me, solo or in pairs, intent on wherever it was they were going. Did they have any idea how lucky they were? I thought about how I was secretly one of them, or at least I could be, if only I were to make one little check mark on my acceptance letter and walk it over to admissions. That day, that very afternoon, before the deadline passed.

So I did it.

It was so simple. I wrote the deposit check and handed it over before I could change my mind. I wandered absently out to the square and sat on the first empty bench I came across, its surface cold through my jeans, watching the crowds pass by until I was wracked with shivers. What had I done? What had I been thinking? Could I undo it? Could I stand up, turn around, make a bee-line back to admissions, and tell the lady behind the desk it had all been a big mistake, a moment of insanity?

I could. The truth was I didn't want to.

But what on earth would I say to Hence?

Couples live apart from each other all the time, I told myself, thinking of Cindy, a girl at school whose older boyfriend had gone off to UCLA last September. She never stopped talking about him—his phone calls, his letters, the reunion they'd planned for spring break. Distance seemed to make their relationship more glamorous, more intense. "Being apart taught us how much we belong together," she'd said, not to me exactly, but to the lunch table at large, flushed with what looked like happiness.

Not that I completely trusted Cindy; she seemed to protest a bit too much. But one thing was undeniable: She and her boy-friend were still together. So maybe the choice I'd made wouldn't break Hence and me apart. The more I thought about it, the surer I was that it wouldn't, that nothing could. Nobody had ever loved anyone the way I loved Hence. And I knew beyond doubt that he felt the same way about me.

I wandered in the direction of The Charles Hotel, where I hoped to find a room for the night. Why shouldn't I follow my dreams while Hence followed his? Four years wasn't such a long time. Once I graduated, we could live wherever he wanted. I would go with him when the band was on the road, the way he'd imagined it. Between tours we'd live in our sun-filled apartment with books, cats, and guitars, happily ever after, world without end, amen.

Hence had to understand. He just had to.

Catherine

When the train pulled into Penn Station I couldn't go straight home to Hence. Luckily, The Charles Hotel had had an open room, and I'd spent the night pacing its mauve carpet, anxiety mounting over how Hence would take my news. Before I told him, I needed to talk through the decision I'd just made, to try out my argument on a calm, logical, nonjudgmental ear. Jackie was back from her trip, so, naturally, I went to her house. When I knocked on her door she opened it and immediately threw her arms around my neck. It was unseasonably warm, so we sat together on the steps of her building, just the two of us, like we'd done so many times before. She couldn't wait to tell me about her trip and her decision: She'd liked George Mason, but D.C. hadn't felt like home, so she'd decided to go to Columbia to be closer to her mom.

But even with big news like that, it wasn't Jackie's style to go on about herself for very long.

"What about you?" she asked. "Why are you dragging around a duffel bag? Are you and Hence moving back into The Underground? And why do you look so weirded out?"

That was my Jackie. She always could read me. Sometimes I thought she should forget all about art and go into psychology— she'd be a natural as a therapist. I took a deep breath and told her everything from start to finish, and she didn't say a word until I was all the way through. When I told her how I'd checked off yes and turned in the form, her eyes got even rounder than usual. After I'd finished my tale, she just sat there, hands on her knees, looking amazed.

"Say something," I begged. "Have I made the biggest mistake of my life?"

"What do you think?"

"I don't know. One minute I think, *Of course I have to go to Harvard.* The next minute I'm thinking, *Hence will never understand what Harvard means to me.* I've tried explaining it to him, but it's like talking to a rock." Maybe I sounded harsher than I meant to, but it was the truth, wasn't it?

"Doesn't he want you to be happy?"

"I don't think he worries about whether or not I'm happy. Since he joined Riptide, it's all about him." Again, harsh but true. "He's going places, and that's fabulous. But seriously, Jack, I'm starting to hate hanging around on the sidelines. I mean, I don't mind going to rehearsals and shows and being supportive, but I need more than that. I have to have my own life, too—my own career."

"Of course."

"Lately I almost feel like a groupie." I'd already told Jackie all about Nina and her blond friend—the spandex, the miniskirts, the high-pitched screaming.

"You're a girlfriend. There's a difference."

"Is there?" I asked. "Those girls Andy and Stan bring home after a show—are they girlfriends or groupies?"

"Hence isn't like that," Jackie said.

"He's not as bad," I said. "But still…I saw the look on his face when Nina was waving her gazongas at him."

"Hence has *you*." Jackie played with one of her dangling earrings. "He doesn't need Nina and her gazongas."

"But what about when I'm away at Harvard and she's here, following him around like she's a poodle and he's a bone?" I hugged my knees. "He's going to be so mad at me when I tell him about Harvard. You haven't seen him when he gets like that."

"I can imagine. Even when he's not mad, he can be a bit… intense." For a long time, the only sounds were the swish of traffic and the laughter of kids bouncing a basketball down the street. "I know you don't want to hear this, Cath—I hate to even say it— but maybe you need to let go."

I was too astonished to even answer.

"Hear me out. I know how *in love* you are. But if he can't understand your whole Harvard thing…if you can't be apart from him without worrying he'll start sleeping with groupies to get back at you…"

"That's not what I said."

"Isn't it? Because that's what I heard. Plus, you're afraid to tell him a simple thing like where you're going to college. It shouldn't be like that. He should be as supportive of your dreams as you are of his. Is he?"

"No," I admitted, my voice sullen.

"Then maybe you should break up with him."

"You're right." The sunlight was suddenly too bright for my eyes. I bent to rest my forehead on my knees, thinking about all that Jackie had said. As silence fell between us again, I heard sounds of a scuffle, sneakers slapping against concrete, car brakes screeching, a driver cursing out his window.

I straightened up and saw the surprise in Jackie's eyes. "I am?" she asked, sounding so amazed that I couldn't help laughing.

"You're right that I shouldn't be afraid of Hence. I should be able to talk to him."

"Oh." Jackie sounded disappointed, as if she'd actually thought I might be considering breaking up with Hence.

A little miffed now, I continued. "I need to go tell him about Harvard so we can get the argument behind us. I'll find a way to make him understand."

A sudden breeze lifted Jackie's hair. "I had to speak up," she said softly. "Don't hold it against me, okay?"

"I know Hence can be...unpredictable. But I could never break up with him. There should be a word for something that's beyond love, something this strong." I closed my eyes. "It's like my heart is made out of Silly Putty and he can stretch it all out of shape just by saying my name...."

"You should work for Hallmark," Jackie said. "There's your career path."

I gave her shoulder a playful slug. Then I threw my arms around her. "You always make me feel better."

And the insane thing is, I did feel better. Right at that moment, when my life was crumbling to dust, I felt better than I had in weeks, so charged up and ready that I went straight to the apartment, hoping I'd find Hence there. I planned to lure him out for a walk so we could talk things through in private. When I got in, all the guys were out, so I ran downstairs to check the rehearsal space. Empty. No big deal; I figured they must be at the studio. Either way, Hence would be too busy to talk to me, so I believed I had time. I took a long, hot shower and put on some clean clothes. If anything was different about the apartment, I didn't notice.

The whole way to the studio, I hummed to myself, swinging my arms as I walked, because of course Hence would be there, and of course I'd find a way to make him understand that he was my life and my future. I'd make him see that all the things I needed to do were for us both, so we could live out our dreams together.

"Hello?" I let the door slam behind me. I heard familiar voices in the mixing room. I found Andy, Stan, and Ruben in a huddle, looking pissed. "Where's Hence?"

"You tell us," Stan said.

"He didn't show," Ruben said. "We were supposed to start work almost two hours ago."

"We thought he must be with you," Andy said.

"This isn't like him," Ruben added. "Did you guys have a fight or something?"

Only then did I realize that something was very wrong. I left without a word, and ran the whole way back to Jackie's house.

"What is it? What happened?" She unlatched the door and I burst in.

"Right after you were talking about how I should break up with Hence and I said you were right, did you notice something out in the street? Some kind of commotion?"

The look on Jackie's face told me she knew exactly what I was asking. "Oh, no. Oh, Cath. You don't think...?"

"He skipped out on a recording session without calling in sick or anything, and he wasn't at the apartment."

"Where else could he be?"

"First answer me." I grabbed her by the shoulders and pressed my forehead to hers. "Think hard. What was it we heard?"

"I didn't look up. We were so busy talking. But I did hear something...maybe someone running down the street. A car slamming on its brakes, and some yelling."

"What if it was Hence running away from us? Could it have been?"

Jackie winced, and I released her shoulders, realizing how hard I'd been squeezing them. "It could have been," she said. "Oh, Cathy, I hope it wasn't."

From Jackie's house, I called the apartment, but there was no answer. Five minutes later I phoned again and Stan picked up. "He's not here," he said. "His clothes and guitar are gone."

227

I tried calling the police to file a missing persons report, but they practically laughed at me. "You know how many boyfriends go missing every week?" the sergeant said just before I hung up on him. So I headed to the apartment, trying to work out where Hence might have gone, but besides the apartment, the studio, and the rehearsal space, I couldn't think of a single place. I wondered if maybe he was on a bus back to wherever it was he grew up, but that didn't seem likely, given how he'd always acted toward his past, like it was a huge black hole that threatened to suck him in if he so much as talked about it.

I couldn't go back to the apartment and sit by the phone, just waiting. I tried wandering the streets around Chelsea, thinking luck would bring me to Hence just as it had brought him to me so many months earlier, hoping maybe I'd bump into him—but what were the odds of that? Finally, I went to our favorite diner. I ordered a cup of coffee that I couldn't drink, and sat in front of it as it cooled, trying to think of a plan. The idea that Hence was walking around somewhere, angry, hating me, knowing I acted behind his back and thinking I was about to break up with him— it was too horrible to contemplate. Somehow, I had to track him down and explain.

Catherine

For the next three days, I sat by the phone, willing it to ring. I didn't dare step away from it long enough to shower, sleep, or eat. While I waited, I wrote obsessively in my journal, trying to straighten out my scrambled thoughts. When she heard what was going on, Jackie's mom agreed to let her come sleep over at the band's apartment, something she never in a million years would have done otherwise. The guys were almost as worried as I was. Days and nights, they wandered through lower Manhattan, hitting his favorite coffee shops and nightclubs, talking to everyone Hence had ever met on the club scene. On the third day, I overheard Andy tell Stan that if Hence was blowing off a chance to record he was probably lying in a ditch somewhere. He probably wouldn't have spoken so frankly if he'd known Jackie and I were in the next room listening, but Andy's words had the ring of a terrible truth.

"God wouldn't be that cruel," I whispered to Jackie, to keep from dissolving into utter despair. "To let Hence die thinking I didn't love him." Dad had never been into organized religion, and I hadn't been to church since Mom's funeral, but the next morning I dragged Jackie with me to Our Mother of Good Counsel for the nine thirty mass. Before the service we lit candles for Hence. *Let him be safe*, I prayed silently, over and over, the whole time the priest was talking. *Give me a chance to explain. Please, God, just give me five minutes with him.* After mass, there was nothing to do but the same pathetic thing I'd been doing for the last three days.

Stare at the phone.

Will it to ring.

Another night passed. Then another day. Then another night.

Then, for the first time in what felt like forever, something like hope. Ruben came screaming up the stairs to the apartment. "I've got a lead! I've got a lead!"

"He's alive?" I threw my arms around Ruben, and he hugged me back, hard.

"I hope so." That morning, Ruben had tracked down the bouncer at Max Fish. "He thinks he saw Hence there last night." Ruben's words came so fast they ran together. "At least he saw some guy who looked like Hence, talking to that girl with pink hair. The slutty-looking one who's always up against the stage with her blond friend."

Nina.

After that I knew what I had to do: figure out where she lived and track her down. From what little I'd seen of her, I could bet she'd made it her business to know exactly where Hence was and what he was doing. And if she wouldn't tell me, I would have to follow her night and day until she led me to him.

As much as I despised her, I needed her help.

That night, after Jackie went home, the guys and I split up, hitting club after club, trying to track down Nina. At the first few places I tried the bouncers and bartenders, thinking maybe they'd seen the girl with the fuchsia hair. Some of them had (because who could miss Nina?), but none of them knew her full name or where she lived. Finally, in a little hole-in-the-wall club on Warren Street, I found someone who actually knew her. Jerry, the rumpled bouncer, gave me the name of a guy who used to be Nina's boyfriend: Dane Slater, the drummer for Pineapple Crush. He wasn't hard to track down; by some fluke, his phone number was listed in the white pages.

So I stayed up all night, calling every half hour, letting it ring off the hook, but he didn't pick up until the next day at a quarter to noon. His voice was husky, like maybe I'd woken him up. "Why should I give you Nina's number?" He sounded suspicious over the phone. I couldn't tell whether he was being protective of Nina or if he disliked her so much that he resented even having to hear her name.

It turned out to be the latter. When I explained that my boyfriend had gone missing and that he'd last been seen talking to Nina, Dane laughed derisively. "Your boyfriend's in a band? And Nina is sniffing around him? And you say he's been missing for a week?"

I didn't like the implications. "It's not like that," I said, because I thought it couldn't possibly be. "I have to find him. Please help me."

For what felt like an eternity, the line was silent. "What do I care?" he said finally. "She's not my problem anymore." And he gave me her last name and her phone number. "She lives on Avenue B, over a pet-supply store. That's all I can remember." And he hung up without so much as saying good-bye or wishing me luck.

Not that it mattered. I had a phone number! So I called, but the line was disconnected. Good thing I had an approximate address. I ran the whole way to Avenue B. I knew Nina wouldn't be thrilled to share Hence's whereabouts with me, but now that I knew he was alive and close by, I would find a way to convince her to help me. We were both women, and we both cared about Hence; shouldn't we be able to put our heads together?

I walked block after block, until I found the pet-supply store; sure enough, Nina's last name was taped under a doorbell in the entryway. I took a deep breath and rang it. No answer. I counted to ten and rang it again.

"Yeah?" It was her voice all right, even through the static.

"Can I talk with you? Please?"

"Who is this?"

"Catherine Eversole." And though I had a feeling she would recognize my name, I continued. "Hence's girlfriend."

To my surprise, she buzzed me in. I climbed the stairs to the fourth floor and found her waiting for me in the doorway, dressed in a sheer black lace slip. It seemed like a strange way to answer the door, but, hey, it was Nina, so why should I be surprised? Her fuchsia hair was mussed, and she smelled like stale Obsession.

She beckoned me in, an inexplicable smile on her lips. I had time to register the décor in her living room—lamps covered with fringed scarves, a large painting of a fleshy, redheaded nude that could have been Nina herself, and framed, signed posters of Hüsker Dü and The Cult. The remnants of a meal—beer cans and pizza crusts—were strewn across the table. Under a jumble of laundry, a red velvet sofa was barely visible.

I stood there for a moment, stupidly expecting her to act civilized—to maybe sweep aside the laundry and offer me a seat, to ask me why I was there and how she could help. Instead, she stood with her hands on her hips, looking me disapprovingly up and down, as if I were the half-naked one. Her eyes on mine, like one feral dog challenging another, she called to someone in the other room: "You've got company."

In the silence that followed, I could hear my heart pounding in my ears.

"In there." With a long purple fingernail she pointed to a closed door and I knew all at once that I'd found Hence. Not only was he alive, he was one room away, and in a second I would throw my arms around him. I'd explain everything and get him to come

233

home with me, and our life would be even better than before because he would know about Harvard and would forgive me anyway. But even as these thoughts flooded my head, my feet refused to budge. I guess they understood before the rest of me that something was terribly wrong with this picture.

When I didn't move, Nina moved for me. She threw open the door to her darkened bedroom. At first I couldn't see who or what was in there.

"Come on." She grabbed me by the wrist and pulled me into a room so small it was almost all bed, a dark, airless den that stank of sweat and perfume. She flipped the light switch and I felt the air leave my lungs. There, amid a jumble of blankets, lay Hence, naked, covered by nothing but a sheet.

Had I expected him to be happy to see me? He wasn't. His eyes were cold and full of distrust. They bored straight into mine, and I had a crazy thought that maybe this wasn't Hence after all, maybe this was just some angry stranger who happened to look exactly like him. Someone who hated me without even knowing me, who had made up his mind to never listen to a word I had to say.

We stayed frozen like that, staring at each other, until his beautiful lips twisted into a smirk and he lifted his hand and crooked a finger, beckoning at something over my shoulder. For a moment I thought he was inviting me to lie down, and I started to move toward him, but Nina breezed past me in her flimsy slip and climbed into the empty space beside this stranger who was Hence. She looked at me and laughed, as if my presence in her bedroom was hilarious, and he joined in laughing with her. As if I weren't even there, she leaned over and started noisily kissing him, and he let her, their tongues down each other's throats, by the looks of it; like they were putting on a show for me. Or worse—they didn't even care that I was there, watching.

The kiss went on for what felt like a million years, and though I knew I should leave, I couldn't seem to move. Her purple taloned hands grasped his shoulders, and then ran over his chest, but his hands weren't on her; they were beside him on the bed, each making a fist, clutching the sheet like it was something he wanted to crush.

And then Nina pulled back to murmur something in his ear. He nodded, his eyes still closed, and she began to nibble his neck. And over her pink hair, he opened his eyes to make sure I was still there, his gaze hard. As Nina kissed her way down his throat, pausing to nuzzle his chest, he stared past her at me. A challenge.

When she dipped lower, to his stomach, he was still staring defiantly into my eyes.

I knew without a doubt they would have kept going like that, her head moving lower and lower, his eyes on my face going colder and harder, for as long as I stayed there watching. But finally, thank God, I found my feet. I tore away, leaving the apartment door swinging open behind me, down four flights of stairs to the street below, and even as I ran I thought Hence might come after me to say that it was all a joke, he didn't really mean it, he was just trying to show me how much I'd hurt him, he could never love Nina the way he loved me—could never love anyone the way he loved me. That this whole terrible thing had been a mistake.

Like an idiot, I waited, trembling, out on the street, but he didn't come after me. Cars passed, a bicycle messenger swerved to miss me and sped off, an old woman pushing a shopping cart slowed to look me over with eyes that broadcast curiosity and pity. None of it meant anything. Finally, I tore myself away, heading for the only place I had left: Jackie's house. I huddled on her front stoop, cold and miserable, waiting for her to get home from wherever she'd gone, though I had no idea what I would say to her, how I would give voice to what I'd learned about Hence. I certainly couldn't go back to the apartment and tell the guys; I couldn't stand the pitying looks they would give me. They would try to be nice, I was sure of it. They would say something comforting about what a dick Hence was being, but I knew their loyalty lay with him and not me. There was no way I could stay in the apartment with them for even a minute longer. I hoped I could move into Jackie's house until I could breathe again.

While I waited on Jackie's steps, night fell and the streetlights switched on, their cold blue light falling on the sidewalk. *Hurry home, Jackie*, I kept thinking. *I need you.*

Chelsea

I sipped a papaya-mango smoothie at the juice bar café while I
read my mother's journal. From my table, I could lean forward
and peek out the window for a view of The Underground, but for a
long time there was no sign of Coop. Finally, a van pulled up and
Rat Behavior piled out onto the sidewalk; I recognized them from
pictures I'd seen online. The tall one with pale skin, black hair,
and a long nose that looked like it had been broken once or twice
was Stan Hodicek, Riptide's former drummer. He ran to Hence
and the two of them executed one of those manly hugs, clapping
each other on the back. After that, they talked for a long time. I
mostly leaned back so Hence couldn't catch sight of me, but every
sixty seconds or so I'd sneak another peek. Talking with his old
bandmate, Hence looked more animated and less sullen than I'd
ever seen him. After a while, he and Stan strode off somewhere

together. Figuring the coast was clear, I hurried across the street and slipped in the front door.

Cooper was directing a swarm of roadies. He didn't exactly look happy to see me. "Didn't I tell you to wait at the juice bar?"

"It's okay," I said. "I saw Hence leave."

"He could come back at any second."

"I don't think so. He and Stan looked like they were headed somewhere to catch up."

"You could tell that just by looking at them?" Coop had a black smudge on his cheek. I wanted to reach over and wipe it away, but I was pretty sure that would have annoyed him even further. "Get across the street. I'll come find you when I've got a free second," he said, brushing past me on his way back out to the truck.

I should probably have done as he said, but instead I found myself wandering deeper into the club's dark interior. It looked like Cooper and the staff had been busy cleaning all morning; the kitchen sink was free of dirty glasses, and the bar had been thoroughly stocked with cocktail napkins and those little plastic stirrers. So I pressed on, and found the door to Hence's office ajar. Though it maybe wasn't so wise, I couldn't help myself; I slipped in and switched on the light. The hole he'd punched in the wall had been patched, and the room had been tidied up.

I wandered over to the wall of eight-by-ten glossies of musicians from the seventies to the present, like a time line of bands, some I recognized and a whole lot of others I didn't. Looking at them made me wish I hadn't been exiled from The Underground, with all its noise, neon, and excitement. How would I ever return to my ordinary life in the suburbs?

238

"If Hence comes back and finds you staking out his office..." Cooper's voice from behind me brought my musings to a screeching halt.

"I didn't touch anything." I held out my palms to show they were empty. "I wasn't snooping."

"Then what are you doing in here?" Cooper massaged his temples, like I was giving him a headache.

I gestured toward the glossies. "Looking at the bands. Wishing I knew more about music. Wishing I hadn't been exiled to Brooklyn."

He dug his hands in his pockets and looked intently at me through the shag of his bangs, waiting for me to say more, but I wasn't in the mood.

"I'll go," I said. "I know this is a big day, and you're busy. In fact, I'll go back to Jackie's. You can call me later...or just text."

"Stop," Coop said. "Listen. I didn't drag you all the way here so we could pick a time to meet up tomorrow."

"Why, then?"

"There's a place where you can watch tonight's show without being seen," he said. "From the mixing room. It has a smoked-glass window. Nobody will be able to see you. Hence sometimes watches from there, but he won't tonight."

"You want to sneak me in during a show?"

"You *need* to be here tonight. Hence is going to join the band onstage. He hasn't played since the last time Rat Behavior came through town, and he'll try to beg out of it, but Stan will insist. You've got to see him. Onstage. The way he used to be."

"But what if Hence finds out?"

Coop lowered his voice. "I'm starting to like living danger-ously." Despite the sly look in his blue-green eyes, I couldn't help thinking that maybe he wasn't completely kidding.

"Seriously. You could lose your job."

"Only if you get caught. Stay out of sight, and come around to the back just before the show starts." Now he was walking me toward the door, looking both ways before ushering me out. "I'll be busy, but I'll keep checking for you, so don't leave."

That night, Coop sneaked me into the mixing room, a chamber so dark, musty, and tangled with wires it seemed like the kind of place rats might burrow in. I took a seat on the heavy table beside all the equipment, cross-legged to keep myself safely out of reach of ver-min. I was excited—not only was I going to see another show, I was doing it on the sly. Plus, I'd get to spy on Hence.

I could see and hear really well from my little nest—I could even feel the buzz of excitement from the growing crowd, to the point where it was hard to sit still for the warm-up bands and the roadies shuffling instruments and equipment in between sets. It would have been so nice to have someone tucked in the dark beside me, to share my sense that something exciting was coming.

The main room filled up slowly. Just when I couldn't sit still a minute longer, Rat Behavior took the stage, and the buzz of the audience escalated to a roar. There were four of them—two pale, wiry, near-identical guitarists; the stocky, bearded bassist; and Stan Hodicek, tall and lean, his black hair mussed and spiky, who waved here and there at faces in the crowd before settling in behind his drum kit. Stan shouted, "One, two, three, four!" and the band launched into its first song, a blast of sound—grungy guitars and a booming bass that sent the crowd bouncing up and down to the beat. Forgetting about the *actual* rats I'd feared might be running around the room, I slipped down from the table and danced a little in place as I listened.

The next song was as good as the first. As I lost myself in the noise and the beat, I still paid special attention to Stan. After all, he'd known my mother. He seemed good-natured and goofy, grinning as he slammed away at his drums, and I mused about how if only my mother had fallen in love with him instead of Hence, maybe things would have gone better for her, and she'd have had her happy ending. Maybe she'd be here now, waiting backstage with a smile on her face.

But of course I never would have been born.

Before long, the show drove all other thoughts out of my head. Rat Behavior was more than just good, and I resolved to download all of their music when I got home. Maybe I'd slip Coop some money to buy me a T-shirt from the merchandise table. When I saw Larissa again, I could act all nonchalant about how I'd seen Rat Behavior at the legendary Underground. Oh, and, incidentally, that I was descended from rock-and-roll royalty.

The band played full throttle for so long that even I was starting to feel wrung out. Just when I was wondering if maybe Cooper had been wrong about Hence joining the band onstage, Stan slipped out from behind his drum set to address the audience.

"Tonight..." He repeated the word a few times, waiting for

241

the crowd to simmer down before continuing. "Tonight a special guest will be joining us for a few songs—one of the greatest musicians I've ever had the pleasure to work with. No. Scratch that. One of the greatest musicians in rock and roll. Period. He gave it all up to play host to hundreds of up-and-coming bands, to give them a leg up and all of us a venue for hearing the best music out there. He doesn't get up onstage much anymore, so anytime he does, it's an event."

Throughout the night, there had been a low-level buzz of conversation between songs, but now Stan's words echoed in the sudden stillness. "So please welcome my old friend…and yours… Hence."

The applause was so loud it startled me. I pressed my forehead to the glass window, trying for a clearer view, wishing I could be right in front of the stage. From where I was sitting, I could see the look on Hence's face as he strapped on his guitar—solemn, as though this were church and not a nightclub. If I'd expected him to change into black leather or silver studs, I'd have been disappointed—he was his usual self, in a white button-down shirt with the sleeves rolled partway up and an ordinary pair of black pants. He looked out over the crowd like he was taking inventory and smiled. Had I ever even seen him smile before? Certainly not like this, a flash of teeth like the beam of a lighthouse cutting through fog.

"Stan overstates my case." Hence waved a hand at the crowd, signaling them to stop clapping, but the noise only got louder. As he stepped to the mike, I held my breath, thinking of how much my mother had loved his singing. Could he really be as wonderful

242

as she'd believed? Given all the buildup, I thought his voice would have to be a disappointment.

But it wasn't. It was bigger and deeper than I'd have guessed, with a range I couldn't have imagined. I recognized Riptide's big hit, with its lyrics about being lost and homesick and finding love, only to lose it again. I knew the song better than I had realized and could sing along with the chorus, except I didn't want to miss anything, so I didn't. The song was upbeat but the lyrics were sad, and as Hence sang, an openness—a sweetness—stole over his face. Launching into a complicated guitar solo, Hence looked almost surprised, as if he hadn't been sure he'd still be able to play with such ferocity. Stan took a drum solo, and Hence stood, arms crossed, watching with evident pride. Was this what he'd been like before he'd gotten so bitter?

The song ended and the band launched into one I hadn't heard before, about riding a Greyhound bus into New York City, trying to catch a break and make it big. The second verse contained lines about wanting to "escape the eyes of a one-horse town, escape the ghosts who drag me down." And something changed in Hence's voice when he belted out the third verse, about escaping the palm of his father's hand and the devil in his face. By then I was sure he'd written the lyrics. He looked down at the ground as he sang, barely acknowledging the crowd, as though the words still had the power to hurt him.

I wondered: Had my mother ever heard this song? It seemed to answer all the questions she'd had about Hence's past. Maybe she was hiding out in a one-horse town herself, listening to Riptide's one and only CD and wondering what had ever happened to her old love. I smiled to think of it. Just then, Hence looked up, his eyes trained in the direction of my window. I caught my breath and ducked, sure for a split second that he knew I was watching. But of course he couldn't know. When I could breathe again, I let myself return to the window.

When the song drew to a close, while the crowd whooped and cheered, Stan jumped out from behind the drum kit to clap Hence on the back. I thought that might be the end, but Hence returned to the mike. "We're going to play one more," he said. "A new one." He lifted his hand to start strumming, but he froze. "The lyrics were written by, uh..." A funny look crossed his face. For a moment, he seemed lost for words. "Somebody I used to know. I've hung on to them for a long time—since I was eighteen, when Riptide was getting started."

A man in the crowd shouted "Hell, yeah!" and there was a smattering of applause.

"And just this week, someone...something moved me to finally set them to music. I...um...hope you like it."

And the song began, a slower one this time. He didn't have to say her name for me to know who had written the words. Had Cooper known about this? If so, why had he kept it from me? But a moment later, those questions didn't matter. I struggled to catch every word, but I missed a lot:

If the shadows sweep me from the table,
crumbs upon your floor
will you gather me like something
something out the door,

244

will you cup me in your hands
and carry me away,
keep my name upon your lips
to whisper when you pray?
I'll something something press you
like a violet in my book,
and something something something
in the music of the brook,
something something something something
blankets that we share
long after you have left me
to these four walls blank and bare.

Had Mom written those words when they were happy together, or in that time when she knew she'd have to choose between Hence and the future she'd dreamed for herself? The song—its lyrics and its tune—was so sad it made me ache for her...and for him.

As I listened to her words in Hence's deep, mournful voice, I kept forgetting to breathe. And when the song drew to a close, I jumped down from the table and fought my way out of the tangled wires I had forgotten were there. What I was about to do was borderline insane, but I couldn't stop myself: I burst through the door and past Cooper, who looked completely surprised to see me. Though I was risking his job and Hence's wrath, I couldn't seem to stop myself. I ducked into the main room, through the milling crowd, working my way toward the stage. As Hence stepped down into the shadows, I needed to be right in front of him, so I was.

What I had to say rushed out before I had time to think better of it. "There's something you have to know," I shouted, desperate to be heard above the applause. "About what you thought you heard my mother say. On the steps of Jackie's house. When you ran away from her."

At the sight of me, Hence looked utterly shocked. He opened his mouth as if to speak, then shut it again.

"What you heard wasn't what she meant," I shouted.

Hence gave me an urgent look, as if I were telling him I'd found a ticking bomb in the back room. Ignoring the fans who waved for his attention, he led me by my elbow through the stage door and into the back of the club, hurried me into the relative quiet of his office, and locked the door behind us. I sank to the chair in front of his desk, but instead of sitting, he stalked back and forth.

"You should have stayed to listen to the rest of what she had to say," I concluded. "You should have let her explain."

"How could you know about any of that?" In the fluorescent office light, Hence's face looked as white as paper. He couldn't have seemed more rattled if I'd told him my mother's ghost had come back to tell me the story of their beautiful relationship and its ugly end.

"I found her journal." I told him about the hiding place in the hollowed-out book and how I'd been afraid he would take it from me before I could finish reading it. Of course I was still running the risk that he'd confiscate it, but somehow that didn't matter as much as setting the record straight.

Why hadn't I realized it before? This was what my mother would have wanted me to do.

"She tried to tell you," I concluded. "She looked everywhere for you, so she could explain. She tried to file a missing persons report. She even lit candles in church. And when she did find you…you know." I couldn't finish that sentence, but the look of shame that crossed Hence's face told me he knew exactly what I was talking about.

"Please," he said in a choked voice. "You can't know how I wish I could go back and undo what I did to her. I've wished it every day since it happened." He looked at me with something like hope in his face. "Would you show me the journal? If I promise not to take it away from you?"

How could I trust him? And yet, I wanted to. I dug for it in my pack, thinking quickly. "First, you have to know that Cooper had no idea I was in the building. I sneaked into the club this afternoon. Just now, when he saw me, he tried to stop me…."

"You're a terrible liar." Hence didn't sound angry. He took the journal from my hands and brought it up to his face, inhaling deeply, as if he could smell her on it. "I remember this," he said, wonder in his voice. "Catherine brought it with her everywhere she went. When the band was recording, I'd look up sometimes and find she'd slipped away. She'd be curled up in a corner, writing furiously."

"You can read the whole thing later," I told him. "For now… let me show you." I flipped toward the end. "There."

He let me read over his shoulder as he devoured each page. When he'd read as far as I had, I stopped him. "So you see. You should have listened."

"I know," he said. "At first I was too angry to think straight.

And by the time I realized my mistake, she'd married your father. They'd had you…" He stopped, his voice cracking as though the wound were still fresh.

I waited for the rest.

"I sent her that postcard. I was going to make it all up to her. Then I got to The Underground and she was just…gone."

Disappointment swept through me. I'd been so sure I was telling him something new and life-changing. I gestured toward the book. "I guess this doesn't mean anything to you, then."

Hence looked down at the open book, then back up at me, baffled, as if I were speaking some alien language and he was trying to pick out familiar words. "Of course it does. It means…a lot. It's like getting a piece of her back." To my surprise, he shut the book and put it in my hands "What happens next?"

"I haven't reached the end yet. I've only got a few pages left."

"You finish it first," he said. "I'm afraid of what I'll find in there."

"I'll bring it to you when I'm done," I said. "It shouldn't take me long. It's a matter of making myself finish. I don't really want it to be over."

"I know," he said. "It's all we've got left." He got to his feet and started toward the office door. For a few minutes, I had forgotten about the world beyond that door, about the last of the customers finishing their drinks and heading out into the night, about Stan and Rat Behavior and even Coop.

"Are you going to say good-bye to your friends?"

"I can't talk to them right now," he said. "You can tell Cooper I'm not angry. Have him tell Stan I'll be in touch."

"But where are you going?"

"For a walk," he said. "To think."

As I watched him go, a thought occurred to me: *Maybe I should be worried.* He might be about to do something rash—throw himself off a bridge or a rooftop. But why should I even care? What was he to me, anyway? Some guy who wished my father had never married my mother. And yet, as messed up as it was, I did care.

"I'll come with you." I scrambled to my feet.

He looked at me absently, his mind already elsewhere. "No," he said. "You stay here."

Okay, so he didn't want me tagging along. "I'll get Coop," I said. "He'll go."

"Don't worry. I won't do anything crazy." He hit the light switch.

"You're sure?"

He nodded, and my hand shot out to grab his arm. "Wait. I have to ask you something. When did she write that song?"

"She meant it to be a poem," he said. "I don't think she saw it as lyrics. She wrote it toward the end of our time together. It was a birthday present for me. She even baked me a cake—chocolate with caramel frosting." His smile was rueful. "It was the best cake I've ever tasted."

"But that song was so sad."

He nodded. "After I ran off, I thought it had been her way of telling me she was planning to leave me. I was glad I'd beaten her to the punch."

"What happened to the one you wrote for her? The one you named after her?"

"I could never finish it. At first there weren't any words that could capture how she was. How amazing. And later I was too hurt and angry."

"But you don't have to be angry at her anymore," I said.

Hence dug his hands into his pockets. "No, I guess I don't."

Suddenly I felt awkward. "You'll tell me more about her? I really want to hear more. Everything. Anything."

He hesitated.

"I don't mean right now," I added hastily. "Will you, though? When you're ready?"

He nodded and was gone.

I lingered in the hallway, unsure what to do next. That's how Cooper found me. "What just happened?" He was pale with worry.

"It's okay," I said. "He's not mad at us."

"He's not?"

"I showed Hence my mother's journal," I said. "Now he's going for a walk. Can we sit down somewhere?" Exhausted, I followed Coop up to Hence's apartment, sank into his deepest armchair, and accepted a can of ginger ale. "Do you have any chips? I'm starving all of a sudden."

"First tell me what got into you. Hence could have freaked out."

"I know I shouldn't have, but when he sang my mother's song, I couldn't help myself." I filled Coop in on the details of how Hence had heard only part—the worst possible part—of my mom's heart-to-heart with Jackie, and how he'd paid her back.

250

"I tried to tell Hence I sneaked into the club all by myself. He didn't believe me, but he isn't mad...."

"I'm not mad, either," Coop said.

"You're really not?"

"You did the right thing. He had to know the truth."

Relieved, I followed Coop into the kitchen, where he dug through the cupboard and came up with a box of oyster crackers. I tore into them. "You should have seen the look on his face when I ran up to him."

Coop grinned. "I can imagine. Are you going to share those?"

I handed the box over. "There's hardly any left." I followed him out to the living room and we both stood at a window that looked down on Houston.

"I wonder where he is," Coop said.

"He promised he wouldn't do anything drastic."

Coop looked doubtful.

"He's okay," I told him. "He has to come back to read the rest of the journal, right?"

Coop sat down on the couch and I collapsed into the love seat across from him, hugging the nearest throw pillow to my chest.

"If he does come home, he'll find you here with me," Coop observed.

"And accuse us of the high crime of being alone together?" I put my feet up on a nearby ottoman. "I don't think he will. Not after tonight."

"Neither do I." Coop shut his eyes but kept talking. "I've been thinking. Before the show I talked Hence into giving me the day off tomorrow. Of course I didn't tell him what I needed it for—"

"Really?" I interrupted. "That's fantastic."

"But wait." Cooper held up a hand. "I was thinking maybe we should tell him where we're going."

"Why would we do that?"

"As long as you're coming clean with him, why not tell the whole truth? Maybe he would want to come with us."

"Come with us? Why would we want that?"

"Quentin doesn't sound like the most stable guy in the world. Did you ever think he might not be thrilled to see us?"

I grabbed another throw pillow and rested my head against it. "He's my uncle."

"He could be dangerous."

"He'll be happy to see me."

"Right. Maybe he'll throw you a party."

"Besides, he hated Hence. *Despised* him. He'd take one look at Hence and slam the door in our faces." I shut my eyes. "Seriously, Coop. Don't, don't, don't tell Hence. Okay?"

"Okay, okay." Coop sounded sleepy.

What felt like a few minutes later, I woke with a start, scared to find myself in a strange room. Somebody had spread a throw over me. I stared into the darkness until my eyes adjusted and I recalled where I was. That was when I noticed the soft current of someone else's breath in the room and remembered Coop.

A swath of light from the streetlamp outside fell on the couch, where he lay on his back, blanketless, arms crossed for warmth. I let the sound of his steady breathing calm me, and then I got to my feet and tiptoed closer. Asleep, he looked unguarded, vulnerable, his eyelashes making dark crescents on his cheeks, his lips curled upward as if he was dreaming about something happy.

"Mmph," he mumbled, crossing his arms even tighter. He really did look cold. I grabbed the throw and covered him with it. He uncrossed his arms, the curl of his lips turning into a full-fledged smile.

While I hovered over him, half praying he wouldn't wake up and half hoping he would, a crazy thought popped into my mind: *What would happen if I leaned in and gave him a kiss?* Would he kiss me back, still thinking he was dreaming? What kind of kisser would he be? Rough and clumsy? Or gentle and sweet?

And what would he think if he woke all the way up and realized it was me he was kissing?

Cooper mumbled again and rolled onto his side. I snapped upright, coming to my senses. What was I thinking? I didn't have those kinds of feelings for Coop, and even if I did, I couldn't risk acting on them. After all, I needed his help. I couldn't afford to make things all weird between us.

I knew I should take the train to Jackie's. But I hadn't thought to call and tell her where I was going, and she might be furious at me for taking off without leaving so much as a note. It was certainly too late to call her now; it must be at least two in the morning. Was Hence back? Probably not; he'd have woken us if he'd come in. Returning to my love seat, hugging myself for warmth, I willed myself not to worry about Hence, or about what lay before us in the morning. I slowed my breath till it matched Cooper's and I was calm enough to fall back to sleep.

Catherine

In the days that followed, I worked out a plan. I would leave for Cambridge as soon as I'd turned in my last final exam. There was no reason to stay in New York beyond that. Graduation was for girls with families. Jackie and her mom understood why I needed to go, though they kept insisting their house was my house and I could live in their guest room forever if I needed to. But the narrow little room with its brass bed and potpourri aura brought back a thousand vivid memories of me and Hence together. I'd wake up hopeful and happy from dreams of him, but the knowledge of where I was and why would come rushing back, and my mouth would fill with bile.

Besides, the fact that I might bump into Hence—or, worse, Hence and Nina—on the street made me want to run away screaming. So I stopped going out unless I absolutely had to. I hurried to school in the morning, did my work, and hustled straight back to Jackie's for the rest of the day.

In the long hours between school and bedtime, I made plans and phone calls. A friend of Dad's from college had gone on to be the dean of students at Harvard. He pulled some strings and got me into a dorm that would stay open during the summer for students with internships. He even offered to help me find an internship of my own, maybe something in publishing, although I didn't much care if it was in public relations, plumbing, or pancake-flipping. Anything would be better than staying in New York.

I didn't see the guys in the band anymore. When I called to tell them I'd found Hence, Stan had handed the phone to Andy, who thanked me for the news and quickly found an excuse to hang up. Hence rejoined the band and they forgave his disappearing act. While I didn't think they knew exactly what had passed between Hence and me, they knew it had been bad, and, with the possible exception of Ruben, they knew whose side they were on.

I learned all this when Ruben came to Jackie's house to pay me one last visit. He said he was sorry for how things turned out and that he thought Hence was making a huge mistake and acting like a major jerk. In his zebra-striped jumpsuit, he looked comically out of place on Jackie's mom's couch, holding a glass of her iced tea on his jiggling leg, the ice cubes clattering noisily. "That Nina chick is a mess," he told me apologetically. "He doesn't really care about her. He's trying to get back at you."

"He told you that?"

"He didn't have to. When she's speaking, he rolls his eyes. Not that I blame him; she's dumb as a post."

"It isn't her brain he cares about." I fought back the mental picture of the two of them kissing in Nina's bed, her mouth on his skin, and the way he'd looked at me, reveling in the pain he was inflicting. But it was like building a wall of sand to keep the tide from rushing in: worse than useless.

"She's nothing compared to you," Ruben said kindly. "And he knows it."

I shrugged, feigning indifference. I had thought about making Ruben my messenger, having him tell Hence that he'd misunderstood what he'd heard, that I needed to speak to him and clear things up. But when I opened my mouth to ask, there was Hence's face again, cruel with his hatred of me. Was I really going to stoop that low, begging him to hear my side of things?

"I don't care what he does," I told Ruben instead. "I'm out of here. As soon as I finish my classes I'm on a train to Boston. Tell him I'm thrilled to be starting my new life as a Harvard snob."

And I meant it—well, the part about being on my way out of New York City, anyway. Like Dad's favorite Janis Joplin song said, *freedom* was just another word for nothing left to lose. Now I was so free I could drift like a balloon over the rooftops and out to sea, and hardly anyone would care enough to wave good-bye.

After I'd taken my last exam and exchanged tearful hugs with Jackie and her mom, there was one thing left to do. From the front window of the café across the street from The Underground, I kept watch until I was sure Quentin had gone out for the night, and then, journal in the deep front pocket of my sweatshirt, I climbed the creaky fire escape up to my window. Up in my room for what looked like the last time, I slipped the journal into its

256

hiding place, grieving for it as I said good-bye. I couldn't bear to take it with me. A reminder of Hence, of Dad's death, of Quentin turning into a stranger, it was a part of the life I had to force myself to forget. If I ever saw it again—and the odds were good that I wouldn't—it would be because a miracle had happened and I'd come home.

Chelsea

Cooper's whisper woke me. "Rise and shine, Chelsea. Let's get rolling." My eyes popped open, everything coming back to me all at once: the concert, my conversation with Hence, and—most vividly of all—the impulse I'd had to kiss Cooper. "Shhh. Hence came in a couple of hours ago. We don't want to wake him." Cooper was bending over me, so close I could smell the shampoo he'd used. Dizzy, I shut my eyes. When I opened them, he was gone.

I sat up, buried my face in my hands, and exhaled with relief. The night before, I hadn't done the first thing that popped into my head, for once. I hadn't kissed Coop, and he would never need to know I'd had such a crazy impulse. "Hence is here?" I asked when he returned.

"You were sacked out when he came in." Damp-haired and

barefoot, Coop swept through the room, straightening it up. "You can shower in the apartment. I'll meet you in front of the club."

By the time I'd dressed and taken the elevator downstairs, Coop was waiting beside a double-parked silver Jaguar Coupe with a box of doughnuts and two coffees. Much to my surprise, when he pressed the button on his key chain, the car's lights flashed.

"That's your car?"

"Ha. Don't I wish? It's Hence's." Coop looked cheery and energized, as if he'd had a full night's sleep in a comfy bed instead of four hours on a couch. He dug in the pocket of his jeans and dumped sugar packets and creamers in my hand. "I don't know how you take yours."

"Hence is letting us use it?"

"I told him I needed to drive you back to Brooklyn and run some errands. He wasn't upset to see you on the couch, by the way."

"Amazing." In the Jag, I fixed my coffee and laid claim to a powdered-sugar doughnut while Coop programmed my uncle's address into the GPS system. A line of cars gathered behind us, drivers swearing at us out their windows.

"I'm going, I'm going," Coop muttered.

As we pulled away from the curb, I put my feet up on the dashboard. Even if we were on a serious mission, this was a road trip, wasn't it? I might as well enjoy it. And so what if I'd started having bizarre feelings about Coop? They would pass. In the meantime, I'd act like my usual self around him, and maybe he wouldn't notice.

"Are you going to give me one of those?" Coop interrupted my interior monologue. I handed him a jelly doughnut and he made a face. "Not that. One of the glazed chocolate ones."

259

"What did you get jelly for if you don't like it?"

"I thought you might." Which was exactly the kind of nice thing Coop was always doing, come to think of it. I thanked him.

He stole a quick look at me before focusing back on traffic. "You've got powdered sugar on your nose."

Cooper changed lanes, passed a slow-moving Buick, and fiddled with the satellite radio, settling on an alternative station. Grungy guitars blasted through the speakers.

"Is this the kind of music you play?" I asked him. "Alternative? I've never understood what it's supposed to be an alternative to."

He didn't answer. Maybe he thought I was criticizing his taste in music? I began again. "How did you start playing?"

That worked better. "I picked up my best friend's guitar in ninth grade. I'd tried other instruments before that. In fourth grade, I played the trumpet. Then there was the year my mother wanted me to play the clarinet. It just wasn't me."

Had Cooper ever mentioned his family before? If he had, I couldn't remember it.

"But the guitar was you?" I prompted him.

"It felt right in my hands," he said. "I taught myself a couple of chords and never looked back."

"Where did you grow up?" I asked him.

"Beavercreek, Ohio."

I laughed. "Is that a real place?"

"As real as *Marblehead*, Massachusetts." And he drew the name out so I could hear how ridiculous it sounded.

"Does it have creeks? And beavers?"

"It's a suburb of Dayton," he told me. "Maybe beavers lived there once. Is your head made out of marble?"

"Why did you leave it?"

"So I could be your chauffeur."

"Seriously," I said. "What made you run away from home?"

Coop laughed. "I left after I graduated high school. I wouldn't call that running away from home." He fiddled with the radio presets. "I wanted to see New York City," he said. "Find out if I could make it in the music scene. That old cliché. 'If I can make it there, I'll make it anywhere.'" He sang that last part. "My mom's a Frank Sinatra fan."

"So you weren't trying to get away from your family?" I thought of Hence and his unspeakable past.

"My family's okay," Cooper said. "They wanted me to go to college. Dad was gutted when I didn't. He's still worried I'll never find my place in corporate America. He calls me every other day to nudge me about it, but he isn't an ogre. He wants what he thinks is best for me, even if it doesn't match what I want for myself."

I thought of my own father, probably worried to death about where I'd gone and whether I was okay, and felt a twinge of guilt for leaving him without a word. "Don't you want to go to college someday?"

"Sure," he said. "I took a class at CUNY this spring. And I'll be taking intro to psych in the fall."

"Hence gives you time off from the club?"

"Of course. Anyway, school's got to take a backseat to my job, at least for now. And my music. I've got an audition lined up next week."

"You do? I mean...that's great. I hope you get it."

Coop resumed playing with the radio, then gave up and connected his iPod. We'd completely left the city behind. The countryside around us sparkled in the sunshine, and the Jag was practically the only car on the road. I leaned back and listened to the music. It was nobody I'd ever heard before, but kind of fun—bouncier and more playful than the stuff we'd had on earlier. I relaxed in my seat and rolled the window up so I could hear better. Halfway through the second song I asked who we were listening to.

"What do you think of it?"

"He's got a nice voice," I said. "And this song is quirky, but catchy. Who is it?"

Coop didn't respond, but the look on his face—and the red splotches on his cheeks—gave the answer away.

"It's you? No way! You're actually good." I meant it as a compliment, but realized too late that it might not have sounded that way.

"'Actually'?" But Cooper was smiling to himself, not seeming to mind.

"I didn't realize," I said. "Is that you on the guitar?"

He nodded. "I play lead."

"Who's that you're playing with?"

"Beavercreek. Don't laugh—that was the name of my old band in Ohio. The bassist, Pete, built a recording studio in his basement. You can hear it's not a very professional recording, right? This was our demo."

"What happened? Why aren't you with them anymore?"

262

"They didn't want to leave Ohio, and I wasn't going to stay. No big drama…we're all still friends."

"But you need another band," I said. "Maybe you should start one of your own."

"Maybe I should," Coop said, but he didn't sound serious. "You play an instrument?"

I felt myself get flustered. "I don't have any talent," I said. "And I'm not just talking about music. My dad says I never give anything my all."

"Sounds like something a dad would say." Coop's voice was matter-of-fact. "Anyway, I've seen you in action. I think he's wrong."

I drew myself upright and folded my legs. "That's nice of you."

"I'm not being nice," he said. "You're spunky."

Embarrassed, I reached for the GPS. "I wonder what Coxsackie, New York, is like."

"Is it a real place?" Cooper quipped, cracking me up. "Seriously, though, I looked at a map. Coxsackie is one town over from Climax, New York."

"It would be."

After that, we talked about who gets to name towns, and wondered why they didn't pick names like Alice or Steve. One moment I was thinking how comfortable we were together, and the next I was wondering if we were destined to always be just friends. Stealing a look at him out of the corner of my eye—his hands on the wheel, his profile, his shaggy brown hair all crazy in the cross-breeze—I wondered how it had taken me so long to notice how cute he was. The inside of my head was a jumble of thoughts. I was working so hard to not betray any of them that at one point I must have fallen silent for a while, and when Coop said something to me I had to ask him to repeat it.

"I said, why don't you read me the rest of your mother's journal? You brought it, didn't you?"

Of course I had. I reached into the backpack under my seat and tugged it out. But I hesitated. "There are only a few pages left."

"You have to read them sometime. Besides, we need every bit of information we can get, don't we?"

Buoyed by that "we"—he could as easily have said "you"—I turned to where I'd left off. The sections she'd written as a teenager had ended; now she was writing from The Underground, after she'd run away from my father and me. Just as I'd guessed, she'd come home to find the club boarded up—*like seeing an old friend in a full-body cast*, she'd written—and had climbed up the fire escape and through the fifth-story window. She wasn't surprised she'd beaten Hence back to New York since that morning's paper had mentioned a transit strike in the UK. What *did* surprise her was the state of her old room, which was exactly as she'd left it, down to the bed that hadn't been stripped since the night she and Hence had run from Quentin's gun. *I pressed my face into the pillowcase and inhaled, hoping to catch Hence's scent, but it had faded.* She wrote about being shocked by the changes her brother had made in the club downstairs: *hideous iron chandeliers, a red marble floor, walls covered with stuffed deer heads staring mournfully down at me. It's horrifying. But who am I to judge the mess my brother made of The Underground when I've done the same thing to my own life?*

There were a few pages about my dad, about hoping he wouldn't stay angry with her, because at least she'd never deceived

264

him; he'd known all along she was damaged goods. Riptide's big hit had been playing everywhere, and the tabloids were full of paparazzi shots of Hence on the town with Nina, and she had been so lonely and miserable. Going on a date with a nice guy like Max had been her way of moving on. And then she had gotten pregnant, and marrying Max had seemed like the only sensible choice.

After that, reading the journal got harder. There was a long part about how my dad couldn't compare to Hence. He was kind, responsible, a good father to me. But his kisses weren't Hence's kisses. His hands on her body weren't Hence's hands. I turned from Coop as I read that part, so he wouldn't be able to see my face, but I kept reading. There was so little of the journal left. I couldn't skip a word.

She described going to the mailbox and pulling out the postcard with a picture of The Bat Cave and Hence's familiar crooked handwriting on the back. *My heart started pounding, somehow knowing before my brain could that the card was something momentous. I read the message over and over till I had memorized every word. I thought I must be dreaming. I told myself I couldn't go to Hence. Think of Max, I told myself. Think of Chelsea.*

Then came the hardest part, a passage about me—*my little girl, my only joy these last three years*—about how once she'd reunited with Hence, she hoped Max wouldn't make it hard for her to see me. *But even if he does,* she wrote, *I'll come up with a plan for getting her back. I'll hire a lawyer if I have to. I won't let anything keep me from her.*

And though I hadn't reached the journal's end, I closed it, unable to go on.

"Chelsea?" Cooper stole a glance at me from the corner of his eye. "Are you okay?"

At the sound of his voice, I couldn't hold back the tears anymore. He pulled over to the side of the road and shut off the ignition. Before I could gain control of my voice, he leaned across to my side of the car and put his arms around me. "Say something," he urged.

"She was coming for me," I said between sobs. "It says so. Why didn't she come back?"

Cooper didn't answer, but he kept holding on until I had cried it all out.

"I need a Kleenex," I said finally. That was an understatement. My nose was running something fierce.

"Use my shirt," Cooper said. I laughed—an out-of-control half sob, half chortle—and he released me to dig between the seats for a stray doughnut-shop napkin. Wiping my nose and pulling myself together, I took my first look out the window in a while. We were in the mountains. A tractor trailer rumbled by, shaking the car.

"Why are you so nice to me?" I asked when I could trust myself to speak. "Lying to Hence, not getting mad when I ran out from the mixing room last night, even though you told me to stay hidden, and I could have gotten you fired..."

"It wasn't such a big deal."

"It was," I said. "It totally was."

"I like you." Cooper didn't look at me when he said the words. "I thought it was brave, what you did last night, telling Hence what he needed to know, even though he might have blown up at you. I like how you always say exactly what's on your mind, no matter how…"

"Thoughtless?"

He held out another napkin, and I took it. "That wasn't what I was going to say." He met my eyes with an expression on his face that stole my breath.

"What?" I asked. "What were you going to say?"

"I forget." He leaned over again. This time I twisted in my seat to meet him halfway. He brushed back the hair that had fallen into my eyes. Before I could think of what to say or how to react, he was kissing me as though everything that had ever happened in our lives had led us to this moment.

I tightened my arms around Coop and kissed him back, his lips on mine more thrilling and gentle than I could have imagined. Who knows how long we stayed like that, his hands in my hair, the air around us scented with powdered sugar. Cars and trucks blew by, sending shudders through our car. A cascade of car honks from a passing van full of college-age guys finally brought us to our senses.

"Wooo-hoooooooo!" one of them shouted, waving his arms out the window at us.

"Get a room!" another one yelled.

Cooper pulled away, frowning up the road after them. "Jerks," he said.

"No kidding." I grabbed his shoulders and tugged him close. "Never mind them. Kiss me again."

And he did, his sweet lips exploring mine for a few more minutes. But then he pulled back. "I've been wanting to do that almost from the first moment I met you," he murmured.

"Really?" Could I have inherited some of my mother's magnetism after all?

"Really." He touched my chin, tilting my face up toward him, but this time he kissed the tip of my nose. "But we should get moving. We've got a mission to execute, remember?"

"I remember." And the pleasant thrill that had run completely through me was replaced by foreboding. I buckled my seat belt.

"Is there more?" Coop said as he turned the key in the ignition. "In the journal? If you feel ready to read it..."

There was more. While my mom waited for Hence to arrive she'd had nothing much to do but write about where Hence might be and what the two of them would do once he finally arrived. *I can't sit here waiting anymore,* she'd written. *I need to do something.... But what?* Being in her childhood home made her ache with longing for her mother, for her father, even for Q. *I keep remembering the way he used to be, floppy blond bangs and freckles on his nose, always wearing his favorite striped rugby shirt, black and yellow like a big bumblebee. We used to be so close,* she wrote. *Maybe it's not too late.*

My throat dry from reading out loud, I took a swig from one of the water bottles I'd tucked into my backpack and turned the page. *I can find him,* it said. *I know his new address must be somewhere in the office... maybe on the bill of sale for the club. I'll go downstairs and look. I've been so cut off from my past, but now I can set everything straight, and by the time I return, Hence will be here waiting for me. Maybe by tomorrow night we'll be together, in this very bed where I'm lying right now, under these rumpled sheets, warm and whole.*

Little book, I'm putting you back in your hiding place for now. Wait there for me, and I hope I'll be filling you with happy news soon.

I turned the page and gasped.

"What's wrong?" Coop asked. "There's more, right?"

But the few remaining pages were blank. I had reached the end.

"This isn't good," I said.

"I know."

"I'm scared." I meant I was scared of what I hadn't wanted to believe but had feared all along—that my mother was dead. But Coop heard something else in my words.

"We can turn around," he said.

I thought for a moment, running through everything I knew about my uncle Quentin. He'd run off to live by himself in the woods, with an expensive gun collection and a vendetta against Hence. My mother had gone to see him and had never been heard from again. I *should* be scared—and not just for my mother.

But we weren't even fifteen minutes from his house. We'd come all this way. And I had to know the truth about my mom.

"Keep driving," I told Coop.

For the rest of the ride, neither of us said a word. The robotic GPS voice directed us off the highway and onto a twisting two-lane road. Before long the pavement ran out and the Jaguar was climbing a steep dirt road, sending up a cloud of dust.

"You have reached your destination," the robot voice said, and a second later the dirt path stopped dead. There was nothing in sight—just trees and more trees.

"Over there." Coop pointed to the left. I strained to see what he was looking at and caught sight of a log cabin about a hundred yards off, almost hidden by tall pines. I unclasped my seat belt.

"We don't have to do this," Coop said.

"I have to. You can wait in the car. You should. If I don't come back in an hour or so…"

Coop reached for his own seat belt. "No," he said. "I'm going with you."

"Wait." I hugged him in the awkward space of the front seat, pressing my face hard into the clean-smelling cotton of his T-shirt, as if I could draw courage from his body into my own. But there wasn't time to linger. We had to let go of each other and knock on Uncle Quentin's door before he noticed our car and came out to catch us off guard. "Let me go first," I told Coop.

He nodded and followed me up the steep path into a clearing. I'd been expecting a broken-down shack, but my uncle's log cabin was big and new-looking, not at all like the hideout of a crazed survivalist mountain man. We paused on the porch for a moment. I took a deep breath and pressed the doorbell. No answer. I tried again.

"He'd need a car way out here," Coop observed. "But there isn't one near where we left ours, and there's nowhere else to park."

"That's fantastic." Relief washed over me. "This way we won't have to deal with him at all." I gestured toward the windows on either side of the front door. "I bet at least one of these is unlocked. Or even the door." Not that I'd break and enter under normal circumstances, but the chance to poke through my uncle's house without having to confront him was too good to resist.

"You're kidding, right?" Cooper lowered his voice to a whisper. "There could be someone in there. A wife or a girlfriend. Or a pit bull."

I pressed my forehead to a nearby window, trying to see into the darkened room on the other side—a living room, by the looks of it. "Nobody's home." I was so sure of it I didn't bother to whisper.

"How can you know that?" Coop sounded exasperated.

"I just do." I turned the doorknob. Amazingly, the door was unlocked. I stepped inside. "Are you in?"

Cooper sighed. "This is a really bad idea," he said. But he followed me.

The living room was straight out of an L.L.Bean catalog, with a rough-hewn coffee table strewn with that day's *Wall Street Journal*. The air smelled faintly of woodsmoke. A stuffed deer head glared down at us from the fireplace's stone chimney. Apart from the newspaper, the only evidence of anyone having recently been there was a blue stoneware mug on the coffee table. I picked it up and swirled the bit of coffee left in the bottom. It still looked and smelled fresh.

Beyond the living room stood the kitchen, its gleaming aluminum appliances and glass cabinets like something from an architectural magazine. "Either he's a neat freak or he has a housekeeper." I opened the fridge and stood there for a moment, analyzing its contents: five bottles of beer, a large block of cheddar, a Tupperware container full of what might have been chili, and many jars of mustard.

"What do you expect to find in there?" Cooper was starting to sound exasperated. "Shouldn't we be moving a little faster?"

I shut the fridge door. He was right, of course, but my nerves tingled with electricity, as though some important discovery waited nearby. Off the kitchen, a hallway led to a room with an enormous flat-screen TV, a pool table, and a bearskin rug, but not much of anything else. A narrow door looked like it might lead outside. I pressed my ear to it a moment, listening for a dog, and pushed it open. It creaked as I reached inside to flick the light switch.

In contrast with what we'd seen of the rest of the house, this room was stacked floor to ceiling with a maze of cardboard boxes that probably hadn't been touched—much less dusted—for years. One end of the room was a graveyard for old sports equipment—a mountain bike, snowshoes, skis, and what appeared to be lacrosse gear.

"Look." Coop pointed to a large photo on the wall, one of those formal family portraits with everyone dressed in their matchy-matchy best. I recognized my mother right away, looking amused, as though she were thinking about crossing her eyes and sticking out her tongue. She must have been about twelve, though if she'd been in an awkward adolescent phase, it sure wasn't visible. Her glossy hair was pulled back in a French braid. At her side posed a good-looking, slightly older boy in a button-down shirt, his blond hair feathered back. Quentin. The wicked little smile on his face made it seem like he'd cracked a joke the moment before the picture was taken. Behind the pair of them stood a beaming man—the grandfather I'd never seen before. I wanted to study their faces, but Coop had already moved on to a glass-fronted cabinet against a wall. I took a step back from the portrait just as he let out a low whistle. Seven guns—hunting rifles, I supposed—stood neatly inside the cabinet.

"You still think it's a good idea to be sneaking around your uncle's house?"

"We knew about the guns." Something else caught my eye: To my right, in the darkest corner of the room, was a bookshelf built of planks and cinderblocks. These were the first books I'd seen in the house, and the sight of them triggered an alarm in my brain. They were old and dusty, probably remnants of Quentin's boyhood—a collection of Jack London stories, a cluster of Hardy Boys mysteries, and some Hemingway novels. I scanned the titles, looking hard for I'm not sure what, until suddenly I knew. I fell to my knees and started opening the volumes one by one, putting each one back as soon as I'd made sure it was an ordinary book.

"Help me," I told Cooper, and he dropped beside me and started searching the ones I hadn't reached yet.

"What are we looking for?" he asked.

But there wasn't time to answer. Right smack in the middle of the makeshift bookcase, I found it—a thick textbook, the letters on the weathered spine all but worn away. The minute I laid my hand on it, I knew it was different. Heart pounding in my ears, I pulled it out and revealed its hollow core. "My mother," I whispered, barely able to get the words out. "She was here."

Inside was a tightly folded sheet of paper, yellowed with age. A shopping list in familiar handwriting: cherry tomatoes, romaine lettuce, bananas, oatmeal, pancake mix. I turned the page over and found more of her handwriting, but smaller, as if she was trying to cram a lot of information into a small space.

Maybe nobody will ever see this, but I'm writing it down any-way, hoping someone who isn't my brother will find this book someday, maybe at a flea market or a garage sale, and open it up. If you're reading this, you are that person. Please keep read-ing. This is important.

My brother, Quentin Eversole, of Coxsackie, New York, is holding me in his house against my will. He pulled a gun on me and forced me into a storage room and locked the door from the other side. So far, I've been here one night and most of a day. For a long time I could hear him sitting on the other side of the door, keeping watch, but I haven't heard him in a while. I think he's left the house. I'm going to listen and wait a bit to be sure, and then I'm going to break the window and climb out. I'll try to find a house to make a phone call from. Quentin has guns—rifles and handguns. And he's not himself anymore. I can't reason with him. Believe me, I've tried.

So if you find this, please do me a favor. However many years have passed, could you make sure this note gets to a man named Hence? That's his whole name. He lives in New York City, at a nightclub called The Underground; the address is 247 Bowery. He doesn't know where I am or that I'm trying to get to him, and I don't want him to think I got impatient and gave up. He has to know I love him . . . that I never stopped. If I don't get back to him, he needs to know I died trying. And please tell him to find Chelsea no matter how grown-up she is and explain what happened and that I love her with my whole being. He'll know what that means.

Whoever you are, please bring Hence this letter. Maybe

you'll ring the buzzer to The Underground and I'll open the door. Maybe I'll be an old woman by then and I'll tell you, whoever you are, that it all turned out okay, that Chelsea, Hence, and I have been together for decades and we had our happy ending. I'll give you a big hug and a monetary reward and cook you dinner and be in your debt forever. But in case you ring the door and I'm not there, in case I never got there, could you please tell Hence I wanted to be with him so much it hurt? And please contact the authorities and tell them about my brother, Quentin. He's dangerous, so please don't confront him yourself.

In desperation,
Catherine Marie
Eversole Price

Hands trembling, I stuffed the piece of paper into my pocket. My legs felt limp, barely able to hold me up. I wanted to sink to the ground and absorb what I'd read, but Coop, who'd been reading over my shoulder, grabbed my hand. "We've got to get out of here," he said.

We hurried toward the main part of the house and were almost to the front door when—just my luck—we heard the sound of a car rumbling up the dirt road and pulling to a stop. Cooper and I looked at each other in panic. Should we retreat and try to find a back door to slip out of? Or would we wind up trapped, as my mother had been? Better to get out of the house, even if it meant facing the enemy head-on. We didn't have to exchange words; we both dove for the front door just as it opened. There in the doorway loomed an older, taller version of the boy in the photograph—still blond, broad-shouldered, and clean-shaven, a couple of grocery bags clutched to his chest. Though he must have seen our car in the driveway, he looked as shocked to see us in his living room as we were to see him.

Coop threw his hands in the air to show they were empty, and I followed suit.

"Who the hell are you?" the man exclaimed. He sounded almost as scared as we were. "What are you doing in my house?"

Coop tried to speak. "Um," he began. "We...uh."

But this was my uncle, and my problem to solve. I took a step closer. "Uncle Quentin?" I asked.

He looked from Coop to me, and his blue eyes got even wider.

"I'm your niece. Chelsea Price. Catherine's daughter. We came for a visit. It was such a long drive, and I had to pee." I gave him a bashful smile. "And you weren't here, but the door was open, so I told Coop you probably wouldn't mind if I used your bathroom." The lies kept popping into my head, one after another. "I hope that's okay."

Quentin's Adam's apple worked. He set his grocery bags on the floor, not taking his eyes off my face.

"I found your picture in some of my mother's stuff, in a box in the closet back home. I asked my father who you were and he told me. So I came here to meet you. Because we're family, right?" And I made myself stand on tiptoe and throw my arms around his shoulders. This man had killed my mother—I was absolutely sure of it—but I pushed that knowledge from my mind. The most important thing at that moment was that I convince him we meant him no harm.

276

After a heartbeat or two, his arms tightened around me. "You look so much like her," he said in a small voice.

I pulled away. "Everyone says that." The smile I gave him was genuine, because after all, my ploy seemed to be working. I didn't dare glance at Coop, for fear his expression would give us both away. Instead, I took a better look at Quentin and saw that he wasn't quite as young-looking as I'd first thought. His tanned skin was leathery, his blond hair shot through with white.

He seemed at a loss for words. "Chelsea," he said finally, his big hands dangling at his sides. He reached for me again. Another hug. Now that the immediate danger had passed, I noticed his smell—a mix of laundry detergent, coffee, and sweat that made me queasy. I wanted to shake myself free, but instead I counted to eight until he let me go and bent to retrieve his grocery bags.

"You want help with those?" I asked hopefully.

"You shouldn't ever let yourself into someone else's house," he said as he disappeared into the house. "You could get mistaken for an intruder." His voice floated from the kitchen. "You could get yourself shot."

Coop and I exchanged a look. Should we make a run for it? But a moment later, Quentin was back in the living room. He gestured toward Coop. "Who's this?" he asked me. "Your boyfriend?" His voice got a lot less friendly. "Is that his car in the driveway? How does a kid like him get a car like that?"

Instinct told me the answer he wanted to hear. "This is Cooper. He's a friend. He drove me here. It's his dad's car." I stole another glance at Coop. His hands were working themselves in and out of fists, unsure how ready they should be for confrontation.

Quentin cocked his head toward Coop. "You shouldn't go for a drive alone with some random boy. I don't care if he's your friend. You never know what a guy is thinking."

Seriously? I fought not to show the annoyance I felt. "He's not some random boy. He's a good friend. He's perfectly trustworthy."

"He'd better be." Quentin looked from me to Coop, who raised his palms in a *Who, me?* gesture.

"He is." I cast around for the next right thing to say, wondering how soon I could plausibly excuse myself and Coop, especially since we'd supposedly driven all this way for a family reunion. Would we have to make nice all afternoon and stay for dinner? I wasn't sure I could do it.

Quentin relented. "Come into the kitchen." It was more of an order than an invitation.

We complied, watching as he started putting his groceries away. Peanut butter. White bread. Dill pickles. Shredded wheat. "Can I help?" I asked, like a dutiful niece.

No answer. I pulled up a seat at the kitchen table, and Coop followed my lead.

"You need something to eat?" Quentin's tone was friendlier now. "I could heat you up some of my venison stew. You know what venison is, don't you? Deer meat. I've got rabbit in my freezer downstairs, too, and squirrel."

"No, thanks. We're good." Squirrel? Really? Coop was struggling to look casual, but his face was a shade paler than usual.

Groceries stowed, Quentin sat down beside me, pulling his chair closer than was comfortable. "You didn't know I was a hunter, did you? I hardly have to go to the grocery store. I even know how to field-dress my kill. There's nothing like being self-sufficient. It's the best feeling in the world."

"That's great," I said, thinking of Bambi and Thumper. "You must be really proud." Luckily, the words didn't come out sounding sarcastic.

"You hunt?" Quentin asked Coop. "You should. Every man should know how to fend for himself."

Coop didn't answer.

"I'm not just talking about food, either," Quentin continued in my general direction. "Any man worth his salt knows how to protect his home against intruders." Eyes narrowed, he shot a glance over at Coop, who was looking down at his folded hands.

"Just a man?" I made my voice playful. "What about me?"

Quentin shrugged. "I could teach you. That father of yours probably hasn't ever held a gun in his life."

Not that he'd met my dad. He was right, though; Dad wasn't a big fan of guns. When I was younger, he gave me all sorts of speeches about how if I was ever visiting a friend and I found out there were guns in the house, I should come straight home and tell him. The memory made me swallow hard. What would he think if he knew where I was right now?

"A father should teach his kids to shoot," Quentin added. "Daughters *and* sons."

"Did my grandfather teach you?"

But my question turned out to be a misstep. Quentin's face clouded over. "He should have."

"I guess he wasn't much of a hunter," I said. "He lived in New York City, right?" I figured I'd better play dumb; as far as my uncle knew, I'd come straight from Marblehead to his house in Cox-sackie, and he didn't need to know otherwise.

"That cesspool." His voice was sullen now, too. "A law-abiding person really needs a gun there. Backstabbing rats, just looking for a chance to steal what's yours." He turned to Coop. "I could teach *you* to hunt." It sounded more like a threat than an offer.

To distract him, I forced out a laugh. "We're from the sub-urbs. It's pretty free of backstabbing rats."

He glowered. "You never know."

"But let's not worry about that," I said. "We have so much catching up to do, right? I want to hear all about what you've been up to...."

The muscles in his face relaxed, and for a moment, I thought I'd successfully changed the subject. Then he reached under his flannel shirt and pulled out a handgun. "Here's my prize posses-sion," he said, holding it up like we were having a happy session of show-and-tell. "It's beautiful, isn't it? It's a Wilson Combat Tacti-cal Elite M1911 in .45 ACP. Cost me more than four thousand after I had it all tricked out." He gave it a loving look. "I use Hor-nady TAP 230 grain jacketed hollow-point bullets. More stop-ping power."

I nodded as if I understood any of what he'd said. What could I do but humor him? "It's very nice." Maybe he'd forget to be angry?

"Nice?" He sounded insulted. "You call this nice?" He held the gun in both hands and squinted like he was aiming at an imag-inary target. He chuckled, lowered the gun, and leaned confid-ingly toward Coop. "Women! She calls my gun nice!" I guess he thought they'd share a laugh about how fluff-brained girls are, how they don't understand important things like hollow-point bullets, and I was working to swallow a sarcastic comeback when I noticed the expression on Coop's face. He was concentrating intently, but his eyes weren't on the gun, and they weren't on my uncle's face. He was staring in the direction of the living room, his head cocked, and I realized he was hearing something. Then I heard it, too. But before I could register what it was—a car pulling up the dirt road and braking abruptly—Quentin had jumped to his feet. "Now what?" Gun still in hand, he disappeared into the living room, with Coop right behind him. What could I do but follow?

I arrived just as the front door flew open, and though I'd have sworn our situation couldn't get any stranger, it did. Hence—of all people—strode into the room, hair disheveled, brows knit together. He took it all in at a glance—me, Cooper, Quentin, the gun—and inhaled sharply. For a long moment we all stood there looking at one another, processing this new development. Then Hence sprang into action, slipping past Quentin's gun to position himself between us and my uncle.

"Let these kids go." His voice was low and steady. Did he think Quentin was holding us hostage, and he was some kind of action hero saving the day? *We had it under control*, I wanted to protest. We would have talked ourselves free, wouldn't we? But the ice in Quentin's eyes and the way he spun to train his gun on Hence made me think maybe it wouldn't have been so easy after all.

"Your problem isn't with them," Hence said. Behind his back, he motioned for Coop and me to get behind him. For a crazy moment, I wanted to laugh. This couldn't really be happening, could it?

But Quentin's posture was stiff. "You." The one word said it all. *You. My enemy, my nemesis, the guy I've been itching to kill for twenty-plus years. Standing in front of my gun.* The smile that crept across his face was hideous.

"That's right. You've got me where you've always wanted me. So you might as well let the kids leave." Hence's voice was oddly calm, as though he were making the world's most obvious and reasonable observation. He made a shooing motion behind his back, telling us to get away, but Coop and I stood frozen in place.

Of course Quentin got angry. "I don't take orders from you." For emphasis, he pointed the gun first at Coop's face, then at mine, then back at Hence. "What if I feel like shooting all three of you?" He smirked, enjoying the moment. "I'd do it, too. Don't think I wouldn't."

Just humor him, I silently pleaded with Hence. *Let him be in charge.* Hence might not be my favorite person in the world, but I didn't want to see Quentin shoot his head off. Not to mention the fact that Coop and I would most likely be next, now that Hence had blown our cover.

But Hence had his own ideas. "Let them go now. Then you can settle your score with me." He gestured toward me. "She's your niece. Your flesh and blood. You don't want to harm her."

"Don't tell me what I want." Quentin's face went purple. "You think I wouldn't kill my own flesh and blood?"

The words chilled me.

"I don't think you've got the guts." Hence spoke quietly. He

282

turned a little, squaring his back toward the front door, and Coop and I moved to keep behind him. Again, his fingers motioned for us to take a step backward. I did, but Coop stayed put, shooting me a quick sidelong look that said, *Go*. But I couldn't leave him there. I wouldn't.

Quentin's voice rose. "You don't think *I've* got the guts?"

"You're a spoiled little boy with the money to buy a gun collection." Hence spoke through gritted teeth. "That doesn't make you a killer."

What was he thinking? Did he *want* Quentin to blow his head off? And could he really not put two and two together? Exasperated, I blurted the words out: "He killed my mother." Okay, so maybe it was a tactical error, but Hence had to know the truth. She would have wanted him to know.

That certainly got everyone's attention. Hence took his eyes off Quentin's gun to look at me. A stunned-looking Quentin was staring at me now, too.

"It's true," I said, more softly.

There was a long moment of silence while each of us digested the situation.

"That's right," Quentin finally said. At the sound of his voice, Hence whipped back around. "I killed Catherine to keep her away from you. And now it's your turn." He threw back his head, the sound of his laughter unnervingly boyish. "This whole thing is perfect."

"Yes. It *is* perfect." Hence's voice was surprisingly steady. "You wanted to keep Catherine away from me? If there's anything beyond this life, you'll be sending me right into her arms."

What was he saying? Was he crazy? I turned to exchange a look with Coop. He'd been standing right beside me, but he'd taken a few steps to the side. I saw him reach behind his back for the stand of fireplace tools. His fingers closed around the handle of a poker, and he inched it up slowly, so that it wouldn't clink against the other tools and give him away.

Quentin was too focused on Hence to notice. He cocked his head again, considering Hence's declaration.

"If there's life after death, you're going to hell," Quentin said.

"I'm going to Catherine," Hence said. "Straight to her. Go on. Pull the trigger. Send me to her." Once again, he motioned for Cooper and me to leave while we still could. "Do it."

I took one giant step backward, but Cooper took a step forward, and then another, so that he was right behind Hence, the two of them a few yards from that trembling black gun.

"You'd be doing me a favor," Hence said. He motioned again in my direction and Coop shot a look over his shoulder, urging me to comply. What was he planning to do with the fireplace poker? Would he threaten Quentin with it, trying to distract him from Hence? Wouldn't a gun trump a poker? I swallowed hard, hoping Coop knew what he was doing. Trusting that he did. As if I had a choice.

Coop threw me another look. I took one step back, and another, and then remembered the phone in my pocket. Maybe I could slip into the kitchen, out of sight, and dial 911. Would there be a signal way out here in the woods? It seemed unlikely. Wouldn't Quentin have a landline somewhere in the house? I hadn't noticed a phone, but I hadn't been looking for one.

I inched sideways toward the kitchen without taking my eyes off the gun.

"If she's dead, I don't want to live anymore." Hence's voice was cool and matter-of-fact, like he wasn't daring his enemy to blow his head off. "Go ahead. Give me what I want." He leaned in closer.

"She's dead all right." And to my surprise and horror, Quentin's eyes welled up with tears. "I didn't . . . I didn't want to . . . but I had no choice." With his free hand, he swiped at his eyes. "She didn't give me a choice." The gun wobbled.

I moved toward him, thinking maybe I should pretend to comfort this man—my mother's brother. My mother's killer. Could I distract him with kindness?

But Quentin flinched and tightened his grip. "Don't crowd me." Now the gun was aimed right at my face.

"She's not the one you want to hurt. Let her go. Let both kids go," Hence said.

"Don't tell me what to do." Quentin was shouting now. "I'm the one with the gun!" He took a threatening step closer to Hence. "You came into my house and ruined everything. You took away my father and my sister. . . ."

"I took away your father?" Hence sounded almost amused.

"With all your music bullshit, like you were the son he always wanted. He never cared about my things . . . my lacrosse games or my swim meets. He hardly ever made time for me. But you . . . with your *guitar*." He said the word mockingly. "You took my father. And you took my sister. . . . You made her love you. . . ."

While Hence distracted Quentin, I had been moving little by

little toward the kitchen. When I got to the doorway, I looked quickly around for a phone, but couldn't see one.

"Catherine had a mind of her own," Hence was saying, as if it were important to set the record straight. "Nobody could *make* her do anything she didn't want to do."

There hadn't been a phone in the storage room, but there might be one in Quentin's bedroom. Its door was open directly behind me. If I made a break for it, would he start shooting?

"You took her away from me...." Quentin's voice was breaking now. "You defiled her. You couldn't keep your filthy hands off her...." He shut his eyes and shuddered. When he opened them a second later, his expression was flat and cold. He glared at Hence a second more. The gun clicked in his hand—a noise I recognized from movies, from the moment just before someone pulls the trigger.

Coop lunged toward Quentin, swinging the poker in both hands, aiming at his outstretched arms. The whole thing seemed to happen in slow motion. I had time to think of many things— how brave Coop was, how startled Quentin looked, how I should probably hit the floor—but not enough time to do anything about it.

The gun fired as it burst from Quentin's grip, flew across the room, landed, and spun around. Coop dove for it. In that split second, I saw Quentin hurl himself toward the gun, but Coop got there first. With shaking hands, he trained the weapon on Quentin.

"Stay back," he commanded in a voice I'd never heard before. "Don't move."

Quentin's body froze, but his eyes darted around the room, as if he was looking for a way out or for something he could use to get his gun back. My eyes on his face, I reached for the poker, retrieving it before he could and nudging it under the couch, out of his reach. "You'd better not try anything," I said to Quentin.

A low sound—a groan—brought my attention back to Hence. He was sitting on the floor, his hand clutching his left shoulder, up high, near his chest. There was blood—a lot of it. He stared at Quentin in what looked like disbelief. Then he grimaced in pain.

I dropped to my knees. "He's been hit," I told Coop, stating the obvious. "Don't move," I said to Hence. Hadn't I seen someone on a cop show say the same thing to a gunshot victim? Or maybe it was a car-accident victim. Did it matter?

"He needs a compress. Some kind of cloth. And we need to call an ambulance. Is there a phone?" Coop barked the question at Quentin.

Quentin didn't answer.

"I may not be a gun expert, but I know how to pull a trigger," Coop said through clenched teeth.

Quentin gestured toward the door reluctantly. "In my bedroom. On the bedside table."

Though I moved as fast as I could, it felt like I was running underwater. The 911 dispatch lady tried to keep me on the line, but once I'd given her the address—thank God I could remember it—I dropped the phone, leaving her to talk to the air. I grabbed a flannel shirt off the dresser and raced back to Hence.

"The ambulance is coming." Praying the shirt was clean, I wrapped it around his wound and knotted the sleeves as tightly as

I could. His blood was warm on my hands, but there wasn't time to care.

Hence was talking. "I should have called nine-one-one on my way over ... had them meet me here ... but I didn't think ..."

"Shhh," I ordered. "Does that look right?" I asked Coop, gesturing to my makeshift bandage.

But he couldn't take his attention away from Quentin for even a second. "Tie it as tight as you can get it."

Hence looked intently at my face as I yanked the sleeves with all my might. A memory popped into my mind: my mother putting a bandage on my skinned knee, her face hovering above mine, warm and reassuring. So I said what she would have said: "You're going to be fine. It's just a nick."

"But I *want* to die," he said, his voice matter-of-fact. "I'm going to die."

"Not just yet." I pressed down on the bandaged wound. "Cooper needs you. I need you." That last bit seemed urgently true to me now. "You've got to live."

Hence closed his eyes and moaned, as if I'd sentenced him to life without parole.

"He looks pale," I said to Coop. "And sweaty."

"Is his forehead cold?"

It was.

"Get blankets," Coop said in his new take-charge voice. "He could go into shock." He barked at Quentin. "Where?"

"In the bedroom closet," Quentin said. "On a shelf."

I found a pile there, and grabbed them all. I draped one across Hence's chest, another over his legs.

"Maybe he should lie down?" I looked at Coop.

He nodded. "I think you're supposed to elevate his legs."

I helped ease Hence onto his back, then rolled the last two blankets and propped them under his shins. "There," I said, but now his eyes were closed. "Look at me." I grabbed his hand and held it tightly. "Talk to me."

"I don't want to."

"But you have to." Wasn't I supposed to be keeping him conscious? Then a question occurred to me. "How did you know where we were?"

"Jackie. When you didn't come back last night, she figured you found Quentin's address." He paused, cringing in pain. "So she called the club."

I checked the makeshift bandage and saw that he was bleeding through it, the red startling against the plaid flannel. Should I run for a fresh shirt, or stay here and keep him awake and talking? Both seemed urgent. "What's taking the ambulance so long?"

Hence closed his eyes again.

"Wake up." I squeezed his hand. "Tell me things about my mother. You knew her better than anyone."

"Catherine." Hence's eyes shot open, like he'd just remembered something crucial. He craned his neck to look at Quentin. "Where did you put her?"

Coop shook the gun at Quentin. "Answer him."

Quentin hesitated for a moment. "There's a dump. Not far from here." And he flushed, looking, for a fleeting moment, almost human.

"You threw your sister's body into a *garbage* dump?" Coop's

289

voice rang with disgust. "What kind of monster…" He caught sight of me and fell silent.

My mother was dead. I'd pushed that fact out of my mind in the struggle first to stay alive, then to help Hence. I shook off a wave of wooziness. When I looked down at Hence, I found him staring intently up at me. We exchanged a look, the two of us whose hearts had been punctured by the news. He moved his lips to speak, but I shook my head. There was nothing either of us could say.

But after a moment, he spoke anyway. "I have to tell you."

"It's okay," I lied.

"No. It's not." He inhaled sharply. "The Underground. It should be yours. I was planning to change my will.…"

"What?" This was the last thing I could have expected. "Stop talking like that. We're not going to let you die." I squeezed his good hand again.

"It belongs to you," he said. "To your family." He looked around. "Where's Cooper?"

"I'm here," Coop reminded him. "Keeping an eye on this one." Hands still shaky, he gestured toward Quentin with the gun.

Hence turned back to me. "I left him the club and my savings. But I want him to give the club to you. When you're old enough."

"You're not going to die," Coop said. "Cut it out."

But Hence didn't listen. "Don't let Cooper run the club. Close it down if you have to. Or hire somebody. He can't run it."

This order shocked me. "But…why not?"

"It's too much…distraction," Hence said. He called up to Coop as commandingly as he could. "As soon as you can, quit," he said. "Give it to her. I want you to concentrate on your music."

290

"Stop talking like that." Cooper's voice had lost its newfound authority. "The ambulance will be here any minute."

"You've got talent," Hence said. "Don't waste it like I did." He looked me in the eye. "Let him live in my apartment as long as he needs to."

"*You're* going to live in your apartment," I said. It all seemed so crazy. Hence wasn't going to die of a little shoulder wound.

"If you say so." His expression changed, softened. "I thought your mother would do this for me." His hand was cold in mine. "Hold my hand when—"

"You aren't going to die," I said again, less certain this time.

"I'm glad it's you," he said. "If it couldn't be her."

I moved my lips to respond—to thank him—but nothing came out. For once, I was speechless. Instead, I did something I never would have imagined myself doing. I brushed his hair out of his eyes, then bent and kissed his forehead. His skin was damp against my lips. I felt him shudder.

"Catherine?" he asked, his voice trembling.

I drew back and saw the joy on his face.

"You've come home."

I didn't answer. Should I tell him the truth? Would it be so wrong to let him believe I was my mother? I squeezed his hand and noticed the flannel bandage was completely soaked with blood. I was about to pull free and run for another shirt when we heard the sirens, speeding toward us, growing louder.

Chelsea

Coop and I rode in silence in the backseat of a patrol car, neither of us saying much. We'd long ago lost sight of the ambulance that was rushing Hence to the hospital. It had run the first red light we came to, leaving us in the dust. I felt exhausted—achy all over, my body too heavy to move—but I held it together until Coop sighed, put his arms around me, and pulled me to his chest. Then I lost it, dissolving into hysterics, soaking the front of his shirt. I had been so sure my mother was out there somewhere. I'd been counting on a happy ending that would never come. And the thought of how she must have died, the brother she loved staring her down and shooting her... Had she begged for her life? Had she suffered? Had she thought of me?

Each question brought a fresh wave of misery. Coop tightened his grip and hung on while I wept a monsoon of tears.

"I'm sorry," I said when I could speak. After all, he had his own sorrows and worries. "I'm such a wreck...."

"Shhh." Coop dug around in the pocket of his jeans and pulled out one of the napkins from his long-ago stop at the doughnut store. I blew my nose in it and collapsed against the vinyl seat. Pale and worried, Coop kept craning his head, looking for signs that we were getting closer to the hospital, but for a long time the police cruiser passed nothing but trees. Everything had happened in slow motion: the EMTs strapping Hence to a gurney and putting him in the back of the ambulance; the cops handcuffing Quentin and dragging him off; more cops taping off the crime scene, telling us we couldn't ride in the ambulance and that we shouldn't drive ourselves. One finally offered to take us, but said we'd need to be questioned before we could leave the hospital. Not that we were even thinking of leaving; the idea of abandoning Hence and driving back to The Underground was unimaginable. And knowing what I knew about my mother, could I ever go home to Massachusetts? How could I bear to look into my dad's face and tell him how she died?

At the hospital, we were ushered into an empty exam room, a surreal place to be answering questions about our relationship to the shooter and the victim and where the gun had come from and what we were doing at the scene of the crime. The cop—a youngish guy whose collar looked about a size too tight—took pages and pages of notes, and asked us the same questions seventeen different ways. I wanted so badly to close my eyes and shut out all the ugliness of the last few hours, to sink into sleep and maybe—please, God—wake up and find it had all been a dream. But the questions went on and on. I was starting to think the guy would never let us go when he put his pen on the table, stared gloomily down at his notes, and looked back up at us. "You can go out to the waiting room and find out how your friend is. We'll be in touch."

The ER receptionist looked down her pointy nose while Coop tripped over his words in his hurry to spit our story out. "You're related to the patient?"

"We're his kids," I piped in. In a way, it was sort of true, wasn't it?

She clicked a few buttons on her computer and waited an agonizingly long time for news of Hence's condition.

"Mr. Hence..." She squinted for a better look at the strange name. "Mr. Hence is still in intensive care. According to this, he's being stabilized."

"Can we see him?" Cooper asked.

"Not until he's out of the ICU. Have a seat right over there and we'll call you when—"

"Is he going to be okay?" I interrupted. "He's going to live, right?"

"I can't answer that." She didn't even bother to say it nicely. "His doctors will be out to speak with you when they're ready." That was all she would say.

The chairs in the waiting room were an awful shade of beige, and the magazines all dated back to when I was in middle school. I tried sitting down, but I couldn't seem to keep myself from jumping up, pacing around the room, and returning to hover over Coop. He'd sunk into a chair and sat there looking stunned.

"Can't we do anything?" I asked. "Give blood or something?"

I'd never had to hang out in an emergency room before, and the place creeped me out.

Coop stared at the dingy carpet. If I felt this anxious about Hence, who I had barely liked until a day ago, how must he feel? Hence was his boss, his friend, his hero, and, in a way I'd never noticed until now, his family.

I made myself sit down beside Coop. I took his hand, trying to send warmth and hope from my body into his. Holding hands seemed like the only useful thing I could do.

"Hence is tough." I made myself sound more certain than I felt. "By the time they let us see him, he'll be yelling at the nurses. He'll take one look at you and demand to know what you're doing here when there are amps to polish and toilets to plunge."

Coop tried to laugh, but it came out more like a cough.

"How did you know all that stuff about elevating his legs and wrapping him in blankets?"

"My mom's a nurse. She made me take first-aid classes as soon as I was old enough. She said someday I'd be in a crisis and be glad I knew what to do."

Thinking about mothers—anybody's mother—hurt. I swallowed hard, linked my arm through his, and rested my chin on his shoulder. "You were good. You jumped on that gun like a superhero."

He gave me a sad smile. "You were pretty cool and collected yourself."

"Only in the sense that I didn't throw up." I took a deep breath, inhaling his Cooper-ness. "Um, about those things Hence said…"

"Which things?"

"About the club...about you giving it to me. That's just nuts. When he's better, I'm going to tell him how crazy it is. You should be the one to inherit The Underground. When he dies of old age."

Cooper kissed the top of my head. "He's trying to undo the mistakes he made," he said. "We have to let him."

That's when we noticed the doctor walking toward us. Cooper jumped to his feet, and I followed. In this new slow-motion world we'd fallen into, there was time for me to say a quick, silent prayer—*Please let it be good news*—and time for me to realize from the grim look on the doctor's face that my prayer was too late, all before he opened his mouth to tell us how sorry he was.

Chelsea

Somehow Coop and I got through the next hour. Hence's doctor tried to give us the gruesome details—a shattered clavicle, a fragment of bone traveling to nick the brachial artery—but all my focus was on staying vertical. I held on to Cooper's arm—the one solid-seeming thing in the room—and concentrated on taking deep breaths. Once I was absolutely certain I wouldn't faint, I felt the return of that cool, detached feeling I'd had when Quentin's gun was pointed at me. It allowed me to listen and speak, and do things I'd never have thought myself capable of.

"Would you like to see him?" a nurse asked us. My normal reaction to that decidedly not-normal question would have been to run screaming out into the night, but Coop said yes, and how could I let him go through such a terrible thing alone? When he walked into that hospital room, I was right behind him.

Seeing the body was not as horrifying as I would have thought. Though the face had his strong nose, his full lips, his brows and two-day beard, the body in the bed seemed much smaller than Hence had been, more like a wax figure of Hence than the man himself.

We stood there for a long time, not knowing what to do or say. Coop drew up a chair beside the bed, so I did the same. In the oppressive quiet of that room, I could almost hear the silent good-bye he was saying. I tried to think my own farewell to Hence, but the words hardly made sense. *Thank you for loving my mother. Thank you for bringing me Coop. Thank you for your songs.* The next thought that popped into my mind seemed more sensible, so I spoke it out loud. "Thank you for saving our lives."

Coop looked up, startled, like he'd forgotten I was there.

"Do you think he really meant it?" I asked. "About not wanting to live anymore? Wanting to be with my mother?"

Coop thought a moment. "I do. I think he meant it."

"Do you think he's with her? Do you believe in all that?"

"I don't know. Do you?"

"I'm not sure. But *she* did, I think. She went to church and lit candles when Hence was missing. She prayed he was safe. She must have believed in *something.*"

"Maybe whatever we believe is what happens," Coop said.

"Maybe." It sounded as plausible as anything else.

We fell silent long enough for a hundred questions to crowd into my brain. "What should we do now?"

"First we leave this room."

"Are you ready?" I allowed myself a last glance at the figure in the bed.

"He's not really here." Cooper stood. "There's no point in staying."

After the police took us back to Quentin's cabin, Cooper drove us home to Manhattan through a darkness barely broken by streetlights. "I can make arrangements from The Underground," he said out of the blue.

"There's nobody else to do it?" I asked. "No close friends?"

"He had friends," Cooper said quietly. "Stan, and some others. But I'm the one who has to...the one who should..."

"Right." I fiddled with the climate-control buttons. "I can help." Not that I knew the first thing about arranging a funeral.

Then there was the other heavy, complicated business that surely would have to be dealt with. Hence's will. Returning to Coxsackie to retrieve the car he'd driven to our rescue. Testifying at whatever hearing or trial would decide my uncle's fate. Would there be a search for my poor mother's body? The idea made me shudder. I thought of my father, not knowing and suddenly having to know that she really was dead. Would I be the one to tell him? Again I felt weak. Exhausted.

"Chelsea." Coop's tone was gentle but grave. "You know what you need to do."

"I do?"

Coop didn't elaborate. He didn't have to. For a minute or two I sat there feigning ignorance, trying to ward off the future. I sighed and checked my phone. "There's no signal out here. I'll call my dad as soon as we get to The Underground. He's going to be furious." Even as I spoke that last bit, I knew it wasn't the whole truth.

"I'm pretty sure he'll be relieved to hear your voice. He might even forget to be mad."

"I'm going to have to tell him about my mother." The threat of being grounded for life was nothing beside the awfulness of having to deliver that news.

"He probably already knows," Cooper said. "Don't you think the police have called him by now?"

He was right, of course. I grabbed his arm and the car swerved. "We have to find a pay phone. Dad must be on his way down here to find me. What if we pass him on the highway?"

"Check your cell again. The exit signs have been getting closer together. I think we're almost back to civilization."

My phone had a few more bars. I took a deep breath and made the call to my father's phone. He answered on the first ring. "Chelsea?" In his familiar voice I heard a mix of hope and fear. I pressed the phone so close to my face that it beeped.

"Dad?" Like a little kid, I said his name again and again. "Dad. Dad." Without expecting it, I was bawling, too out of control to even speak, but my dad held the line and waited me out. After that, the conversation went as Coop had predicted. Dad wasn't mad; he didn't scream and make threats. But he did make sure I knew what a scare I'd given him. He said the police had been searching for me, contacting practically everyone I knew at school, grilling Larissa repeatedly. "I kept picturing you in trouble, needing me, and me not being there to help you," he said, sounding teary. By the time he apologized for making me use a cheap, untrackable phone, I was feeling way worse than if he'd yelled at me.

"Don't apologize, Dad." Somehow I couldn't speak the words above a whisper, but at least I was saying them. "It's all my fault. I never should have run away. I'm sorry."

"It doesn't matter," he said. "All that matters is that you're safe." His voice got fainter. "Hold on," he said. "I've got to go through a toll booth...." He explained that I'd caught him rushing to Logan Airport; he'd been planning to talk his way onto a flight to Albany or Westchester County or whichever airport would get him the closest to Coxsackie.

"You should fly into New York City," I told him.

"That's where you are?"

"That's where I'm going." I gave him the address of The Underground.

"You'll be safe until I get there?" As if I hadn't spent the last few days without him looking after me.

"I'll be safe. I promise." I looked over at Cooper, who was staring intently at the road ahead. "I'm with a friend."

"Promise me that you won't disappear again. That once you get to that address, you'll stay put."

I gave my word, and was saying good-bye when he stopped me.

"Wait. Chelsea. Just...well...what I'm trying to ask is, was I really such a terrible father?" Though steady as always, his voice sounded smaller than I'd ever heard it. "I left you alone too much, didn't I? Is that why you left?"

My heart twisted in my chest. "Of course not, Dad. You're a good father—a wonderful father. It's just…I needed to find out about Mom." Saying her name made me remember, with a sudden sinking feeling, the important thing I needed to ask him. I struggled for the right words. "They told you? About what happened to her?"

Dad sighed, as he always did when I mentioned Mom, but this time I couldn't blame him. "They said her brother confessed to… murdering her."

I was crying again, too hard to speak.

"Oh, honey. I'm so sorry about all this. I was wrong not to tell you, not to be up-front about her. I thought you'd be happier if you didn't have to wonder about where she was."

"But what about you?" Had a small part of him believed she might be alive somewhere, waiting to be found? "How are you?"

"I'm sad," he said simply. "I'm just sad."

"I know." I was crying again. "Oh, Dad, I'm so, so sorry."

Was he crying, too? His breathing on the other end of the phone was jagged, but his voice sounded calm and controlled. I loved him for that—for how hard he was trying to stay strong for me. Thinking of the things my mother had written about him, I couldn't wait to hug him and tell him how much I loved him. After all, didn't he deserve someone who *really* loved him, who hadn't just been faking it?

I hung up knowing that before long I would be home in Marblehead. I thought of my bed, with its polka-dotted comforter, and of the warm glow of the Chinese paper lanterns hanging from my bedroom ceiling. It was a strangely satisfying concept: my life, back to normal.

But then I thought of Coop. I glanced over and caught him in the act of looking away from me, back to the road. Had he seen me smile at the thought of seeing my dad again? Did he think I was happy to be going back to Massachusetts, so far from him? Might he even be relieved to see me go?

"Coop," I began, struggling for the right words. "What happens next?"

He didn't answer.

"With us, I mean. What happens to us?"

"What do you want to happen?" His voice was neutral, impossible to read.

"We're just starting to get to know each other." Again, my words came out in a tiny, choked voice. "I don't want this to be over."

For the second time that day, he swerved to the shoulder, braked to a halt, and gathered me into his arms. "It doesn't have to be. Massachusetts isn't that far from New York. I'll visit you. Or you'll visit me."

"Like my father will ever let me out of his sight again."

"If you introduce me to your dad, I'll make a good impression. Parents like me."

"I hope you don't mind being chaperoned," I said. "My dad's always been overprotective. I bet he'll be even worse now."

Coop sighed. "How long till you graduate?"

"A whole year. Forever."

"Well, you'll have to come visit The Underground, now that

it's yours. You can drop in every so often. Keep an eye on the place."

I shook my head. "Seriously. You can't give me The Underground. What do I know about running a nightclub?"

"If you want, I'll teach you everything you need to know."

I thought about that for a minute. Me, the owner of the legendary Underground, living in New York City, getting to decide which bands to break into the big time? If I hadn't been so tired and homesick, it would have sounded exciting. Of course, I would have to finish high school first, then college. Maybe I could go to school in New York City—NYU, maybe, or Fordham—close enough to The Underground to learn the business, to see if running my own nightclub was what I wanted to do with the rest of my life.

"And if you don't want... Well, it's still your family home. It'll be waiting for you until you're ready. And I'll be there." We kissed, and it was different this time, knowing we'd be far apart before long—sadder and even sweeter.

Before I was ready, Coop pulled back. "We'd better get going. We can't let your dad reach the club before we do." He checked over his shoulder before returning to the highway. "I don't want to get off on the wrong foot. Not if I'm going to impress him as good boyfriend material."

According to the GPS, we were still an hour from The Underground. I settled back into my seat, thinking hard. There must have been a thousand things Coop and I needed to say to each other while we still had time alone together, but, limp with exhaustion, I couldn't think of a single one. Instead, I yawned loudly.

"Tip the seat back," Coop advised. "You can sleep. I don't mind. Take my hoodie for a blanket."

I rummaged in the backseat and found it—warm and soft and smelling deliciously of Coop. I pulled it over me, shut my eyes, and enjoyed the feeling of floating at sixty miles an hour through the countryside, drifting in and out of sleep.

What happened next could only have been a dream, though it didn't feel like one. I leaned back to watch the landscape speed past, and, drenched in moonlight, the hilly roadside dipped and swelled, its undulations soothing. Wind tossed the tops of the trees just beyond the shoulder, and I noticed two distant figures walking hand in hand along the edge of the woods. Though it was a perfectly ordinary sight—a slender girl, her long hair whipping around her, and a tall, angular boy—it struck me as extraordinary, almost miraculous. I thought to point them out to Coop, but couldn't seem to find my voice. For a long time we approached them, then, too quickly, we were flying past, close enough for the car's motion to send the girl's hair whooshing back from her face.

I turned in my seat for a better look and caught my breath at how lovely and familiar their two moonlit faces were, even as they receded and grew as distant as twinned stars. As I stared, they turned right and vanished from the roadside into the dark woods. *Turn back!* I wanted to urge Cooper, but the words wouldn't come to my lips, and the highway was hurtling us on toward our futures and, anyway, there could be no turning back.

AUTHOR'S NOTE

It would degrade me to marry Heathcliff now; so he shall
never know how I love him: and that, not because he's
handsome, Nelly, but because he's more myself than I am.
Whatever our souls are made of, his and mine are the
same....

Those words, spoken by Catherine Earnshaw, the heroine of
Emily Brontë's *Wuthering Heights*, thrilled me the first time I read
them. I was seventeen and shy to the point of barely being able to
speak to boys I liked, but I dreamed of someday feeling that same
connection with someone—a love so intense it could last for the
rest of our lives, and beyond. I fell in love with Heathcliff, and
with *Wuthering Heights* itself—a love that led me, quite a few
years later, to write *Catherine*, my own take on Brontë's novel.

Wuthering Heights is the kind of thick, delicious book that transports a reader to another world—the remote and windswept moors in which ghosts walk and the living are as harsh and cruel as the weather. So when I set out to write a modernization of *Wuthering Heights*, I needed a setting as exhilarating in its own way as England's Yorkshire Moors. I decided on Manhattan's Lower East Side, mecca to artists, musicians, and writers. The raw energy and excitement of New York's underground music scene seemed like the right environment for a modern-day Heathcliff and Catherine.

Once I picked a setting, the plot of *Catherine* began to fall into place. My Heathcliff would be an aspiring punk rocker, hot tempered and wounded by an unspeakable past. And Catherine, a nightclub owner's daughter, would be talented, spirited, and a bit spoiled. Like the characters who inspired them, they are flawed and sometimes selfish, but capable of an intense and electrifying love.

Of course *Wuthering Heights*, with its multiple narrators and multigenerational sweep, is more than just a great classic love story. When the love between Heathcliff and Catherine is thwarted, their lives are twisted out of shape like the wind-blasted trees on the moors. This blighted love casts a shadow over the lives of their children. As much as anything else, *Wuthering Heights* is the story of how Catherine's daughter finds her way out of that shadow and into the sunlight. It was important to me, in writing *Catherine*, that the story unfold over the course of two generations—which is how the character of Catherine's daughter, Chelsea, came into being. Though I could never hope to approach the richness and complexity of *Wuthering Heights*, I wanted Catherine's story to be told in more than one voice: her own, and that of a daughter struggling to unravel the mystery of her mother's disappearance.

Wuthering Heights has haunted the imaginations of readers for generations. Like Heathcliff, who begs Catherine's ghost to visit him so he can feel her presence once more, I return again and again to *Wuthering Heights*, eager to be haunted anew by its characters. Writing *Catherine* was my way of returning to that ghost-riddled landscape—of stepping into Catherine and Heathcliff's story, however fleetingly. I hope that readers who enjoy my retelling of Brontë's great novel will be inspired to return to the original—or, maybe, to read it for the first time, and allow themselves to be swept away.

ACKNOWLEDGMENTS

Thanks to my editor, Julie Scheina, who smoothed my path with patience, generosity, and know-how. Thanks also to Amy Williams, agent extraordinaire, and to Ann Green, Ted Fristrom, and Jamey Gallagher, who provided feedback and encouragement.

Extra-special thanks to Eric Coulson, who lent me his considerable expertise on guns and gunshot injuries, and to Dan Courtenay, owner of the venerable Chelsea Guitars. Thanks to Jesse Malin and Bowery Electric for a jolt of inspiration and a glimpse into the real thing.

I'm also grateful to Denise Duhamel for her memories of the Hotel Chelsea circa 1989, and to my Facebook brain trust for their input on all sorts of cultural ephemera: Ali Barsanti, Alli Hammond, Diane Wilkes, Ned Balbo, Shenandoah Lynd, Chris Bamberger, Melody Lindner, Lori Askeland, Cindy Gagnon

Raschke, Lydia Ricker Butler, Laura Pattillo, Daisy Fried, Cecilia Ready, Victoria R. Palmer, Beth Kephart, Monique St. Amant, Susan Sink, and Ann E. Michael, among others.

Finally, hugs to Andre St. Amant, for his willingness to share me with my imaginary friends.

Where stories bloom.

poppy

Visit us online at
www.pickapoppy.com